EARL LIVINGS
THE SILENCE INSIDE THE
WORLD

Earl Livings
The Silence Inside The World

Peggy Bright Books

Contents

The Silence Inside the World   ix
Dedication   xi

1	Beyond the Last Gate	1
2	Two Gifts	11
3	Stone and Blood	19
4	The Service of Names	31
5	The Soul Mirror	39
6	Blood Seeds	47
7	The Striking of Shadow	55
8	The Story Game	67
9	Zane's Story	77
10	Jessie's Tale	83
11	Remesh's Account	87
12	Murga Flight	95
13	Of Crooked Signs	101
14	Leap and Echo	109
15	Matters of Trust	119
16	A Vow for Fate	129

17	Broken Hope	139
18	The Ice Temple	151
19	Above the Abyss	161
20	To Meddle	173
21	The Cave of the Scylarii	179
22	Serpent Song	187
23	The Design in Stars	193
24	The Sentinel Tree	205
25	Shultar's Secrets	215
26	The Next Breath	227
27	Only Chance	241
28	The Garden of Play	247
29	The Death of Shultar	257
30	A Vision of Rescue	265
31	Facets of Awe	273
32	Birth of a God	279
33	Closer to Home	287
34	The Call of Dust and Flame	301
35	The Sacrifice	313
36	To Unravel Herself	321
37	A New Poise	327
38	The Gem of Synrath	335
39	Another Juncture	343
40	Prelude to a Death	353

41	The Song of Unknowing	367
42	The Rule of Fate	375
43	Sparks Weaving	385
44	Always Choice	395
45	A Surge of Silence	403

Glossary 413
About The Author 417

The Silence Inside the World

by Earl Livings

Like a long-legged fly upon the stream
His mind moves upon silence.
W B Yeats, 'Long-Legged Fly'

Peggy Bright Books
2021

The Silence Inside the World. © Copyright Earl Livings, 2021.

First published by Peggy Bright Books, 2021.
www.peggybrightbooks.com.
Please direct all enquiries to editor@peggybrightbooks.com

All rights reserved. Without limiting the rights under copyright reserved above, no part of this publication may be reproduced, stored in or introduced into a database and retrieval system or transmitted in any form or any means (electronic, mechanical, photocopying, recording or otherwise) without the prior written permission of both the owner of copyright and the above publishers.

ISBN 9780992512576

Edited by Edwina Harvey.

Cover illustrator Manabu Takeda.
https://www.instagram.com/manavuart/

Two Edged Sword Clipart | i2Clipart - Royalty Free Public Domain Clipart

A catalogue record for this work is available from the National Library of Australia

Peggy Bright Books. Proudly publishing square pegs for round holes.
www.peggybrightbooks.com

For Chris Millar,
who now walks the sacred road,
and for all other healers and dreamers

1

Beyond the Last Gate

The way-gate slams, with the deep rolling sound
of a cavernous bell struck once, so deep
the long cadences shiver the bone's core.

The woman flinches from a dream of light
so intense she remembers nothing but
her grief quickening as she whirled away.

She blinks. The wavering starlight shows trees
and gravestones braided with shadows. She starts
to turn. Darkness engulfs her from above.

She is reminded of a feather cape
she once made, but this smothering is thicker,
wilder, a whiff of bile, more like a beast

thrashing its meal. She feels no breath from it,
recalls her father locking the hall cupboard,
her hot breath against fur coats, his command:

'Stay there until you learn how to behave
like a child of God instead of a whore.'
Just ten years old, all she had done was spread

her new church dress for everyone to see
and smiled for her mother. What is a whore?
Splinters of ice jag through her consciousness,

form dark maws that suck light from memory
till breath and sense begin to whimper-fade
no matter how she struggles, how she prays.

Then hands grip her arms, shake her. Darkness falls.
Her mind stumbles like every child alighting
from the merry-go-round. Hands hold her tight

as she hauls breath through posture, sense and thought.
Strong hands. Without the just-clench of her father
wrenching her from the packed and humid gloom:

'Never do that again. God does not love
those who wallow in filth. They go to Hell.
Go to your room. You will not eat today.'

She shakes her head, then hears a deeper voice,
and tender, not her father's: 'Can you stand?
Are you all right?' Tilting her head she shudders

at the dark shape before her. He lets go,
steps back. She hugs herself, regards his poise,
the hooded cloak, the knee-high leather boots,

the dark breeches, tunic, vest. He is tall,
wiry, a hint of stealthy elegance.
A bulging sack hangs behind his right shoulder.

She wonders what saga she now is dreaming,
what new distillation of her strained studies
is tainting thought and vision, recent pain.

She trembles at his wary stillness, notes
deep worry lines on his dark, angled face,
grey eyes like veiled mirrors that follow her

but allow nothing past, as if protecting
a deep fragility, or worse, a core
of emptiness. She wants a simple truth.

He removes his cloak, wraps it around her.
'You stood like a statue, then you began
to twist and thrash about, clawing the air

'as though drowning, and when I grabbed you, shadows
slid from your body and slithered away.
I fear this graveyard is not safe for us.'

The thick cloak is lined with fur and she welcomes
the warmth, not knowing till now she is cold,
has bare feet, wears only a thin nightdress.

Her knees buckle as she looks about her.
He goes to help, but she pushes him off.
'Who are you and what am I doing here?'

Hitching his sack, he smooths his long, dark hair.
'I know I have been here before. Each time
is never the same, the people, the landscape,

'the path we follow. Memory for me
is wayward, like leaves swirling in a river.
Of two things only am I sure, my name,

'and that we must travel this sacred road,
learn what we can before we reach its end.
That gate will not open for us.' He pauses.

'My name is Zane.' His hand is warm and gentle,
calloused edge, knuckles. A fighter, she guesses.
'Mine is Jessie.' He bows slightly, then points

to her scant clothing. 'What do you remember?'
His voice is command-strong, yet frayed a little,
as from fatigue. She closes her eyes, sees

other snippets of childhood: the rose sparkle
of water spray she hurtles through again,
again, her mother urging her, then quiet

when her father appears; the serene owl
one night in her tree, its vanishing wink;
the whispered snatch of story-time, with dragons

that tickled, trees that talked, and singing swords
that opened the white way to paradise;
her cramped tears in the middle of the night

with her parents shouting, then that slap-silence.
She slides herself from under these stark moments,
strives to recall her time before this place,

tells him of bare grey walls, fusty aromas,
something tight at limb and chest, how blood tastes.
Like one who also knows of brutal secrets

his face remains impassive as he nods.
Pulling the cloak tight, she looks at the hill
behind the stone wall: 'I want to go home.'

The hilltop is efflorescence, all curves,
shapes, textures, all shifting angles and colour,
a vast chameleon hiding in nothing.

Sometimes it seems a hovel of mud huts,
other times a metropolis of gleam
and moving shapes of smoke and strangling flame,

machines flitting about towers like moths.
The activities of man and man's structures
make no sound, wonders seen through jellied air.

Suddenly there is a tremor beneath
their feet. Jessie hesitates, starts to run,
stops when she sees him standing still, eyes closed,

head craned as if tuning for distant notes.
A moment later, another vibration,
which spirals through her body, and her atoms

scatter, like dandelion clocks she blew
while sitting against her favourite tree
as a child, an hour of peace for each puff.

After the third tremor she breathes again.
Nothing seems to have changed, though Jessie feels
a tantalising vigour in her being.

Raising her hands in front of her, she gasps,
keeps turning them around. Where Zane is dark
of feature, like deep water in a cave,

she is wan, though hazed with blood radiance.
Jessie brings her hands closer, is amazed
by deep traceries of veins visible

through her translucent skin. Now she remembers
her white hair, her pale blue eyes that flash red
or purple in bright light, her frailty,

how she was deemed a judgment on her parents
for past sins, a test of faith, for her also.
A pale witch they called her, not just her colour,

but her manner, the projection of pride,
choosing to sit with tree and grass and air
and not play or read or converse with others.

She knew more than they. The patterns of lines
would tell her things about the world. A vein
abruptly throbbing would signal a summons

from her father. A spasm on her thigh,
a visit from other brethren, or worse,
the minister, who often stared at her

from the bedroom door. A twitch in her palm
and she knew to leave the house before dawn,
stay all day with her tree and watch the wind.

When her mother left them, she searched the patterns
all over her body for any clue
to the reason, found only jumbled lines.

As she drops her arms and turns towards Zane,
the steel and ivory gate behind them
creaks open and a bulbous mass of shadows

avalanches through, whirls and splits to hammer
the quick-shut gate, the stone wall on each side,
re-gathers into a heaving black hulk,

surges forward. Dozens of twisted faces
leer or wink at them, then vanish within
the roiling tangle of misshapen bodies,

limbs at awkward angles, the stench of slime,
flecks of stagnant colour. Shadows of statues
and headstone detach themselves, slink towards

the foaming mass, which swells with jeers and moans,
then splits around the two companions, joins
behind them, slowly begins to press inwards.

Zane chant-gestures and a bone staff appears
in his hands. He swings at each fetid limb
that stretches towards them, pivots and strikes

again, again, each blow a crimson blaze
that shrivels the limb; but too many reach
towards them, and each one that touches stuns

skin and nerves, till the whirling man is lurching
into his blows and Jessie is shriek-huddling
like a small child inside a raging mob.

A sizzle-rush of air engulfs them all.
The dark mass collapses to either side
of a dazzling female being, hair swaying

in waves of black, red, white about her poise
as she floats down the path, skin fair then dark,
the air filled with a shimmer of lute music.

As she passes, tendrils of hair stroke them,
healing their wounds, while others fling away
foul remnants the creature left as it fled.

She pauses, nods at them in turn, then glides
down the winding narrow path to the archway
with its broken emblems of flight and chasm.

Jessie's body is still twitching with static
from the goddess's touch, her breasts and belly
tingling wildly, but Zane sprints after her,

demands she stop and face him. His speed blurs
Jessie's vision, yet the goddess glides swifter
than he, no effort, no glance back. He stops,

gapes, drops a hand. When Jessie reaches him
Zane is shaking with confusion and urge,
as though this goddess were lure, sorrow, secret.

She waits till his posture straightens, then asks
what was happening and why. He walks on
without answering. She pulls him around,

ignores his glare and raised staff. 'Answer me!'
He breaks his staff in two. The pieces vanish.
'We have to go. Those shadows may come back.'

Jessie crosses her arms. He sighs and points
to the slowly rising vapours of rose
and orange light circling the far horizon.

'The tremors signal *Glymsen*, the new day.
I've seen so many dawns here, none the same.
As for that creature, all I can say is

'this land will always seek to challenge us.'
His tone is urgent, his gaze cold. He shrugs,
turns, strides towards the broken light ahead.

2

Two Gifts

Jessie studies the graveyard she is leaving:
no flowers left by mourners, no trimmed lawns,
no foraging insects, no swooping birds.

The headstones lie in drifts of dust, inscriptions
weathered beyond repair. Gloom muffles all
so that even singing would choke and fade,

if anyone could remember a song.
A chill snakes along her spine and the thought
of walking on her grave catches her throat.

Once it leaves the graveyard, the path becomes
a narrow road covered in the same dust.
There are no footprints. The light is so dim,

perspective so warped, she bumps into Zane
before realising the shape she sees
is not a road-curve shadow but his back.

Zane shows her the sign suspended above
a bridge damasked by mist. Scored on red wood
are lines of script that change like flame whenever

she recalls the alphabet of each tongue
she knows. Rubbing her eyes, she hears inside
her mind a female voice say, 'Trust in this,'

but still the script moves. Zane touches her shoulder:
'Something about silence. Can you read it?'
She sigh-shrugs, so he peers again, moves forward.

The instant he mounts a step the air chills,
the mist swirls. A male voice booms from within:
'Can't you read? Now take a wish and be judged.'

Zane plants his other foot, his voice the stealth
of an old hunter. 'No one judges me.'
'Don't be too sure of yourself,' says the mist.

Zane glares, takes another step. 'Show yourself.'
From deep below the bridge a whistling starts,
rises louder, shriller, the closer, faster

it comes, a concatenation of frenzy
as air tumbles, colours shatter, breath teeters
to the crescendo of a thunder-blast,

then abrupt silence. When their vision clears,
before them stands a monk in tattered robes,
ascetic body tinged like a moon halo.

He smiles, bows, then offers his begging bowl
with his left hand, his right limb a stump only.
Jessie stands before him. 'What did it say?'

He rattles the bowl. 'Some things only open
to wisdom after all else is well tested.
That's why we travel. Take one and be judged.'

She peers within and sees a broken shell,
a leather pouch inscribed with triple spirals,
a long, bent nail, crimsoned by rust or blood,

a green feather, a globe of crystal filled
with spinning flakes of gold. She takes the pouch,
which is heavy, hums softly at her touch.

The monk turns back to Zane, whose arms are crossed.
'Not choosing is a choice.' He waves his stump.
'And not all choices lead the way we think.'

Zane snorts his disdain. 'No one judges me.'
'Except yourself.' The monk grins. 'Take a look.
You have nothing to lose, this time as always.'

Zane smiles as he chooses the nail. Before
the monk can return the bowl to his robes,
Zane cuts his palm and drips blood into it.

The monk nods as he fades into the mist,
a slow spinning mass that draws to a point
above their heads, then wink-swallows itself.

The bridge is made of wooden struts and pylons,
but its planks are shafts of quivering light.
As Jessie opens her gift, Zane steps up

to a swarm-frenzy sounding far below.
The light beams bend with his weight, and he sees
between them a colossal maw of darkness,

like looking from the bottom of a well
at a stark black sky, the sides swiftly folding
back its mass to a mountain underneath.

Zane breathes a sudden ease that he will know
what lies past all darkness, or cease to know,
if only the light beams would weaken further.

They stay firm. In disappointment he steps
across the bridge, sits at a nearby bench,
rubs his palm, wonders about endless quests.

Jessie inspects the gem she found, is startled
by the rainbow shapes inside that spin-tumble
at a slower rate than she rolls the jewel

between her fingers, and by the sensation
of living warmth it exudes. She puts it
back into the pouch, steps onto a beam

that instantly becomes a wooden slat.
When she reaches the apex of the bridge
she spies the glide-glow of their goddess saviour

in the distance, the luminosity
reclaiming and filling the shifting landscape,
shields her eyes as the radiance erupts,

a thousand bonfires lit at once in front
of a giant cauldron of focussed mirrors.
Seconds later, eyes still stinging, she senses

a strange eagerness quicken step and breath.
She notices too how the fringe of light
at the horizon has stopped climbing, leaving

most of the sky filled with stars, though all things
are now visible, clearly emanating
their essence, even Zane, whose darkness glimmers.

From high overhead comes a sound like crows
in fierce debate. Jessie feels she could leap
into the sky and join them, and their cries.

Zane heaves himself up. She watches him shift
his sack and wonders what stories it holds.
As they stride down the road, she pats her pocket,

tries to recall more of her former life—
nothing, as if remembrance were a candle
being always snuffed out before her eyes.

If not her past, what of this bizarre present
that trigger-echoes images of fable?
Something about rulers of sun and moon,

something about hidden jewels of the soul,
something about blood sacrifice and hope.
But why recall stories instead of life?

Jessie soon loses count of hills they climb,
a way to measure time where nothing moves
except themselves, no sun but narrow band

of varied light that rings the world and leaves
a frosting on everything but the living,
her nimbus a firefly's afterglow.

Finger at throat, Jessie can barely feel
a pulse, more like sludge stirred by random flutter
than beat of vital force. She strains against

the mounting fact of death: the fields of briar
and thistle; silence under foot; the constant
squeeze-weight of cold that steals beneath her skin

to smother breath, carriage of bone and sight;
her lack of memory; though now she knows
this afterlife is nothing like rote lessons

drummed by cane, purple glare. This is not hell,
nor heaven, nothing like those sacred vistas
revealed in ancient texts upon her desk.

And here, a strange companion, so unlike
anyone she would ever meet, except,
perhaps, in dream…She stops, stares after him,

scans his face when he turns to hurry her.
The spinning chasm in her belly says
she's known a dream-incarnation of him.

But when? She closes her eyes, tries to force
her mind down traceries of recollection.
One of them persists: a boy skipping pebbles

across a surface speckled by green light,
the lure of solid radiance within
waving and clutching water weeds, the strain

of reach through clinging liquid, abrupt plunge,
limbs clawing for air, one final burst, gasp
as light and breeze again touch skin, the thanks.

She senses Zane peering at her. 'The more
we walk,' she says as they move on, 'the clearer
become some memories. What about you?'

He does not answer. Whenever he shuts
his eyes to probe the murk of his mind, all
he feels are ghost inklings that bring disquiet,

the belief he has planned this path before
and may again, the thorny intimation
his plans will ruin far beyond intent,

futile havoc for those he hates and loves.
Deeper thrusts of will pierce the gloom, but show
images shuffle-merging endlessly:

constant discord of battle-cry and sobbing,
smoke haze, blood tang and fever, whirling stars,
no constant thread of self, no hint of reason.

Zane does not answer, does not look at her.
Jessie scowls, then notices how his aura
ebbs and flows like a dispute; turns away.

As they walk, the grey dust billows about
yet does not choke them, even though it enters
mouth and nostril. Silences enfold them.

3

Stone and Blood

They round a bend and see a huddled form
beside the road. It does not move as they
approach, does not flinch when Zane touches it.

A strangled hissing rises from its throat,
like hot, hammered metal plunged into water.
As Jessie turns its head, she sees a gaze

like eye-holes of some statue, but without
the trick of light that summons life to marble.
The man is cold to touch. Her stomach spasms

as she starts to cover him with her cloak.
Zane admonishes her, wants to move on.
She glares her defiance till he relents,

draws a circle around the man, unhitches
his sack and takes out a lyre unlike any
Jessie has seen or read about. He plucks

the strings, long, glossy, magic-wound red hair,
and corrects the tuning, flame notes, eyes closed.
He sits beside the circle, starts to play.

Jessie perceives the air swirl into shape,
an embodied darkness that brings to mind
recollections of sermons and rank depths.

She shudders, but is drawn to sway within
the binding rhythm, the resurging song,
the erupting visions that cleave the will.

The music swells from simple four-beat measure
to lavish melody-skeins of fire, wind,
flow and pause as Zane's deft fingers explore

the lean boundaries of chaos and stasis,
his voice a low counterpoint to the pitch
of his strings, the wild pace-turns of his playing.

Within moments, Jessie sees what Zane sees
behind closed eyelids. She hears him command
the man back from the depths, is just as shocked

when new eddies of darkness coalesce
into two lofty shapes of wings and shadows
that hint at hidden spheres of light and heat

and are flaying at each other with whips
of fiery darkness. First one then the other
staggers under the blows, but when Zane casts

a ball of light at them, the taller one
hisses then streaks skyward and disappears.
The other folds its immense wings and waits.

Throughout the battle, Jessie isn't sure
if the beings are present in mind only
or also in the circle with the man.

Zane stops playing, gestures the sign of locks
reversed: 'Who are you?' The dark being laughs
and Jessie thinks of magpies carolling.

'Your magic has no effect on me, yet
you need only recall where first we met.'
Jessie feels Zane struggle, sees rapid scenes

of combat with sword and flame against men
and creatures concocted from man and beast,
sees voluptuous women held in globes

suspended over mist and gaping lakes,
but is not sure if these are history
or spinning phantasms of lust and spite,

or if they are the same in this strange world.
She loses contact as he plunges deeper
into his story, yet still she can see

the winged being, who has been watching her
all this time. She hears a child singing nonsense
rhymes, finds herself crying. She sees tears, too,

in the star-shimmer orbs of the weird creature
and realises Zane is again speaking,
though with strained voice. 'We met one night outside

'my village. You were searching for those lost
from the star realm and I was practising
the laying out of sand songs'—a pause, and

Jessie again hears singing—'with my sister.
You are Rynobar, a *hoya*, though you
never harmed us, unlike other star-demons.'

'And you are Zane the Immortal, denier
of gods and life, though not when first we met.
I do not think you will succeed this time.

'Or ever. What is behind life can never
vanish, though we have argued this before,
which you always forget, and will again.'

Zane chuckles. 'And what of your search, my friend?
Found those lost *hoya*?' Rynobar spreads out
its wings, presses its palms together, bows,

and fades from sight. Zane studies this new absence
that echoes behind his eyes, packs his lyre,
smudges the circle, watches Jessie massage

the cold limbs of the man till he awakes,
then helps her lift-prop him against a boulder.
His face is round, with almond-shaped brown eyes.

His mane of brown hair drip-straggles with sweat,
like an over-taxed athlete, though his belly
and thick frame would belie such a pursuit.

After blinking a few times he stares wildly
around him, folds himself into a ball,
starts to rock. Jessie coos to him, calms him,

tells him how they found him beside the road,
and asks how he came to be there, says nothing
of the scars she saw as she massaged him.

'My name is Remesh.' He pauses to search
his memory, blanches, says nothing more,
rocks a little as he stares into space.

Zane pulls Jessie aside. 'We should leave him.
He'll slow us down.' She points to the smudged circle:
'What about Rynobar?' Zane starts. 'You saw?'

'Not everything. What does it want with him?
And what is a star-demon anyway?'
Zane shrugs. 'No one knows. Not even themselves.

'In my world, *hoya* come down at night, kill
anyone who wanders far from protection.
Rynobar was not like that, but was searching—'

Remesh's raspy voice sounds behind them.
'So everyone I meet is on a quest.'
Zane moves towards him. 'And how would you know?'

The man gets up, dusts off his blue and orange
shirt and pants, smiles, does not allow Zane's height
to intimidate him. 'It appears death

'gives one certain knowledge. You both are seeking
an atonement of sorts, though why you bother
is beyond me. Dead is too late. There's nothing

'but the wait for nothing, no formal judgment,
no blessing or curse for life's strategies,
just illusion of company, then nothing.'

Jessie can't accept his words. Death is more
than nothing, though not her father's belief
in punishment or reward, constant guilt.

'So why don't I know what you know?' she says.
Remesh half turns to her. 'Maybe you don't
want to accept you're dead. If you are real.'

Zane smiles. 'What of me, who has never died?'
Remesh shrugs. 'We all have our fantasies.
I'm wondering if you're both part of mine.'

'We all are real,' Jessie insists, then wonders
how to prove a thing so obvious, here
where nothing is familiar, except

thoughts and memories dredged from deep within.
She has felt cold, she has felt muscles move.
Her body is as she remembers it,

colour of hair and skin, smallness of breasts.
Yet, how to know her memory is true?
To pinch her skin, as in a dream, can't help.

Better to accept this place, follow paths
mapped by those who have come before, and if
self-delusion, then nothing leads to nothing.

As if reading her mind, Zane counsels faith.
'No matter what we believe this world is,
or is not, and our destiny in it,

'we are here and have only this grey road,
unless,' and he stares at Remesh, 'we have
a liking for the condition of stone.'

Remesh sniggers. 'And where does this road lead?'
For an answer, Zane edges with his foot
another circle, smaller than before,

sits cross-legged beside it, takes a bag
from his vest. 'I remember the first time
I saw my mother use this, a dawn rite

'all families in my village conducted
to ensure good fortune for the men fishing
on Lake Tarlkarni, for whatever wares

'we needed to ease life. The *murga*, path
of prayer.' He opens the woven bag, pricks
a finger with the point of his small knife,

lets fall three drops of blood into the bag,
shakes it, then pours sand grains onto his palm.
'It is said Ghajat was first formed from these.'

Jessie sits beside him. 'What do you mean?
What is Ghajat?' He gestures around them.
'Ghajat is my world. Maybe this world, too,

'for I sense similarities: *Glymsen*,
the sway of song, the vision-hints of landscape.
Yet I have wandered so long, many lands,

'no matter how many tricks I have tried,
the memory hoard is too vast to hold.
But skill and sight are never lost, if used.'

He sprinkles grains around the circle, hums
a tune Jessie suspects she also knows,
maybe an air her own mother once sang.

The grains form a black outline to the space.
Zane takes some more. 'Before there was a world,
there was only grey sand, and the first Kenri

'sung Ghajat into existence from it.
So we prepare our sand songs before dawn
to renew the world and seek aid.' He casts

the grains over the circle and begins
to chant. Though Jessie can't decode the language,
pictures of sunlit pools and flowers blooming

form in her mind, and she feels her pulse quicken.
She smells the aroma of summer grass,
of soft rain, sees wings emerge from those flowers.

Remesh, however, coughs his disapproval.
'If there was only sand, where did this god
come from?' Zane smiles. 'Maybe the sand itself.

'No matter. The song is the only truth.'
Jessie urges Remesh to let Zane finish
without interruption. They watch as swirls

of sand coalesce into flowing patterns,
change colour with every note of his song,
become a detailed living map, with gorges,

mountains, and a ribbon of road on which
can be seen figures surveying a map.
Remesh jumps into the air, and his figure

does the same. 'That's impossible,' he mutters,
watches as Zane's song defines even more:
a field of red trees, fortress clumps of rocks,

a coastline with lapping waves and low island,
a swamp, a walled garden, abodes of light,
hilltops with swaying trees, how the road passes

a series of ancient craters and ends
at the base of a strange volcano, though
the more fierce he sings, the more details blur.

Suddenly, the air above the map splits
and a small object speeds towards the mountain.
Shadows crawl out of the landscape and follow.

Before they can see what happens, white clouds
shaped like immense beings made from deformed
spheres and cubes fill the space above the map.

They look up, notice white tendrils of mist
about them, and shudder. The map dissolves
to grey sand. Zane bows his head, claps his hands,

then scoops the grains into his bag. He looks
at them. 'I remember her stories now.
This is not Ghajat, but Thexlan, creator

'and final world of all possible worlds.
That mountain is Mt Alkerii, from which
all things arise, to which all things return.

'My mother once told me that Larandor,
First Kenri, came from here, may even be
Thexlan, may yet live deep in Mt Alkerii.

'We should find all our answers on its slopes.'
He puts away his bag of grains, and stands.
'Or a deeper awareness of our questions.'

When Jessie and Remesh query him further
he ignores them, reminds them of the mass
that may be falling somewhere above them.

Back on the road, no one speaks as mist swirls,
as high whispers tug at the ear, and each
wonders what things can ever be judged real.

4

The Service of Names

When the mist dissipates, they find themselves
passing through fields of high, wilted spike-grass.
In the distance they can see a scarecrow

that swiftly becomes a tall, thin-faced woman,
the grass parting before her, a bow-wave.
Her black hair flops across a face that seems

caught between smirk and grimace. She greets them
with a slight nod, regal acknowledgment,
then graces the air with a quick, high laugh.

They see her staff is covered by small skulls
that emerge near the base and spiral-stream
up its length, becoming flesh, gazing eye,

then vanishing with a smile after joining
the snake and bird figures that crown the wood.
Others flow downwards, all rage and despair,

sometimes delight, as they wrinkle and fade.
She is dressed in rags. Eyes sparkle with humour,
the scent of lilac blossoms around her.

She holds her staff, patient poise, acute gaze.
Jessie discerns questions are not in order.
She gives her name and those of her companions.

'Thank you,' the woman says, and strokes her staff,
'but tell me who you really are and why.'
Violet flames dance around Zane. 'Why should we?'

The woman chuckles. 'What have you to lose,
now you have volunteered your names?' She raps
a skull half way along the staff. Zane staggers

as though cuffed by a giant. His eyes blaze,
but Jessie restrains him. The woman nods.
'Names are everything in this world, so be

'careful to rely on them. Now, your answers.'
Remesh hides a smirk. 'I seek to know who
I was.' The hermit taps another skull.

Remesh turns white as knees collapse. 'Too smug.
If you desire to tread this road and live,
you need to know how to address its questions.'

She draws a circle on the road and strikes
the centre three times. 'Here's a hint for you.'
They watch the grey surface disappear, nothing

taking its place. They reel with vertigo,
clutch at each other, at the shredding air,
as they feel themselves fall outside their selves

into nothing there, bodies only mist,
minds the wind that weaves vapour from itself,
the rhythm behind minds a shifting pause.

The staff strikes twice. The travellers fall back
from the sealed chasm, wipe their eyes of sweat,
grip shaking limbs, find breath, find sight, find speech.

Jessie recovers first, receives that gaze
which pierces right through her, but dares not flinch.
'Who are you and what do you seek from us?'

A finger hovers near a glowing skull.
The woman leans forward. 'Not without merit,
though my answers may not help you find yours.

'My nature and my name is one. Guess it
and I will help you on your way.' Zane waits
on the balls of his feet. 'And if we fail?'

The woman smiles like a teacher rebuking
a favoured, frustratingly-wayward, pupil.
'We go our separate ways, nothing more.'

Remesh moves alongside Zane, though his stance
is nothing like the predator-attention
of the fighter, is barely held alarm.

'I don't trust you. I don't believe you would
help us for nothing in return. What game
are you really playing? I say we leave.'

Jessie sees the woman's eyes pity-glisten,
knows now that some give without need of payment:
'No. We have nothing to lose.' Zane agrees,

but the task is almost impossible
without a hint. 'And I don't mean that image
with which you tricked us before. Too dramatic.'

'Each hint will mean one less thing I can do
for you when you win.' Everyone agrees.
'My first hint is that I do what I ask.'

There is silence as each of them recalls
her exact words, though Jessie interrupts
to ask if false answers are penalised.

They won't be. Jessie continues. 'You know
our names, which are everything, yet imply
we do not know our nature as our name.'

She pauses. 'What you ask is to be told
who we really are and why. This you know.'
The woman nods. 'So you want us to know.'

The woman nods again. Jessie's scalp tingles
as images and ideas fire-cracker
each other so fast she gasps, shivers, steadies,

body elation-flushed. 'This is your function,
is the function of Thexlan, of all worlds,
to help reveal what is already known.'

The woman gestures that Jessie continue.
'You are Thexlan, at least its advocate.
As Larandor is for Ghajat. Its symbol.'

Zane joins in. 'But Larandor formed Ghajat.
He's not its symbol.' Jessie faces him.
'In Thexlan, names, symbols, nature are one.'

She turns back to the woman. 'To name you
is to refine your nature. I call you
Enheduanna, my world's first known author,

'who balanced the human and the divine,
as good a name as any, which declares
service to creation, to revelation.'

The woman's laughter quivers throughout Thexlan,
and they are cocooned by the sound. They stare
as all the world flows from her rags and staff,

as laughter issues from each skull, as light
erupts from cavern eyes to glaze each blade
of grass, each curve of rock and hill, to cleave

the gap beneath each grain of mass, from which
each thread of sound and light and texture comes,
the world a prism of all seas of nothing.

'Well done,' she says, the land again distinct.
'I gladly take the name you guess, for now,
and owe you much, three answers for your grace.'

'If you are a symbol-song for all this,'
Zane gestures about him, 'how were you made?'
'I have always been. Besides, we create

'every world we live in. Before I thought
or dreamed, there was no I to know the I,
and after, dream-thoughts cascade into life.'

'So you are a second without a first,'
Remesh suggests, his tone consciously even.
Enheduanna's face shows slight annoyance.

'I will ignore that, which was never meant
to be a question. What is it you really
wish to know?' He closes his eyes a moment.

'Am I dead, and if so, why am I here
and not with the one true God?' Sage eyes soften.
'Your god is always with you, though you sin

'in his name. Those sins prevent you from seeing
his true nature, which is yours.' Remesh scowls.
'Fulfilling my God's word is not a sin.'

'That depends on whether your heart is filled
with your god or you hear him with a heart
turned rock by harsh desire. It's up to you.'

Remesh uncurls his fist and moves away.
'And your question?' Enheduanna says
to Jessie, who bows her head. 'I have none.

'May I ask it of you some other time?'
'Of course. You'll know what to ask at that point,
though you may be beyond an answer then.'

Enheduanna continues the course
she took across the fields. As the staff strikes
the ground and the grass parts, the skulls start singing.

And abruptly she is gone, though the wind
carries a muted musical susurrus
that echoes in their ears for many hours.

5

The Soul Mirror

For some time the road is nothing but hills
each one higher than the last. Though their vigour
is greater here than in their former worlds,

the way saps them quickly, as if the meeting
with Enheduanna asked more of them
than she gave. Soon they top another rise,

are thankful for the flat terrain they find,
can see how the road continues straight, till
it bends around a distant breast of earth.

After a while, as they stride out with something
like a child's abandon to downward slopes,
they feel the road coil itself to itself,

a silk ribbon twisted, its two ends joined.
They fathom the instant as utterly
endless, flooded with the exhilaration

that comes from rolling down a grassy hill
the first time, before the grief of it ending.
The event passes before each of them

knows the others have conceived the same thing,
and they continue their glide-pace advance
without mentioning such a passing fancy.

As they approach the mound they feel the ground
pulsing with drumbeats. Closer, they hear singing
coming from the bare summit where smoke rises

to form a troop of grey and silver horsemen,
their voices like cascades of tiny bells.
When the last rider dwindles to a speck

the sky fills with showers of pulsing orbs
that chase each other in widening circles
to the horizon, and the drumming stops.

Remesh sneers as he faces Zane and Jessie.
'And I suppose you're going to tell me
that those are fairy folk, this mound their home.'

'It seems to me,' Zane says, his tone low, even,
'the drummers, not the riders, are the owners.'
He turns towards its base, which is embedded

with upright slabs of basalt fused together.
He points out how one is mirror-sheened, while
the rest show signs of constant weather-scour.

Jessie recalls the distant brilliance
of the floating goddess that morning, wonders
whether this mirror is result or cause.

Zane steps towards it, but she pulls him back.
Remesh joins them: 'Why do you fear this thing?'
She tells them what she saw, and that she feels

curiosity may prove their undoing.
Zane shrugs, stares into her pale eyes. 'But surely
you want to know about this road, this world?'

She shivers. 'I don't have his certainty
that consciousness fades to oblivion.
Nor do I have faith in sweet paradise.'

Zane touches her arm. 'How do you explain
this place or your presence here? Just a dream?'
She looks upward. 'Yes. Everything a dream.

'But no one who wakes up. Not me. Not you.
Everything not real.' She drops to the ground.
Zane bends down, but she turns her face away.

'Do you want to be a rock like he was?'
He grabs her shoulders, forces her to look.
'I believe dreams contain some part of truth.'

Zane stands back. 'We have no choice. Let's agree
that each of us is alive in this place,
that we are separate and have a purpose.

'If we find reasons to doubt these, then fine.
Until then, let's not waste what souls we have
in futile argument.' The others nod.

Zane moves closer to the flickering mirror,
which is taller than horse and rider, wider
than three abreast, heavier than tradition.

His image shimmer-sways briefly, then firms.
Slowly a milky swirl forms around him,
blotting out the others, the road's reflection.

The swirl grows, divides, forms shapes that become
people and creatures, some bleeding, some screaming,
some open-mouthed, some mouthing their disdain,

his mother, father, sister, brothers, lovers,
foes, mentors, friends, over millennia
of endeavour and failure, sin and grace.

Shivers slice through his spine. Sweat beads his skin.
Breath flutters to a long diminishing,
along with his body, till he is vision.

Zane watches his image move through events
of repercussions with each being, shown
through their viewpoint; how he used them to fathom

only his path of knowledge, a wild wind
seeking its spiral centre, battering
all centres outside its circumference.

He feels himself shatter into the gamut
of emotions he has provoked in others,
becomes the mirror itself and each scene,

as if a drop of rain in a storm-cloud,
the storm itself, the drop about to dimple
the skin of sea, break open to itself.

But then with strain, like bending tree to earth,
he reels in his filaments of mind, wrenches
himself from the darking mirror, and falls.

Zane awakes with his head in Jessie's lap.
The revelations drum incessantly
at his temples: pain wreaked on him, by him,

through him, and the rising fear that he is
destined to live the mirror for all time,
finding no way to break the wheel of life.

Though still groggy, Zane sits up, asks what happened.
Remesh offers his hand. 'You only looked
at the mirror a few seconds then fell.

'You've been unconscious a minute or so.
How did it affect you?' Zane rubs his cheek.
'It showed the repercussions of my actions.'

Jessie hands him his sack. 'What did you learn?'
His gaze at the slab is all the reply
she needs — doubt, burning fascination, awe.

She approaches the mirror, steels herself,
sees a pale figure that quickly divides
into many pale selves, all ages, sexes,

a parade of flesh-roles from gentleman
to temple harlot, each self drawing others
to the contamination of its life.

Like Zane, she suffers all that ever happened
from both sides. Like Zane, she begins to feel
the complicity of pain and release.

She merges with each event, with the mirror,
with the mirror's own image. Grief and laughter
take turns to remind her of fear and fate,

affiliation of lightning with earth,
a liberation path, the quickening
between silver and glass. Like Zane, she falls.

Jessie awakens to the taste of water.
The first thing she sees are Zane's eyes. They flicker
with the afterimages of her trial,

star-bursts and shot-streams and cataract-ripples,
and she sees completely past his blockades,
feels a vigour of affection link them,

knows the mirror has opened them, made them
too raw to counteract each other's rawness,
that emergence from dark into shared light.

Zane props her against a boulder and waits
for Remesh as he moves towards the mirror.
They see nothing but his image stretch out

its hand and touch his, an instant, and then
he steps away, mumbling about his God
again proving itself a disappointment.

6

Blood Seeds

Instantly, the drumming begins again
and the air about the mound hums. The mirror
swarms with dazzle-light and wild forms that change

into wizened female dancers who twirl
about a blazing cauldron, till exhaustion
spurs one then another to leap inside.

Breath and blood resonate deep within Jessie,
the urge to dance till her whole being soars
and yields to the benevolence of flame.

She turns to consider Zane and Remesh,
their outlines becoming distant to her,
like memory of day once sleep arrives.

Jessie steps closer to the mirror, feels
hands restraining her, peers at frantic eyes,
knows dimly that her time is still ahead.

She allows the men to absorb her weight
as they retreat towards the road. They watch
a stream of butterfly-winged maidens spiral

from the top of the mound and float towards
the stationary stars far above, voices
high and mellifluous, like summer birds.

As the music fades, Jessie shakes herself,
says nothing about what happened or why.
No one looks back as they resume their journey,

the distances between them filled with silence
and chains of will o' wisps their passage rouses
from the dust at the edges of the road.

When the wisps fade, Remesh approaches Jessie.
'Where did you meet Zane? In Ghajat, or here?'
She tells him of the gate and the strange city.

'He acts without hesitation,' he says.
Jessie sighs. 'And you act with revealed knowledge.'
Remesh taps her arm. 'And what of you, then?'

She doesn't know. This world has dream-sense only.
There is a road, companions of a sort,
the mystery of what is to be done.

Atop the next rise already, Zane urges
them to join him quickly. They rush to him,
the slope steeper than those before, and gape

at a plain filled with rows of stunted trees
poking through a miasma of stale light
that ripples as trees flicker, without wind.

As they descend, waves of putrescence threaten
a detour—senses and stomachs heave-reeling—
yet fade to minor nuisance at the bottom.

The trees are linked to the road by a network
of wavy crimson lines from base to verge.
Jessie realises each snaking trail

is blood seeping from entrails wrapped around
the limbs of each dead tree. She steps near one
and starts to sink, yet before Zane yanks her

back onto the firm road she hears a voice
much like her own, and thinks she sees a tree
blaze with incandescence and become bare

of flesh before sprouting leaves. When she looks
the tree, silver fir, is still dripping gore.
The afterimage dances before her.

Remesh and Zane stare at her. She is wearing
slacks and boots, tight sweater, large woollen jacket,
Zane's cloak folded on the road between them.

She tells them these are the usual clothes
she wears when bushwalking, that the encounter
with the tree somehow gave her a small grasp

of how thought can become true in this place.
'Just like a *makir* or Dremaan,' Zane comments,
explaining that those who perform the *murga*

are *makirs*, who by tradition are female,
while the Dremaan—especially the Kenri,
who is the dream sentinel of Ghajat—

is as far above the *makir* in skill
of making as the *makir* is above
the rock in skill of breathing. 'Maybe here

we all can be Dremaan, with skill and insight.'
He wonders, though, if his friends' newfound talents
will interfere with his uncertain quest.

He retrieves his cloak. 'Don't do that again.'
She dusts herself down, gestures to the trees.
'Surely this road is not only concerned

'with what lies at its end. What if we fail
to reach it? What if there is nothing there
and we dismiss the only chance for learning

'why we are here by always rushing there?'
Zane paces before her. 'We can't dismiss
our safety.' Remesh grabs him. 'We are dead,

'or still dying, and fading into nothing.
What does it matter what we do or say?'
Zane stares down at him. 'Believe what you will,

'but I have known this world longer than you.
Even if we are dead, I know there is
more than mere nothingness awaiting us.'

Remesh glowers. Zane does not flinch, but widens
his eyes into combat vision, soft focus
on all, lowers his breathing, primes strike-muscles.

Each settles their stance. Each waits for the other.
Each thinks of blows that hurt. Each barely knows
this preening has reasons other than faith.

Jessie starts to interpose, but a voice
subdues them all. 'You haven't changed, Zane. Always
the search for what cannot be found, unless

'you detach yourself from that urge to seek.'
For a moment they think no one is there,
that the road itself spoke, then the air sizzles

around them, body hair on end, hearts racing,
throats dry, extremities sparking, ears popping,
and a gold-skinned version of Zane steps through.

He is dressed in brown tunic, breeches, sandals.
He bows to Jessie. 'Who are you?' she whispers.
'I call myself Gedon, who was forgotten.

'His past. Future. Ideal. And none of these.'
Zane confronts him. 'And why are you here? Now?
I didn't summon you.' Gedon shrugs, smiles.

'Maybe I summoned you, and also them,
to do my bidding, which is always yours,
if you remember.' He laughs, and the road

crumples an instant. Remesh throws his arms
around in exasperation. 'What rubbish!
I was told death would be a simple task.

'There would be a reward for duty done.
But I was fooled. There never was a God,
though I was sure I felt him. Now this nothing.'

His face contorts with despair and confusion.
Jessie moves towards him. He backs away.
'Leave me alone. This is plainly illusion.'

He steps onto the verge and starts to sink.
Jessie and Zane rush to him, but are held
by Gedon's gaze. 'It is his wish. For now.'

By the time he sinks to his knees, the motion
has slowed, and then stops. He appears unsure.
'Now we can help,' Gedon says as he strides

towards the tree on the left side of Jessie's.
He grabs a coil of flesh, stretches it fine,
and wraps it around Remesh, who looks up

in surprise as eddies of blood ooze down
the intestine and slowly engulf him.
The birch tree emits a low-pitched hum, glows

more ruddy, more exuberant, like flame
from a furnace than from a dying candle.
It spreads to Remesh, who sinks to his groin,

though now his face registers puzzle-doubt.
Abruptly, he decides to extricate
himself, using the entrails as a lifeline.

Soon he lies panting on the road, no smears
of blood on him, tree draped with viscera.
'What happened?' Jessie says. He shakes his head.

Zane turns to his double. 'What do you know?'
Gedon wraps himself with another tree.
'I know what you know, and it doesn't help.'

The hazel bursts into a swelling rush
of light and heat. They are thrown to the ground.
When their sight clears, the tree is blood once more.

Jessie checks Remesh, who is shaking wildly
and refusing to talk, then turns to Zane.
'Why is Gedon like you? What does he mean?'

Head cocked, Zane stares at the trees. 'We should leave.'
Jessie helps Remesh to his feet. 'Why now?'
'Because we are never meant to stay long.'

Closing her eyes, she observes a cocoon
of contradictory whims—white affection,
black dread—undone by a serrated edge

of excitement and stupor, yet can't tell
if these feelings flourish inside or outside.
This new unease makes her agree with him.

As the group begins to walk, a breeze gathers
from both sides of the road and nudges them
from behind. Gone completely is the stench,

in its place the distillation of flowers.
They look back and, though the glow is still pale,
the trees are prouder, are wreathed in fine tendrils

that sway and lift within the breeze, then drop
their tips into the streams below, to drink
until they burst and spray the air with seed.

7

The Striking of Shadow

After a while the travellers traverse
a narrow pass that opens to a valley
with palm trees, red sand, thin pillars of rock,

some as high as nearby knolls, same brown colour
but smoother, as though polished by harsh winds
(though now there is no breeze) or by design:

the nearest pillar shows finely inscribed
whorls and circles that resolve into patterns
Remesh and Jessie recognise as phases

of the moon surrounding blank and dark suns.
Other columns have many moons and suns,
or none, different intervals for eclipses.

The pillars are scattered like termite mounds,
hundreds of them, though there is a large clearing
around the central one, which has no pattern

except for seven bands of incised shading,
each of different texture, though equal height.
At its summit is a crystal globe that,

from time to time, fires silent chains of lightning
into other pillars, which hum as one
and shoot flames of iridescent force skyward.

The first time this happens, Zane sees a hole
appear in the third band, shift sideways upwards,
then disappear when the lightning chains fade.

He wonders what will occur when the hole
reaches the summit. Will the globe explode
or will the hole reappear at the base?

An impulse for wild ruin grips him now,
quickening his breath, flush-tensing his body,
battle-cry threatening to burst his chest.

With an effort he controls himself, hopes
no one has noticed his excitement, joins
Remesh and Jessie as they leave this pillar.

After more displays of lightning and flame,
with no clear sign of change to world or sense,
except a subtle shifting of star pattern

or the brief flaring of a star, the group
decides to move on. As they leave the valley,
Zane looks back, sees the pillar shoot a beam

towards them. It strikes him and splits in two,
the strands of lightning whipping about him,
two hissing snakes that then collide within.

The attack is so swift no one else sees it,
and Zane doubts the event, for as the strands
danced around him, he felt no sting of power,

no burning sensations, nothing but ice
at the core of his being, the strands nothing
but fate honouring his ardent song-spark.

A few yards from the valley their ears pop,
skin tingles, nape hairs bristle, air sting-sizzles.
The road in front bulges upward, thins, splits,

stretches horizontally, forms loops, curls,
tresses, shapes itself an enormous tree
through which the road now travels, as if always.

Then starts a muffled hammering, with sparks
showering the road from one side, each spark
splitting into two again and again

before vanishing with crack-wisps of colour.
Peering into the hollow of the tree
Jessie sees the back of a thickset man

working an anvil, short tongs in left hand
holding something against the massive anvil,
right arm lift-dropping a double-head hammer,

corded muscles flexing with double beats.
As he limps without discomfort towards
his deep water trough, the thing he is grasping

seems itself made of the heat waves and steam
that quickly fill the hollow on the plunge.
Looking up, he beckons her and the others

to wait. They watch him inspect his creation,
the wafer-thin object held to forge-light,
smile in satisfaction, wrap it in felt.

He waves them to the hollow opposite,
joins them after cleaning off sweat and grime.
He puts the parcel on an oval table

grown instantly from the floor as he entered
and looks at Zane. 'So, you have come again,
but not to ask me to repair your weapon.'

Zane stares at him. 'What weapon? Who are you?'
The smithy chuckles. 'Your means of salvation,
though only you can do that, when all dies.'

Jessie can't contain herself any longer.
'I'm sick of riddles. Tell us who you are.'
The blacksmith bows. 'My apologies, daughter.

'My name is Dukor, husband-son of Neshxi,
whom Zane has met many times, many guises,
as have you all. Some may think me a god,

'but I am merely a worker of worlds,
a Dremaan, as we all are at some point
during this long homecoming into wisdom.'

Still with a scowl, Jessie steps up to him.
'I am not your daughter. Nor anybody's
now I am dead, as everyone is here.'

Dukor rubs his beard. 'Again, I am sorry.
I called you that because in many ways
the worlds in Thexlan form one birth, one song,

'and I, like all Dremaans, parent and midwife.'
He peers at her from under bristle-eyebrows.
'As for your states of death, forget them here.

'Nothing is as it seems, as with the life
you led before appearing here. Death enters
through those moments you don't attend to life.'

'Then we aren't dead,' Remesh says with relief,
'and this is some foul dream or fantasy.'
Knowing such queries only last forever

Dukor does not answer, but leads them through
a door that was a mere pattern of grain
into a smaller chamber of the tree

lit only by chinks high above their heads.
Mounted at eye-level around the wall
is a collection of large, white, round objects.

As eyes adjust to gloom, they see each plate
is a slowly swirling vapour contained
within a thin border of whorling flame.

'I have seen such frames before,' Zane observes,
'but showing scenes of impossible realms.'
Dukor nods. 'This is my art, to make *Turma*,

'canvases that act as maps and as doorways,
as containers for memories and dreams,
as triggers for things forgotten or lost.

'Many are called to pay the price, but none
can predict what will appear when the work
is breathed upon, or how this will affect

'its owner. And no one can rid themselves
of their *Turma* once bought.' Remesh averts
his eyes from the one he is studying.

'No need to worry,' Dukor adds. 'No picture
will form until you buy it.' 'And the price?'
Remesh says as he returns to his study.

'No more than you can pay, only the breath
that compels a true picture, and the life
you lead once you discover such true breath.'

Zane trails his index finger through the middle
of one disk, watches the milky-white substance,
more like thickened smoke than layers of oil,

follow his motion, creep along his finger,
and slowly start to drag it to the centre,
before discarding it as something foreign.

The finger emerges clean. 'Who or what
decides the breath is true?' The blacksmith smiles.
'That's the secret of my art, as of all.

'But now you might find an answer yourself.'
He fetches the new *Turma*, unwraps it.
'Those on the wall are for one. This, for three.'

Though slightly bigger than his other works,
this one retains the rim of fire, the white
smoky canvas, thin when looked at edge-wise,

of great depth and suggestion when held up
to any light and looked at far too long,
as when staring at one's eyes, nose to mirror.

Jessie folds the felt cloth and turns away
from the whispered summoning of their *Turma*.
'But none of us asked for one of these things.'

Dukor shrugs. 'I was inspired to create
one like this. Now the three of you are here.
Call it fate, if you like, but this is yours.'

He places the artefact on a ledge
that first appeared when he unwrapped the *Turma*.
Zane, Jessie, Remesh reach for it as one,

instinctively taking hold of the rim
with left hands equidistant. They peer into
the swirling depths and, as one, breathe a sigh.

The vigorous motion snap-stills, as though
contemplating the flavour of their breath,
then fractures soundlessly into minute

globules that change colour, that fly within
the fiery frame, that fuse with one another,
flatten, stretch, break and recombine again,

weave themselves into a picture unlike
anything they have ever seen, not even
Zane's sand paintings: a deep landscape of mist,

and rocky outcrops shaped like ragged profiles
of feathered and long-snouted beasts. They hear
the high whistle of wind or bird, the piping

of frogs. They watch a bubble push aside
the scum atop a nearby pool, and gag
when it bursts with a strong whiff of decay.

Wrenching her sight from the scene, Jessie turns
to the blacksmith. 'What is this place?' He shrugs.
'The vision is true to all of you. Maybe

'it represents your common past or future,
maybe a symbol of your common soul.
I make the canvas; you reveal the image.'

She returns to the picture, feels herself
lured in so far she hears a rustle-cracking
of brush behind her, large creature advancing

slowly towards her without haste or stealth.
She spins around, is back in Dukor's chamber,
the others as puzzled and awed as she.

Swarthy face tinged by white, Remesh asks her,
'Besides the mist and rocks, what did you see?'
'Nothing, just a sound' she replies, then looks

at the two men. 'What about you? Sounds? Smells?'
Remesh: 'A cylindrical mass of flies
opening its maw to discharge jewel streams.'

Zane: 'The fright-marvel of my sliding into
a pool of viscous liquid that melts flesh,
then becomes that pool again, without motion.'

Intrigue slants his gaze. 'What's wrong?' Jessie says.
'I remember the day my brothers gained
their boat rights. In celebration and homage

'to Haal, the ancient goddess of the lake,
our father took us to a quiet cove.
I was young and wanted only to play

'amongst the rushes and the trees, or climb
around the headland to find what was there.
My father warned me not to go too far

'but I ignored him, as I did the counsel
of the *Forii*, our ancestral rule-voices.
I found a narrow pool, began to jump

'from one rock to another with the poise
and speed of mighty fighters in the midst
of battle, like those in my mother's stories.

'I slipped and fell much deeper than I thought
a pool on the lake shore could be. I struggled
against tentacles of water and worse

'snatching at my limbs. The flickering surface
dwindled, air bubbles shrank from me, in me.
I thrashed once more, then felt my body hush.

'Before my sight completely dimmed, I saw
a haloed face, dark eyes splintered with fire,
playful cat-gaze, with hint of venom swiftness.

'I awoke on the beach to laughter-scorn.
My father and brothers claimed I cried out
Help as I slid under, and always after

'would chide me when I chose my mother's lessons
before the manly arts of lake and boat,
but I was sure I had called out to Haal.'

He turns to Dukor. 'Maybe these are nothing
but scenes of past troubles, reminding us
of what we hate about ourselves or others.'

Dukor passes a hand across the *Turma*.
'As I said, each shows meaning for its owner.
I suggest you look for a common truth.'

Remesh raps his knuckles against the doorway.
'Zane's childhood adventures are not like mine.
I don't recall anything from my life

'about flies and jewels. Besides, truth is mist,
here, as elsewhere. We have nothing in common.'
As he walks away, Jessie grabs his arm.

'Except having to walk this road. Let's take
the *Turma* and discuss the visions later.
Nothing is by chance, even if bizarre.'

Zane joins them. 'Besides, we have to keep going.'
Remesh nods, and for a short while consensus
softens the taut air that had filled the chamber.

Suddenly, Dukor choke-gasps with amazement.
Turning, they see him dwarfed by a thick pillar
of revolving smoke growing from the *Turma*,

a clicking roar like millions of wrath-hornets.
The pillar bends and widens towards them,
but Zane dodges it, grabs the glowing frame,

and dashes it against the wall again
and again as the column lashes out
like a maddened serpent. The *Turma* bends,

the creature stiffens. One last slam against
the wood and the *Turma* shatters. The pillar
shriek-rears like a thunder-head filled with lightning

then collapses into a stinking vapour
that forces everyone onto the road.
The cloud drifts skyward, slowly dissipates.

'Nothing like this has happened to my work,'
Dukor says. He looks at them with suspicion,
whistles a triple command to the air,

and returns to his vast smithy, which starts
to shrink and slowly fold back into silence
until there is nothing but the grey road.

For a long while they continue to stare
and wonder if they had imagined all,
but for the broken *Turma* in Zane's hand.

8

The Story Game

Jessie says, 'What now?' Zane places the frame
inside his sack and points to where they see
Mt Alkerii, finger-thin in the distance.

'With the *Turma* destroyed, there's nothing more
to discover here. Let's continue on
and worry about any visions later.'

As they walk, the landscape in a brown haze,
with sound of wind running through crevices,
Jessie ponders the lack of sun, drops back

to ask Remesh what he knows. 'I presume
this land of the dead is without the light
of salvation,' he says with a tight smile.

She is not sure if he is serious
or is baiting her. She looks straight ahead,
her voice even. 'What religion are you?'

Remesh looks skyward for some seconds, sighs.
'I once belonged to the Monady Church.'
Her stomach quivers, though there seems no reason.

'I've never heard of it,' she says. He laughs.
'Likely because we are of different times.
Or else different universes, if tales

'of parallel worlds are true, which I doubt.
There is only one world, one God, one way
to rejoin God, one Heaven. So I thought.'

'What way?' She shakes a little with recall
of her father's prayers, messianic glare.
'By helping those who believe in the many

'to find the right way themselves.' Her breath cramps
a little. 'How?' He also stares ahead.
'By any means, which is why I am here.'

Before Jessie can ask him to explain,
Zane joins them, whispers caution. He points out
how a few stars are now starting to wander.

'In Ghajat, the stars only move at night,
and here they seem to act with the same law.
We'd better find shelter, or fear attack.'

Taking some grains from his song-bag, he whispers
a spell of finding and tosses them high.
They swirl into incandescence, then point

towards the hollow of a nearby hill,
before fading and dropping to the ground.
Zane starts to move there, but Jessie stops him:

'So much for caution.' 'We have no choice now,'
he replies, steps off the verge, turns around,
spreads his arms, a sure conceit: 'See, no danger.'

Remesh joins him, and they stride around tussocks
of white, five-petalled flowers on long stalks.
Picking one up Jessie stifles a shriek

as the face at its centre winks at her.
Abruptly, the eye detaches itself
and is borne away by the wind, to join

those other tiny insects gathering
nectar from inner sanctums of the flowers.
Laughing, she follows the men up the hill.

Their shelter is a hut of broken boards
and thatched leaves, just sufficient to keep out
the biting gusts that come with rapid night.

Within the vortices of the wind, Jessie
can hear voices summoning her—the dead,
the misplaced in heart and soul, the forgotten,

those who would call her to a type of death.
She knows, now, that in Thexlan she can't follow
their bright tumult until she knows what follows.

After marking protection signs at door
and window, Zane throws wood on a fireplace
that looks like it has been used every night

for a million years, so deep are the ashes,
their texture like Zane's *murga* grains, their colour
the road's charcoal grey. Maybe all of Thexlan

lies in a vast hearth, and their passage through
just the breeze flicking cinders to complete
their service of breath to the hearth's creator.

Jessie envisages worlds nesting worlds,
but draws little relief from the idea
as wind jostles wall and ceiling for access.

'What is so dangerous out there?' she says
as Zane puts away his fire kit and sits,
lifting palms to the flames inches away,

a faint bewilderment filling his features.
'As I've said, star-demons come down to kill.'
'That's just fear-fantasy,' Remesh replies.

'The stars are furnaces of light and matter.
Nothing exists but what we can touch, measure.'
Zane passes his hands through the fire and smirks.

'Maybe in your world. Not Ghajat or Thexlan,
though I suspect all worlds have the same root.'
Remesh grunts and moves away. Jessie follows:

'How do you explain Rynobar?' He stops.
'Who?' 'One of the two *hoya* we encountered
when we found you. Maybe they were both trying

'to kill you.' He shakes his head. 'If I'm dead
how can they do anything?' Jessie shrugs.
'Maybe they need souls for their furnaces.'

Zane speaks from his seat. 'Maybe they are souls
looking for bodies to possess. I'm sure
Rynobar has proposed such an idea.'

Jessie leaves Remesh to consider this
and sees Zane playing with the flames again.
She sits on a log beside him. 'What's wrong?'

'At the mound and elsewhere I have felt cold
and heat. Here, the flames give light but no heat.
It seems Thexlan is nothing like Ghajat.'

Remesh grins. 'This is the realm of the dead.
You encounter only what you bring in.
Maybe there is no fire in you. Not ever.'

Zane rushes and subdues the plump man quickly,
drags him to the flames. 'Maybe I have more
fire than I need. What about you, Remesh?

'What did you bring, leave behind, never have?
We don't know you.' He grabs a burning brand,
thrusts it towards his face. 'Does this help you?'

Jessie knocks it away, though the blow hurts.
The men move apart. Remesh rubs his face,
takes up a position across the fire.

Zane notices Jessie nursing her hand.
'Let me look.' She glares at him and returns
to her seat. 'Leave me alone. Both of you.'

As the wind dies down footsteps sound outside
the barred front door. There is a single knock.
Zane conjures a staff from a heavy bough.

The second knock rattles the door and frame.
'We are already dead,' Remesh insists,
'so no *hoya* can harm us. Let it in.'

A voice they recognise as Gedon's issues
from beyond the door, and the air gild-shimmers.
'Yes, let me in. You know I can't hurt you.'

Zane refreshes his warding spells. 'You sound
like me, but *hoya* are cunning. Leave now
and feast on less suspecting travellers.'

For an answer, gold slivers of light flare
through the door and Gedon appears, all scowl
and crossed arms. 'How hospitable of you.'

As he moves to a seat, Zane accosts him.
'Why are you plaguing us? Who are you, really?'
Gedon leans back. 'Just a seeker, like you.

'I am you. Or else an imagined you.'
Jessie sits near him. 'Imagined by whom?'
Gedon raises his left eyebrow. 'Good question.'

He takes her injured hand. 'But you are hurt.'
She senses warm assurance in his touch.
He closes his eyes, slows his breathing, passes

one hand back and forth above the bruise, stops.
She feels the flesh tingle, watches it blister
frenetically for a second then hiss,

then wrinkle back into pale skin, marked only
by a pink outline that steadily fades.
'Thank you, Gedon.' She touches the raw skin.

'You said you were forgotten. Why? By whom?'
Gedon considers Zane. 'Another time.
Besides, it is as good a name as any.'

Jessie flexes her hand. 'So what are you?
A god, demon, Dremaan, or something dreamed
by all of us as wishful interlude?'

'I'm not sure if there is a difference.'
He pokes the fire. 'All we can know is this.'
Remesh shuffles in his seat. 'What of God?'

Zane nods vigorously. 'There's always more.
I want to know the why, the how of being,
of meaning. Else existence is a waste.'

Gedon rolls his eyes. 'Always the same quest,
though you never mention the other one,
both hopeless as a sword cutting itself.'

Zane's eyes fill with fresh rage and for a moment
the twin beings lock wills like two great beasts
over territory. Breath and thought teeter,

till Zane laughs, Gedon nods, tension snap-fades.
Jessie and Remesh exchange puzzled looks,
and the room settles into awkward silence.

Turning her body away, Jessie takes
the rainbow gem from its pouch, which had stayed
on her person when her clothes changed. Its highlights

still move mysteriously, but one facet
shows a tree with ten stars in its bare branches,
another, strange maze shapes. She returns it,

takes a quick look around the rundown room,
rummages through dusty shelves, broken cupboards.
Remesh walks over to her, questions her,

tells her the dead do not need any food.
'I feel hunger,' she says. 'So I'm not dead.'
Gedon joins them. 'The habit of your life.

'Still, even here such addictions have power.'
A mist appears in the room, slowly forms
into a servant wearing ruffles, gloves,

standing before a sumptuous banquet table.
Remesh pats his belly, but makes no move
to join the feast. Gedon accepts a drink,

sniffs its bouquet, rolls eyes in mock regret.
'What you eat here you have only brought forth
with your mind, which may not even be yours.'

Zane whirls on him. 'My mind is always mine.'
Gedon turns one palm outwards. 'You are here
because you deny such knowledge and being.'

Jessie tosses aside the tasteless fare,
watches the feast and servant disappear.
'How do we attain such wisdom? With thought?'

'Ask him.' Gedon points to Zane. 'He knew once.'
Zane throws a branch on the fire and sparks shower
all around them. 'As always, you talk nonsense.'

Gedon points to a spark floating in circles.
'Wisdom is not accumulation, but
an unburdening, which is easier

'when you follow that song-spark deep within.
You gave me that, but have forsaken it,
and soon will drag us all into disaster.'

Everyone stares into the flames that jump
and tumble-dance as wind rattles the hut.
The burning wood emits a smell like myrrh.

Jessie bangs two logs together and smiles.
'I propose a game, since no one is tired
and sleep doesn't seem to be needed here.

'It's called *Fable, Lie or Life*, and is simple.
One of us tells a story and the rest
choose if it is unreal, or made from life,

'or something else.' 'What do you mean?' Zane says.
She looks at them over her steepled fingers.
'A story can come from that total tale

'governing all life. Not real to one life,
not false to all. Difficult to do well,
if at all.' Zane leans forward. 'And who wins?'

'The speaker, if the listeners are wrong.
The listeners, when they make the right choice.
With Gedon as judge if we can't agree.'

Zane hunches near the fire so that flames flicker
across his face like hieroglyphs, coughs once,
stretches his neck, then begins in a whisper.

9

Zane's Story

'I was born on the shores of Lake Tarlkarni.
My father was a fisher—and my brothers,
who were nine years older than I—all strong

'in those ancestral voices that guide us.
The *Forii* were never that strong in me,
and my dreams my own. My mother saw this.

'Here, as elsewhere in Ghajat, women sang.
Before dawn, my mother would sprinkle sand
on a cloth, hum a tune of conjuring,

'and the day would bring whatever she sought.
All women were *makir*, but as no girls
were born to us, I was trained in this skill.

'A storm took my father when I was eight.
Some of the villagers saw this as doom
for my mother breaking *makir* tradition.

'They did not shun us, for men often died
on that lake near the mist-edge of the world,
but they were wary. Then, after a year,

'my sister was born. Dimples. Tight blond ringlets
like my father's. Green eyes, not seen in Tarlkar
before then. Olive skin, lighter than mine.

'We named her Kerrilea, the bright joy,
though the others cursed her as *hoya*-spawn,
as if strange births were unlike *murga* gifts.

'At Kerrilea's fifth birthday, my mother
would have started training her, as is lore,
and I would have returned to fisher ways.

'But weeks before, my mother made a garland
of rocks and the ancient lake swallowed her.
I wept to see her, arms outstretched, head high.

'She couldn't hear me because she was singing
to someone in the lake's star-phosphorescence,
someone who was keening for her. My father.

'Lake Tarlkarni forms the edge of Ghajat.
Above that edge is Aimal, Shultar's home,
of groping shadows, crashing, shrieking blasts,

'like cautions told to children before sleep.
Shultar is a Dremaan and, as the mistress
of our lake and land, would demand tribute,

'eight barrels of *sorra*, a purple plant
that grows at the lake's bottom. Failure meant
the casting of lots to see who would die.'

Zane takes a deep breath, stares into the fire.
'My mother was chosen that year. Not chance,
but the terror-reprisals of our neighbours.

'They hated her because they thought a *hoya*
came to her soon after my father's death,
thought Kerrilea a demon who planned

to destroy all those things we love and do.
My mother went willingly. Chose her death.
To save us. To see my father again.

'Two years later the tribute failed again.
Shultar asked for Kerrilea. My brothers
held me back while the headman lit the fire—

'the drawing of lots, the ancestral voices,
never wrong. Her screams haunt me every night.
Her imploring eyes I see every day.'

Once more he pauses, gaze fixed to the flames,
then rubs his eyes, throws back his head, and stretches,
and all know this pause has become an ending.

Remesh claps softly. 'Very entertaining.
Very skilful. But too many misfortunes
to tug at our emotions. I vote *Lie*.

'But what of his distress?' Jessie replies.
'The story feels true, though I can see how
the tragedies seem like they've been contrived.'

Remesh demurs. 'The sadness may be real,
but it is a clever weave of emotion
to deflect our focus from his inventions.'

Zane stands. 'Though the events are from my life,
both of you may be right, in an odd way.'
'What do you mean?' Jessie moves towards him.

'Thexlan is womb and home to dreams, to stories.
I may be a tale myself, a sand painting
woven into words someone tells another.'

Remesh lets out a bellow and then slaps
Zane on the back. 'I might believe your tale
was *Life*, if I accepted Jessie's instincts,

'but your last comments show a skilful jest.
So, a false story. Do you agree, judge?'
Gedon blinks, his mind wrestling with Zane's musings.

'All stories have pleasure, once you unravel
the spirit inside. But I cannot judge
upon this tale till Jessie casts her vote.'

She frowns. 'I believe Zane has told a truth,
yet whether it is history or fable,
his life or essence of all lives…who knows?'

Gedon glances at Zane. 'Because I know
a little of his path, I will judge *Life*,
though others would say *Fable*. Jessie's next.'

10

Jessie's Tale

Jessie looks at each in turn. 'I'm not good
at making up stories. That's why I read
the past and stories that help me forget.'

She sighs, closes her eyes. Her breathing slows.
She rolls her shoulders twice, as though uncoiling
from herself. Eyes flash open, firelight-glitter.

'Around the globe called home is endless space
traversed by ships transporting sleeping pilgrims
who do not breathe. Their focussed dreaming pauses

'the universe-weave, cleaves the emptiness
of vast reach, drops itself through, then reknots
the arc of crossing closer to its goal.

'When a ship touches earth again, its people
awaken from their single dream, unload
seed and beast, channel water, build stockades

'against those hordes who come to repossess
what was conquered. Soon, towns and roads begin
to leach the land of sustenance, of title.

'The pilgrims infest their world, wrestle-war
for wealth they can carry, eat or display,
wreck the elements till nothing remains

'but the ribs of their vessels and the stench
of despair. Others arrive, quickly leave.
Nothing remains. Maybe a beetle rolls

'ripe dung across the land until it reaches
the size of a world.' She sighs. 'Maybe not.'
Jessie smiles at each of them, then leans back.

Gedon nods approval, but not so Zane.
'There is nothing beyond Ghajat but mist,
as here in Thexlan.' 'Not true,' says Remesh.

'In my time craft strive to reach other worlds,
though not in the manner Jessie describes.'
Zane shakes with incredulity. 'And why

'would people destroy the world that feeds them?'
Remesh shifts around, the thought of such greed
reverberating deep-dark within him.

Zane continues. 'Such a race deserves death,
though not the worlds they conquer.' Jessie clasps
her hands. 'My wish too.' Zane narrows his gaze,

wonders if her claim to lack story skill
is a clever ploy to off-balance them
in this game that feels deeper than amusement.

As his admiration steepens, he knows
such cunning tactics call for equal guile.
'As I think about your tale, I recall

'a vision from my distant past of worlds
in mist-swirl formation. Yet I vote *Lie*,
for the story seems a life not yet lived.'

Jessie looks askance at him, but says nothing.
'While this time my vote is *Life*,' Remesh says.
'The storyteller wins again. My turn.'

11

Remesh's Account

'There is a tree with bitter yellow fruit.
There is a man who mourns his lover's death.
There is a god who does not wish to live.

'The man begs his god to retrieve the soul
of his lover. The god agrees, but only
if the man brings him the fruit of that tree.

'The man journeys far, but all those he questions
deny knowledge of the tree. His hope withers
till he meets a dishevelled mage who knows

'how to reach the tree, to be revealed only
for a share of the fruit. The man agrees.
Given a small boat, he is told to sail

'where the horizon folds over itself,
to find an isle of magnificent birds
who will try to stop him taking the fruit,

'for they feed on it. To attend the man,
the mage sends his familiar, a fiery
baboon that speaks in riddles. The man sails.

'At first he must sway the wind to bear him
on the right course. The wind agrees, but only
if the man cremates himself above ground

'when he dies, which may happen any time.
Soon the craft skims the waves faster than birds,
faster even than the bending of rainbows.

'A sun-moon cycle later the man senses
the world drop, and the sea surges a wave
that lifts him far above the tracks of clouds.

'When the boat teeters on the edge, he sees
the island just above him. The wave lurches,
but the wind ferries his craft to the beach.

'Watched constantly by the baboon, its talk
of ghosts in flesh, of demons in disguise,
of maps that only lead to fading maps,

'the man enters the dank and fertile jungle.
All about him are the frenetic cries
and whoops of unseen beasts that even quieten

'his riddling companion. He battles through
dense foliage and rank aromas, tripping
on roots, falling into holes filled with feathers

'and dead leaves, ignoring always the sounds
that seem to say, "Go back, ruin draws you.
Go back, your soul is at risk. Go back, now."

'He spurns phantasmagorias of shapes
and fetid pools, grotesque camellias,
noxious orchids, the zigzagging escarpments,

'and stumbles into a clearing, the ground
littered with shards of gleaming rib and skull,
skeletal hands not always with five fingers.

'The man pants for a long time, hands on knees,
head barely raised. Before him is a presence
like a mountain forest suspended from

'a giant earth pole trailing knotted cables,
a monstrous apparition of a tree
with lily-white flowers and immense clusters

'of yellow globular fruit, spectral sheen.
Around the tree, flocks of rainbow-flecked birds
with long gossamer tails wheel in wide spirals

'before returning to its laden branches
to eat more of the fruit, then quickly launch
once more in rapid cataracts of colour.

'Each time the birds pass near him, their wings flash
keen prisms into his eyes, fixing him
with their brilliance. The baboon's sudden chatter

'jolts him out of his reveries. He straightens,
takes out the brooch his lost beloved gave
with the words, "I will always be near you,

'a halo of scent till we are pure scent."
The birds roost again and watch him approach.
As he stretches out to pluck the first fruit

'he can reach, he hears his beloved's voice.
"Please, my sweet, let me rest among the dead.
You will see me soon. But if you continue,

' "our fate will be to never see each other."
Recalling the wizard's words, he ignores
the voice, plucks three fruits, one for the god, one

'for the mage, and one for himself—he needs
to know the truth. The tree shudders each time
and its birds let loose shrieks that fray the air

'and dull the shine and colour of its fruit.
With their third cry, they surge upwards like flames
in a forest exploding with wild fire

'and disappear into the too-hushed jungle.
Nothing moves as the man bites the first fruit.
The pulp is fine, but the juice is so acrid

'it burns tongue and throat. The man gags but, frantic
to know the tree's secret, he bites again.
Nothing happens. He closes his eyes, summons

'the face of his beloved. Again, nothing.
He tosses away the core and returns
to the beach the way he came. He sails back

'to where he set out, gives the second fruit
to the wizard, who allows him to watch
the ritual: he splits the fruit in two,

'takes out the kernel, pounds it in his pestle,
pours in the juice, cuts his left palm, lets fall
three drops of blood. The brew hisses and bubbles.

'He pours it into a goblet, drinks half,
gives the rest to his pet, who has not spoken
ever since the birds vanished. Nothing happens

'till the familiar begins to chant
a formula in an unknown tongue, while
the mage dances about it widdershins.

'The more emaciated he becomes,
the more the animal acquires the shape
and stance of a human, then beyond-human,

'its features swelling, its body and limbs
thickening and lengthening, like a god,
and in one stride it disappears from sight,

'the wizard now a flimsy sheet of skin
dissolving into dust scattered by light.
After more years of travel and travail,

'he returns to the temple of his god,
near the edge of a chasm. Noxious fumes
rise from beneath, swirl about the huge columns.

'The man steps over the threshold and calls
for the god. "Neti, Neti." Vapours merge
into a massive statue, which consumes

'the proffered fruit whole, attains flesh and breath,
then contracts to human size. The man says,
"What of my beloved?" "Soon," Neti says,

'settling into a cross-legged position
on the temple floor and remaining silent.
When the building judders with sudden thunder,

'Neti smiles at the giant shape approaching.
Now wearing the mage's anger-wrought features,
the god-like baboon towers over them.

'For the wizard had also lost a lover,
had made the same pact. Neti ate the fruit
to become a god but refused to pay.

'The wizard strikes the god and the stone temple
crumbles into the chasm. The man plummets
and feels the fumes ravage his flesh and spirit,

'soon finds himself clothed in feathers, and eating
the yellow fruit of the tree. Other souls
surround him, including the contrite god,

'but nowhere can he discern his beloved,
not in the jewelled eyes of the other birds,
not in the bilious taste of the fruit.'

For a long time the listeners are stunned,
then Jessie speaks. 'The story makes no sense.
What happened to the beloved? And why

'did the god lie? I find the story mean.'
Remesh stands and puts more fuel on the fire.
'Life's like that. Not all tales have happy endings.'

'Whether true or not,' she says, 'I feel cheated.
The man did what he was asked, yet was robbed
of his reward.' Zane calms her. 'But did he?

'No one told him to eat the fruit first. Maybe
it was a drug. Maybe he is still there,
a statue holding a half-eaten fruit,

'the baboon panic-chattering in riddles,
his beloved hovering about him,
imploring him to wake up. I like it.'

Remesh grins. 'And your vote?' They both decide
on *Lie*, while Gedon judges it a mix
of *Lie* and *Fable*. Remesh claps his win.

Gedon stands. 'The night is soon ending, time
to take up our own humble tale. I hope
the road ahead will grant us what we seek.'

He opens the door, smiles, and moments later melts to auric-sheen light that flows so swiftly clouds of dust motes stream-melt into his wake.

12

Murga Flight

Jessie sees Zane put both hands to the ground,
dig fingers into earth, close his eyes, listen.
'*Glymsen* is coming.' He takes out his knife

and song-bag, sweeps the ground clear, draws a circle.
Remesh taps him on the arm. 'What will you
request in this *murga*, another map?'

'Speed and ease of travel. Maybe some answers.'
Remesh points to the world outside the hut.
'Since thought is so strong here, why can't you open

'a direct path from here to Mt Alkerii?'
Zane glances at Remesh, ponders a moment,
then nods his head. 'It might be possible,

'though I'm not sure such a thing has been done.'
He closes his eyes, thinks through all his lessons.
'Both of you will have to help.' He gives them

some grains, sits them around the circle, tells
them to form a clear picture in their minds
of the mountain seen in the *murga* map.

He tunes his lyre. Then, as they sprinkle grains,
he starts playing, instrument and voice spinning
a plea-chant that fills the room with warm mist.

The *murga* grains waver, refuse to gel
into a constant picture, whirl through colours
like all seasons in an instant, then lift

from the ground and speed-swirl into the mist.
Jessie struggles to hold the mountain image
as the mist jostles her and the heat rises.

She feels the floor drop, then vanish completely,
knows herself part of the spinning mist, sees
the *murga* itself open into space,

in which appears a tiny shard of darkness
that rapidly grows, and she realises
they are speeding towards their summoned goal.

Her smile falters as the mist shudder-shifts.
The music lurches, strives to regain tempo,
is cuffed again. The mist ruptures. They fall.

Jessie sees a woman in a bed, wrists
bandaged, older woman holding one hand
and crying, someone else chanting in shadow.

Zane sees a man wearing a robe of suns
hand a small crystal to a pregnant woman,
sees a flower burst out of a blaze-tree.

Remesh sees a woman gather a mob
of children into a small room and sit
singing songs with them as the flames draw near...

After picking themselves up from the ground
they survey their surroundings: no dawn yet,
which means the danger still of *hoya*, or

whatever else interfered with their spell.
They have landed someway along the road,
which here is smothered by thick, motley creepers

and bent-over tall reeds, dense foliage
beyond these on both sides, striated dark
quivering, now becoming still. The stench

of a bone factory, maggots in marrow.
Suddenly, a roar like a million frogs
judders the air, the reeds, the leaves, the road,

draws all into a giant murky membrane
that towers over the group. The rank shape—
world-skin scrunched into a giant fist—trembles,

shreds itself to a rain of haggard creatures
armed with spears, then bamboo shafts spouting poison,
then cross-curved knives that make a whistling sound.

Zane shoves Remesh and Jessie behind him
and surrounds them with a high barricade
of flame that repels creatures who approach,

but does not prevent them from hurling missiles.
He conjures a wooden staff to deflect
the attacks, is stunned to see Jessie standing

with him, using twin fighting sticks to knock
missiles away. She shows great skill and speed,
but there are too many for both of them.

One hits her left temple. The sight of her
spinning from the blow and hitting the ground
so maddens Zane he summons all his will

and fans the flames into a raging vortex
that surges with such speed towards the creatures
they cannot evade their doom. Moments later

there are only slivers of vegetation
on the verge of the road and smouldering
shadows where their strange attackers once stood.

Though there are no ill effects from the blow,
Jessie lets Zane inspect the wound. She finds
the touch of his long fingers strangely soothing

as he cleans the wound, presses the skin flaps
together, applies a salve, and sing-whispers
a healing heat, the precision and flair

of a master craftsman in a bazaar
while a buyer watches the handiwork.
She lets herself relax and, as eyes close,

hears her mother calling her to get ready
for church. She doesn't want to go—no one
else to talk to, nothing to do but listen

to the minister's drone in the hot-cramp
wooden chapel with glory-windows shut,
or those screech-sermons that make her sit up

and shake, knowing her father will test her—
but if she doesn't go, another sin,
her father will use the strap, or do worse.

Her eyes snap open with fear as she thinks
her father is before her with a gag
to stop her screaming, then discovers Zane

holding the cloth he used to dab her wound.
She smiles her thanks and slowly finds her feet.
To his question about her martial skills

she explains a childhood friend taught her moves
and technique drills during the games they played,
though she hadn't thought about them for years.

As for the conjuring of her twin sticks,
she merely thought of them and they appeared.
A smile flickers on Zane's face as he listens.

They only move a few yards down the road
when they feel tiny tremors ebb and flow
through their soles. A stronger series rocks them

and they look up to see a mist-plume spurting
high in the distance to touch stars. It thickens
in the middle, flattens to a wave-ring

racing across the land and ruffling all.
When the wave passes overhead, the land
buckles and tilts, their senses prickle-hum.

After recovering they see the glow
at the horizon is yellow with green,
and a little higher than their first day,

notice too the dancing stars are still moving
ever so slightly, and know this to mean
increased danger from *hoya*. As they walk

two ravens appear from nowhere, dip-sway
in front of them, rock wings as they ascend
to a high branch and watch them, all in silence.

13

Of Crooked Signs

The road travels through lightly wooded fields,
with tiny birds flitting through the trees, or
wheeling above them in great swathes, their circles

of flight dictated by instinct of flock
not leader, single wing beat, bank and soar.
In the distance is the curve of low hills

that are tinged with saffron, like prostrate monks.
Zane sniffs the air. 'There's a faint whiff of salt.
A sea, though it must still be some way off.'

He sees Jessie sniff and scowl. 'What is wrong?'
'The seaside means sun, but my lack of pigment
meant I could never enjoy it. I wanted

'to swim, to be like other girls and boys,
but fun was not my father's faith.' Except,
she almost adds, when she was very young

and he used to make finger-people vanish
then return again, to her glee. 'Because
I feared the sun, the forest was my haven.

'The smell of leaf and fresh earth. The way light
and breeze shapes the soft spaces between leaves
and branches, never the same shadow play.

'Leaf to bough to space, my gaze leapt and paused.
Hours later Father would summon me.
Always I would get home two minutes late.'

'What was your father's faith?' Zane asks. 'A rigid
belief in holy book and pain,' she says,
'though the book only came when I was older.

'If I dared ask questions to point out flaws
in scripture, the pain increased, so I stopped.'
Her voice is bitter. Twitching vein at temple.

Though his father and the village boys taunted
Zane about his *murga* training, their scorn
arose through ancient laws and roles, but not

her father's abuse, more a fault of soul
than an outrage to change. 'What of your mother?'
'She left not long after he joined his church.

'He claimed my affliction drove her away.'
Jessie pauses. 'My dearest recollection
is her hushed voice singing nursery rhymes.

'I liked the one about the crooked man.
Maybe because I'm crooked in some way.'
She pauses again. 'I hate missing her.'

'My mother also sang, humour and wisdom.
Before bed, my sister and I would listen
to tales and fables of Ghajat and Thexlan

'and the wish rings Mt Alkerii flings over
and through Thexlan every morning. How these
renew our world with the dreams of all beings

'in our world, and maybe in other worlds.
Where they were she did not know, yet from them,
she claimed, came tales of birds with wings like shells,

'of massive cities, empires rising, falling
in the tear-blink of an elephant's eye,
gossamer creatures that float in scorched darkness.

'She told how the rings are composed of Orms,
world bubbles from the depths of Mt Alkerii,
which bear answers to prayer and dream and hope,

'and how at times gem fragments of Orms drop
out of the rings, Keth shards, which can be used
to predict the future or find the past.'

Jessie recalls the strange gem in her pouch,
yet thinks it too well-made to be a shard
though what it could be she has no idea.

She looks at him. 'I thought you didn't know
about our task, our journey or our purpose.'
He strokes his chin with his thumb as his gaze

turns inward a few seconds, then he shrugs.
'Maybe all these stories we have been telling
are starting to unlock my past, my plans.'

A sensation of dread knots Jessie's stomach—
whether from the tone of his last two words,
or the strange sight before her, she can't tell.

Their road continues over a small plain
of flat basalt rock in which are incised
swirling lines a drunk engraver would make.

With each new step the area vibrates,
then the rock between the markings slides upwards,
becoming walls of white stone ten feet high,

inscribed with interlaced spirals and crosses,
some crudely slashed and gashed, anger-despair
of other travellers blocked by this trial.

Jessie wonders whose monster they will meet
in the centre of the stone maze, and what
lesson awaits them if they do survive.

She joins Zane at the wall across the road.
'What can we do?' He checks along both sides.
'It's not too wide for us. We go around.'

Remesh agrees and steps off the left side
of the road, disappears as through a door,
which shuts behind him, and completes his stride

to their right, then staggers when he sees them.
Zane walks past him, looks briefly at the verge:
brown dirt, a scattering of milk-white pebbles,

tiny tufts of thin grass, swings his leg over
the ground. The limb vanishes. He leans back
and sees his lower leg emerge from air.

He shakes his thigh, and the suspended foot
wobbles. His probing confirms there is no
severing of the leg, so he moves back,

leans his vertigo against the wall, shuts
his eyes briefly. A hand touches his arm.
He gives a smile to Jessie's concerned look,

then begins tracing the sigils and runes
on the rough stone, some geometric, some
ornate, some finely cross-hatched, some distorted.

'I've seen something like these before, but not
on such a structure. On something much smaller.'
He knocks his forehead against the wall, stops,

turns to Jessie. 'You study ancient scripts.
Can you decipher these?' Remesh guffaws.
'I thought you were a powerful Dremaan.'

Zane spins on him. 'Why don't you help us out,
instead of these useless comments.' Remesh
glares back. 'I know nothing of magic symbols.'

Zane grabs him by the throat and lifts him high
with one hand, even though the man weighs more
than he. Jessie tries to wrench his arm down,

is surprised at his corded strength of muscles.
The struggle continues as Remesh wriggles,
chokes. Zane lets go. Remesh slumps to the ground.

Zane glares at him. 'I don't care what you do,
beat the stone with your hands or head, but help!'
Just as he turns back to the wall, he sees

Jessie standing, head aslant, in front of
a huge inverted triangle containing
smaller and smaller versions of itself.

'You've seen this before?' he asks. 'Not the same,'
she says, 'but such a symbol could mean *woman*.'
As she studies the triangles, they seem

to shift back and forth, rhythm of her pulse.
Her gaze is drawn deeply into their centre,
then her eyes widen. 'I know what to do.'

She turns slightly from him, hunches a little
and plunges two fingers into her groin.
As she thrusts them back and forth a few times

her mind is enthralled by the memory
of passion and patient intimacy,
though her lover's face is hidden by shadow.

She is alert to what she's doing, what
she's remembering, of who's watching, how
a channel of triple energies forms

as she smears the juices into the runnel
of the innermost triangle, and how
power flash-blazes through each nested symbol.

In the instant before the stone within
the outer triangle dissolves, she wonders
if she created the opening, or

merely uncovered what was always there.
In the same instant the lover's face turns
from moonlight memory, and has Zane's smile.

14

Leap and Echo

After checking the door for sign of ambush,
they enter single file, a floating ball
of light before them: Zane, Jessie, Remesh.

Immediately they face a blank wall
and are forced to turn right. A few steps on
is another wall, paths to either side.

The floor is packed dirt, trodden by the passage
of countless pilgrims. The breeze touches them
on all sides, is cool, with sickly-sweet fragrance.

'Which way now, Jessie?' Zane says. She joins him
and takes a deep breath. Her shoulders drop slightly
as she exhales. She draws another breath

into her lower lung, holding it there,
sensing its poised vitality vibrating
through and quickening muscle, organ, skin,

sensing its echo too in the breeze lifting
the fine hairs on her right arm as it rises
of its own accord, points towards the left.

'Once we take that path,' Zane notes, 'we should stick
to the left wall, thus ignoring all paths
that look useful but would lead us astray.'

They walk steadily, left hands touching rock.
As they round their way out from yet another
deep dead end, Zane looks up. The high walls block

the band of light at the horizon, leaving
the wavering stars for illumination,
yet their vision within the maze is clear.

He looks behind him. The others are glowing
with magenta iridescence, thin tendrils
stretching like lifelines between each of them.

As Zane turns back, takes a step, the air chills
and a dark mass hurtles down from the sky
to form a monstrous, snarling, bat-winged creature,

body-bulk of vapour and spider webs,
shell-plate head with long, razor-thin, hooked beak,
clicking claws, a *hoya* unlike his friend

Rynobar of the star-blaze limbs and body.
A cry from Remesh says another *hoya*
has appeared behind them. Zane hurls light-balls

at both of them and pushes his companions
into a small room. He conjures a curtain
of indigo flame at the doorway, but

before he can cast a flame barrier
to protect them from above, the two *hoya*
leap the walls and advance towards the group.

Jessie and Zane conjure their weapons, step
towards the star-demons, who hesitate
at this audacity, then laugh in voices

like glass breaking and loom-charge towards them.
Then another blur of winged darkness plunges
into the room, not to join but to batter

one *hoya* aside and attack the other.
Zane recognises Rynobar and rushes
to help. He throws a bolt of incandescence

at the first *hoya*, follows up with blows
from his staff that keep the creature off balance,
throws a net of fury-light over it,

keeps pummelling until Jessie pulls him
away. The other star-demon is limp
in Rynobar's arms. Zane sees his friend sobbing,

asks what is wrong. 'This should never have happened.
Now stars are moving during daylight hours
and these *hoya* are in league with a darkness

'even beyond us. I can't leave them here.'
Rynobar picks up the other attacker,
unfurls vast wings, soars skywards without sound.

After checking for wounds and speaking briefly
about the strange events, the travellers
decide their only choice is to keep moving.

Two long passages and a dozen turnings
later they come across an open space,
a sunken pool in the centre, no movement.

A thin causeway runs around it, with many
openings to other dark passages,
too many for the left wall strategy.

Remesh slumps against the wall. 'What now, Jessie?'
The battle with the *hoya* having ruptured
her maze-connection, she can only shrug.

Zane tries a *murga*, but the grains refuse
to settle into shape. The probe he forms
circles the space endlessly, tells them nothing.

'If your *hoya* friend were here,' Remesh says,
'it could fly above the maze, guide us out.'
Zane ignores him, because he notices

Jessie no longer listening. He touches
her arm. She doesn't respond. She is looking
intently at the black water that glitters

occasionally with the overhead stars.
Her eyes are shifting rapidly as if
she were striving to snare a fleeting scene,

sear it into mind. All at once she throws
herself into the pool and sinks from sight
without a sound or splash, without a ripple.

Zane dives after her, but finds himself skidding
across the causeway on the other side.
He dives again, but ends up where he started.

He joins Remesh to scan the pool for bubbles,
or other signs of life, then chants a spell
to part the black stillness, reveal her fate,

but nothing happens. 'What now?' Remesh says.
A voice sounds from the passage they just left.
'Though it may take some time, she should return.'

Wings barely fluttering, Rynobar glides
out of the dark and stops in front of Zane,
who greets the *hoya* with a puzzled smile.

'Thank you for your help back there, but what is
this place? Is Jessie safe?' Rynobar nods,
says *hoya* use the pool to devour souls,

though he is yet to find out why they do.
Having gone in by herself, she will have
no choice but to be drawn back to her path.

Although reluctant to talk to the *hoya*
for reasons he can't fathom, Remesh asks
if Rynobar can carry them out, or

at least guide them while flying overhead.
'It is not possible. When seen from high
the maze is a shifting blur of shape patterns.'

'But you found us after taking those *hoya*,'
Remesh says with a harshness that surprises.
Rynobar glares at him with lava eyes.

'Because I was able to drop straight back
to the exact place in the maze I left,
then find and follow your trail from that room.'

With the hope that music will sooth their tensions
and draw Jessie back, Zane pulls out his lyre
and begins to play, in a halting rhythm.

Eyes closed, he restrains his rage at this loss
and lets his fingers tap into pure sorrow,
the sound like cold wind caressing bare trees.

The discords, which shift between muffled sobs
and shrill keening, fill the cavern so nothing
is untouched by their dark alarm and grief.

Then with sustained notes, Zane tries to transform
the seething din of his mind into calm,
like a new shoot breaking through frozen earth.

He barely registers a tiny echo
coming from deep within the music, yet
also apart, like a distant wind chime.

Then Remesh nudges his arm and he opens
his eyes to see the pool stippled with starlight,
waves rippling to the rhythm of his music,

the pattern drawing their gaze across water
to where Jessie stumbles out of a passage
one third of the way around the pool's edge.

When they reach her she has collapsed, face gaunt,
clothes ripped, body shivering, breathing shallow.
Rynobar brushes the others aside,

leans over Jessie, drapes its giant wings
around her till no one can see within.
As the *hoya* chants softly, subdued light

filters through its wing tips, the colour spinning
rapidly through the rainbow as though searching
for an apt tincture for healing. It settles

on roseate light, and while the soft thrumming
echoes throughout the chamber, the glow brightens
and dims as though the tune were a breeze ruffling

the drapes protecting an eternal flame.
After some seconds Rynobar steps back.
Eyes blinking, Jessie declares, 'I'm not dead.'

'How do you know?' Zane says as he helps her
stand up, notes weariness and certainty
in her pale eyes. 'I don't know why I dived

'into the pool. Intuition. And then
I found myself in a bed, could smell Daphne,
my favourite flower, could hear machines humming,

'but couldn't open my eyes, couldn't speak,
though I sensed people nearby.' Her eyes glisten,
for she is sure that one of those hold-squeezing

her hands was her mother, not seen for years.
She massages her forehead as she tries
to make out the other person…the skin

much smoother than her mother's, yet mist-cool.
'Then a weariness crept over my mind,
faster than I could battle. Other people

'rushed into the room. I felt immense pain,
like skin being ripped from muscle and bone,
then woke up outside the maze, though I couldn't

'be sure if it was the entrance we used,
or the exit. I followed the left wall
in a stupor as time circled itself.'

After Jessie rests a while, the group enters
her tunnel, right hands on rock, though each person
feels a keen itch at the back of the neck

as they slowly retrace her journey, more
twists and dead-ends than the way in, more glances
upwards each time starlight reveals their path.

15

Matters of Trust

Just when Jessie is sure the exit is
around the next corner, the passageway
opens into a small chamber, with Gedon

seated nonchalantly on a flat rock.
The gold being looks up at her, then glances
at Zane, Remesh, lingers on Rynobar.

'I see the troupe is whole once again, and,
you have discovered death is not the only
reason to travel the grey road of Thexlan.'

Zane stamps his staff. 'What are you doing here?
What do you want?' Leaning against the wall,
which moulds itself around him, Gedon says,

'You called me here. Or maybe I called you.'
He shrugs, and the rock shrugs. 'It doesn't matter.
We are all here till someone lives or dies.'

Again, Zane stamps his staff in sheer annoyance.
'How can you know what task we face unless
you imposed it upon us?' His eyes narrow.

'Who are you really?' His staff hums with power.
'Maybe you're the one who will live or die.'
Zane smiles, and Gedon returns the same smile,

no rancour, more humour, gaze resolute:
'But you may not survive, and so not know
what meaning lies behind this quest of yours.'

Jessie thinks this banter is more than useless.
'We have to keep moving. Either you have
something for us or we find the maze exit.'

Gedon nods, then stands. 'In fact, I have two.
A warning: Trust no one, not even me.
And this.' He holds out his clenched right hand, waits.

Remesh mutters, 'Again, more paradoxes.'
Gedon lifts one eyebrow. 'To exist is
a paradox of choice, for you to live

'another thing must die. The food you eat,
the boundaries on others your own presence
inflicts.' He lifts his hand. 'So, what's your choice?'

Zane considers the options before them:
'We can't trust him.' Rynobar nods, then says,
'Yet whatever we do he wins. I favour

'defusing his threat now than having it
hang over us. Only by trusting him
do we discover if he is worth trusting.'

Zane bows his head to the star-demon's logic
and steps away. Rynobar locks his gaze
on Gedon, gently touches the clenched fist.

When they discuss the moment afterwards
they all agree the palm was empty when
first unfurled. They all agree a small object

appeared from nowhere, a squat cube of stone
that formed a temple portico, its columns
wrapped in shifting shadows. They all agree

that nothing changed, yet they were drawn inside,
to walk the pilgrim-worn flagstones alone
towards a darkened niche, the air cool, clean.

Rynobar sees a shaft of swirling smoke
suspended above a hollow with wood
laid out as for a fire, but still unlit.

Remesh sees nothing at first, will claim later
there was always nothing, does not know how
to tell of babies the colour of maggots,

each face and voice his own, the words they spoke
confounding him as when he first met truth:
'That time is false, if this time claims the same.'

For Zane, the temple hasn't changed. Again
the niche is empty and again a voice
coming from within commands him to bow

if he aspires to master everything.
Once more he declines, not because the goal
is one he does not desire, but because

he can't abide the thought of someone else
ruling him. He will find another way
to master all knowledge, all power, all.

With each step, Jessie sees clearly, becomes
more puzzled by what she sees, what sees her:
an oval shape resolves into a face,

eyes closed, bare lines, smooth sheen of rock, a smile
drifting between surprise and bliss, awareness
of those eyes watching her with her own eyes.

Then another step, a ripple of mind,
and the sweet sting of rupture as two faces
female and male, blaze and flow, scowl and grin,

appear on either side of that first face,
their eyes open now as more faces part
the dark with ceaseless interplay of light

and music, of movement, and Jessie feels
this rhythmic poise form the body, mind, saga
of her discourse with the dance, feels her being

become the dance, become each pulse of life,
become the open gaze of two lost faces
always turned from each other, until now.

When everyone blinks, Gedon is not there.
All that remains is a small temple model,
which crumbles into sand as they rub eyes.

After long silence, there is hesitant
discussion, more shuffled silence, a question:
'Has anybody changed because of this?'

No one confirms a change, but Zane can tell,
because nothing changed for him, that the others,
tone of voice, shift of bearing, were affected,

and wonders if this had been Gedon's plan
and why. Was trust the issue? What could he
gain from such manipulation of minds?

And how could Zane uncover Gedon's nature
if he still could not understand his own?
He realises this thought is not his,

but comes in the voice of one of his teachers,
a croaky whisper from the distant past—
or the future, another voice insists.

He grabs his head as it fills with the clamour
of advice—father, brothers, and all those
whose wisdom he sought, all those he evoked

within a circle and questioned, all those
whose minds he invaded when they were dying
as he snatched at the art of life and death.

His mind reels within the maelstrom of sound.
He wills everything to silence, but nothing
happens. He applies his will like a sword

clearing a path through charging warriors,
but the melee thickens further and threatens
to engulf him. He sees an opening

and rushes towards it, but is held back.
He releases his will, allows the sound
to bear him through the rushing gap, and comes

face to face with Gedon, who winks, then opens
his mouth into another chasm, out
of which come minute, rainbow-coloured versions

of himself, each of them opening mouths
for more minute versions to burst out, all
singing the advice, but in harmony.

The song bears him into a floating warmth,
a constrained comfort much like he imagines
a child experiences in the womb

though here all memory is his, and light—
soft, fibrous—replaces the dark he knows
exists as a baby grows into being.

He rocks from sharp pain. He opens his eyes
to find Jessie hovering over him
and his cheek stinging from her slap. The look

of relief in her eyes tugs at the music
fading in his invigorated mind,
and he savours the momentary concord.

'Are you all right? What happened?' She helps him
stand. 'I suppose I answered my own question.'
Nothing more is said till they leave the maze

and watch the walls slide back into a pattern
on the road and the surrounding flat rock,
two bubbling flows filling the complex path

from both exits to a hole where the pool
should be. They collide with a roaring sound
and wheeling spumes of smoke. After a while

the pattern fades, the hole shrinks to a mere
depression like a footprint in the middle
of the road, which the dust quickly fills in.

Zane goes up to Rynobar. 'Well, my friend,
you must be eager to resume your search.'
The *hoya's* wings flutter. 'If you agree,

'I would like to travel with you some more.'
Remesh stares vehemently. 'I say, no.
We don't need a *hoya* who'll kill us later.'

Jessie glares at him. 'What a thing to say
after what happened in the maze.' He waves
his hands around. 'It could all be a trap.'

Barely controlling his anger, Zane raises
himself to the balls of his feet and whispers,
'I can vouch more for Rynobar than you.'

Remesh splutters. 'Then what about this search?
How can we be sure it won't bring us harm?
This road has already brought too much danger.'

The star-demon sniffs the air, as if testing
for the source of the man's aggression, or
sensing something ill in his inner self.

Eyes narrow, and the mouth twists with disquiet.
With severe effort, Rynobar relaxes.
'For countless cycles of the *hoya* dance

'I was like others of my kind, but then
began to notice many disappear
from the patterns we make in the deep night,

'and others take their places, forming new
shapes. Unlike my kin, this intrigued me, so
I seek lost stars, first in Ghajat, now here.'

Jessie blinks her eyes, but can't firm the edges
and colours of the *hoya* as it speaks.
One instant it is solid, the next, barely

there at all, only diaphanous shapes
of light that change colour and size as they
float over, slide through, and absorb each other,

like watching through the surface of a sea
the bright and many-coloured creatures living
deep within and occasionally exposing

themselves to the watcher and the night sky.
She can't be sure what gender it is now,
though the curves suggest more female than male.

'What makes you think the lost stars are in Thexlan?'
She watches the fluorescent patterns steady,
the boundaries of the curved body firm.

'As you surely suspect, Thexlan is all
there is, can be, or ever was, disguised,
however, by the gates before our eyes.'

Zane can't recall him ever saying this.
'What do you mean by gates? And what makes them?'
'They are the ways we choose to see the world.

'They are closed to things we decide are not
possible nor worthy of our attention.
They can open wider, but only if

'we wish to comprehend unwelcome things.
I have exhausted my search, so it's time
to find whatever will open me further.'

Muttering that Thexlan is a phantasm
anyway, Remesh gestures his disgust
and walks a little distance down the road.

After glancing at the stars, Zane tells Jessie
and Rynobar to start after the man
while he casts a quick *murga* to check progress.

He then looks back over their line of travel.
In the distance he sees a swirling creature
of lightning splinters and darkness, which glides

then stops every now and then. A grim smile
plays across his face as he hurries after
the others, and the beast catches a scent.

16

A Vow for Fate

The road before them rises gently through
fields filled with purple flowers that give off
a scent that reminds Jessie of the incense

inside a church, though Zane is taken back
to his childhood, to the barrels of *sorra*
harvested from the floor of Lake Tarlkarni.

He shudders, clamps down on the memory
of screams as flames ravage his sister's body.
He clenches fists, renews vows, stares ahead.

Though she has her own images to clear,
Jessie notices Zane's discomfort, starts
to move towards him, is held by a touch

on her arm, a quiet cough. She turns slightly.
Rynobar's face is softened with concern.
'When one heals another, one takes a measure

'of that person's pain, the reasons it happened,
the reasons the person ignores self-healing.'
Jessie sees again how the *hoya's* body

incessantly changes shape and size, sometimes
the contours of a female, sometimes male,
sometimes both at once, or neither, though now

the changes are less dramatic, less frequent,
its form becoming more and more a female.
Rynobar looks back to the vanished maze.

'What happened to you is still happening.
Like him, there are deep needs you must confront.
And such tasks only can be borne alone.'

She glides off before Jessie can reply,
if she could, for her memory is still
fragments of sound, kaleidoscopes of scenes,

hospital and childhood, the niggling puzzle
of why and when, of mother-loss and coma,
what was meant to happen, here, anywhere.

She is not dead, is clearly someplace else
as well as here, this Thexlan Remesh thinks
is a half-way house between life and either

paradise or complete annihilation.
For him, judgement, for her, a dream unlike
any she's ever had, though she can sense

a familiarity, an old secret
kept from her father, who could never value
anything beyond his strictures of faith.

Jessie hears Remesh panting as he strives
to stay ahead. She suggests he slow down
and, when she catches up, asks him what's wrong.

'Whenever I look at Rynobar, fear
wracks me, as though she were my past sins, or,'
he shudders, 'in some way, my future ones.'

She decides not to delve into his sins.
'So what will you do?' His look gives her shivers.
'Stay well away. Hope someone else kills her.'

Too shocked to answer, Jessie merely nods
and moves off a little. Remesh's rage,
righteousness and mania remind her

too much of her father. She couldn't do
anything against him for all those years,
but leave home and never look back, and now

these companions fill her with the same fears,
same sense of helplessness. Should she rage too?
Then she remembers the first time she stretched

from one branch to another without fear,
though the gap was much larger than expected,
the secure confidence of leap and grab

only tapped when there was encouragement,
a presence not a parent but a friend
whose face even now she still can't recall,

whose existence Jessie dared not reveal,
though her mother guessed, her own wistful smile
when recalling imaginary friends.

This friend taught Jessie many other things,
then vanished in a splinter of blood music.
Yet, how could such memories help her here?

Zane looks up to see the others stretched out
along the road. He wonders if their maze
encounters are meant to so divide them.

Did Gedon form the maze, or is he part
of some larger plan? In some person's dream?
Zane hates the thought of being someone's pawn,

but doesn't know how to discover this
unless he fulfils his own quest, the answer
to the corruptibility of life,

the insistence of death, the need for both.
Too many times he has opened a book
that promised solutions, or woven spells

designed to bring him closer to the source
of total knowledge, and discovered nothing
but more questions, more mystery, more doubt.

Maybe the only answer is to end
the search, or the domain of the search, or
the need for anyone to search at all.

A long-forgotten memory snags breath:
a circle in sand, a drum between knees,
a chant over and over to a tune

he was sure existed before time birthed
itself out of the silence outside silence,
the black dragon that sings time's moving breath.

Someone had taught him the tune, but the words
were carved in ancient crystal, in his hand.
though he could never remember the act.

This someone was supervising the rite,
or maybe he was watching himself, once
exhaustion set in and he collapsed, fleeing

his body in delirium, and floating
above it, and looking down at a mirror.
A voice called him and he turned to a fissure

in the sky the width of lightning, the colour
of cold lips. The voice told him to renounce
his quest or else be damned to wander always

in dark disappointment, all love forgotten.
'Only when you accept that gain and loss
are both the same, oasis and mirage,

'that what you seek is only true when neither
plea nor desire, then you will be set free
of contention, though never free of fate.'

The voice was soft, like when his mother sang
the bedtime tales of quiet heroes slaying
those monster foes that ravaged land and life,

and then returned to mortal life, good sons,
loyal fathers, no battle lust to taint
the home, no further gleam for destiny.

But always he bristled at any power
not his own, so dismissed the voice and vision.
He could not live without his need for wisdom.

Besides, he knows himself already damned,
though he has forgotten why, his true fate
to dissolve the means of fate, and not care.

He looks up to see Remesh sprinting back,
screaming at them to hide, for a strange beast
is starting to climb the hill towards them.

Zane directs them to a bracken-filled hollow
and stands guard, balls of lightning in each hand.
His breathing quickens at the thought of combat.

Minutes later, a large, long-snouted creature
with speckled scales and eight stout legs strides over
the hilltop. A wide enclosed pannier

of wood and leather is strapped to its back,
and inside a white-haired man holds the reins.
Two large ravens launch themselves from his shoulders

and circle the companions' hiding place.
Zane gets ready to cast the balls, but Jessie
whispers she senses no danger from him.

The man stops his beast as near as he can
to the hollow. 'No need to hide from me.
Hurry up. We've got a long way to go.'

His voice is low, deep, without any tenor
of malice or duplicity. As soon
as Jessie appears, the man waves at her.

'I have your message. I'm sorry it's taken
so long to answer.' She narrows her eyes.
'What message? Who are you?' The wizened man

whispers to his mount, and the beast kneels down.
'All in good time. Now, climb aboard.' He whistles
to his ravens, who burst skyward, head inland.

'There's enough room for you and your three friends.'
Zane stops her. 'I don't trust him.' She walks past
and climbs one of the bent legs. 'That's your choice.'

Remesh follows her, while Rynobar flies
directly to the pannier. Zane pauses,
then hitches his lyre-bag and joins the others.

'Welcome. My name is Azra, for today.'
Jessie introduces the others, though
the old wizard nods as if he knows them.

'Remesh. So you made it through The Ice Temple.
Sorry I didn't get to you in time.'
Remesh looks askance at him. 'How is it

'you know me?' Azra gestures around him.
'We all know each other in Thexlan, once
we recognise our nature, which is one.'

Azra surveys Zane's calm pose. 'So, you're trying
the sacred path again. How's my good friend
Elgron? Have you passed his water test yet?'

As when trying to answer someone speaking
in a foreign tongue, Zane has no choice but
to lapse into vague gesture, puzzled look.

'A hard path you've chosen, my friend, but one
that should bring you great success. As it will
for everyone here. Always a fine tale!'

He clicks his tongue, and the beast, which he calls
Phaox, gets to its feet, more gracefully
than expected from one of such great bulk.

Azra directs it to follow the ravens,
then sits back in his seat, reins loose, as Phaox
nimbly speeds across the broken terrain.

Jessie taps him. 'Where are you taking us?'
He points to the darkening clouds above.
'My home. To get out of this coming storm.'

He turns to Remesh. 'What of The Ice Temple?
Did you find your key?' They see his right hand
start to move towards his breast pocket. Stop.

Disbelief fills his face, which has turned pale.
'How did you know about that? No one knew.
Except…' He stares wide. Azra nods. 'Ah, yes,

'how is Nikolina? She is my daughter,
though of course, how could you know. I am sorry
she gave you so much anguish. Always was

'a wayward child. So sweet, when things go right,
though often she doesn't see it that way.
Still, your key is bound to be of help later.'

Remesh ignores Azra and hunches deeper
into his seat, eyes blank-staring, face twitching.
The white-haired man looks ahead. 'Not long now.

17

Broken Hope

The landscape they travel over is brittle,
as if a blast of steam has scalded it.
Only here and there a few scraggy trees

or ragged tufts of grass. No animals,
no birds, no habitations. Jessie wonders
about this change from other places seen.

She asks Azra. 'Thexlan has become barren,'
he replies. 'Or maybe it's our own minds
that are bleak, in fallow, Thexlan as bright,

'as vibrant, as it always is.' He clicks
his tongue once more and Phaox picks up speed.
'All this to help us quicken our song-sparks.'

Jessie squints at him. 'I don't understand.'
Azra smiles. 'It's simple, as are all wisdoms.
Do you recall the day you went horse riding?'

Her father had sent her to study-camp,
but the last day, encouraged by her friend—
someone not from school, someone always known,

someone holding her hand after the beatings,
someone always telling fantastic stories
those cold nights her thin blankets weren't enough,

always showing her magic tricks, and always
telling her to listen to her own song—
she sneaked out to visit a riding club.

'Remember how you were scared, and the horse,
named after a great female warrior,
knew your fear, as all creatures can, and wouldn't

'obey your commands. It was only when
you relaxed, when you forgot everything
but feel of leather reins woven through fingers

'and ease of body in stirrup and saddle,
dropping the heels, cocking the wrists, when you
gave her one last pat on her neck, spoke softly

'but firmly, when you kicked her flanks, leant forward,
only then did your ride truly begin,
only then did you recall who you are.'

Jessie doesn't know she has closed her eyes
till Azra stops talking, pulls back the reins,
then whispers: 'There you are. My humble home.'

She opens her eyes. Although it is still
morning, dark tumbleweed clouds fill the sky,
the land a shifting patchwork of their shadows,

except in one valley fountained with light.
Azra waves his hand. The blaze vanishes,
leaving behind a ruddy flickering.

A few strides downhill shows the travellers
that Azra's abode is of dimpled glass,
which glow-prisms the small fire at its centre.

In answer to Zane's raised eyebrows about
the earlier radiance, Azra says,
'A simple trick to avoid getting lost.'

The next shock comes after they disembark
and start walking towards the house, its walls
made of bottles of all shapes, colours, lengths,

stacked orderly one on top of another,
the chimney the neck of a huge decanter.
The door is made of heavy slabs of driftwood.

'Welcome,' Azra says as he pulls the latch.
'Given the look of the weather, we may
have to remain here till tomorrow morning.

'Come, come, it's cosy. I'll make us some tea.'
Walking on a thick, woven hallway runner,
they file past a coat-rack, wooden cabinets,

then enter the middle room, which is furnished
liberally with cushions, couches, low tables,
the small fire casting soft encouragement.

Jessie strolls about the room and examines
the bottles in its walls, some crudely blown,
with twisted necks and bulbous sides, and some

designed with whorls and other complex shapes
embedded in glass, crystal, or clear metal.
Most contain furled pages just as diverse.

Azra appears beside her, air of teacher
with student. 'Ah, you've noticed my collection.
Do you remember now?' She props herself

against a wall as her mind reels with sudden
recollection: sand grinding skin between
her toes, in crotch, under arms, anywhere

clothes rubbed against delicate skin, red now
even with protection of cream, long sleeves,
hat; her tears when skin soon peeled, when her father

admonished her mother for this one picnic,
this one solace for lack of summer thrill,
for any thrill other than Sunday School.

She remembers playing with a girl. Jenny.
They dug holes in the wet sand, made tall castles
like those summoned from dreams—driftwood drawbridges

and buttresses, seaweed for flags, shell windows,
a sprig of blade grass for the magic tree
set in the middle of the inner ward.

She sniffles as he hands her a green bottle.
'Do you remember what the message said?'
She shakes her head as she takes out a scrap

of newspaper with crayon scrawl: 'My father
will kill me and my mother. I'm trapped. Please
help us. Miss Jessica D Willis. Please.'

But where is the other note? It was Jenny's
idea, when they found the bottle in seaweed,
to scribble secret messages behind

bushes so Jessie's mother would not see.
Was she the friend who pushed her to go riding
years later? Why had Jenny disappeared?

She wipes her eyes, glances about the room,
but no one seems to have noticed her anguish,
or are leaving it to their host to handle.

She turns to him, is momentarily
disarmed by the firm gaze, his lambent eyes
almost all pupil, iris a fine ring

of vibrant green. 'Who are you?' He bows slightly.
'Simple enough, young Jessica D Willis.
I am an answerer of messages.

'I find them on the shoreline where I rummage
for supplies, study how sea and sky merge.
When one tells me, I open it and help.

'You do need help, don't you?' She turns on him,
rage rupturing her features, her mouth working
but no words coming for some seconds, till

she squeezes her temples, and takes a breath.
'Where were you back then when I needed it?
My father screamed at us, slapped us, drove us

'into silence and despair, never stopped.'
Her words spew out, her hands beat at the air.
'I was trapped.' She crumples against the wall.

Azra's lustrous eyes fill with moisture. 'Not
totally. You sent a message.' She stares
at him in shock. 'Out of sheer desperation.'

He dips his head, as in partial agreement,
then adds, 'More out of hope. And it was answered.
You do remember who encouraged you.'

She gapes at him. He shakes his head. 'I am
never that young, that gender. Not my role.
But you'll recognise her. If not already.'

Remesh coughs. 'What is he talking about?'
Jessie throws down the bottle, stares at it
when it bounces but does not break, and rushes

outside. Zane makes to go after her, but
Azra holds him back. 'Let her go. This world
is not easy even for those from here

'or from Ghajat, which is closer to Thexlan
than her world. We all need time to adjust.
Thankfully, we have plenty of it here.'

He turns his attention to Remesh. 'Now,
tell me about my daughter.' The man squirms,
then points to Zane, who is sniffing the air.

'What's wrong?' Azra asks him. The Dremaan drifts
around the room, his head at a slight angle,
his eyes narrowed. 'I feel great power here.'

Azra gestures outside his home. 'The storm.
It means a darkness drawing near its peak.
Which is why we came back here. When it fades,

'we can be on our way.' Zane sniffs again.
'Not that. Something much closer. In this room.'
Azra nods. 'I wasn't sure you were ready.'

He ransacks a corner filled with tea-chests,
broken furniture, sailcloth, coils of rope,
lanterns and spars. He extracts a long object

wrapped in waterproof cloth and tied with hemp.
He hands it to the Dremaan. 'This is yours.'
Zane receives it with both hands, and a look

between recoil and hope, then holds it high,
a votive offering of last resort.
With one sharp tug the bindings fall away.

He unfolds the crinkled material
to reveal a matt black metallic scabbard
inscribed with silver runes, sigils and signs

Jessie would identify as belonging
to traditions distant in time and place,
though the sword hilt is fashioned like a creature

no traditions would have seen, eagle wings,
bull head, lion body, the pommel ring—
set between the bull's curvaceous horns—empty.

'Can this be the Thulsword? I don't recall
such metal, such symbols, such workmanship.'
'You won't know unless you look,' Azra says.

As Zane grasps the hilt, his countenance brightens
with anticipation. The sword emerges
smoothly, then his elegant action falters:

the bottom part of the weapon is missing,
broken slantwise across the crystal blade,
which is etched with related scripts, and which

reflects firelight into bursts of spark-gleams.
Zane's shoulders slump. 'I was hoping this time…'
Azra gestures for him to sheath the weapon.

'That task awaits you. Why else are you here?'
Zane straps the scabbard to his back. 'To master
everything.' The man squeezes Zane's right arm.

'That is always your mistake. Now, Remesh,'
he returns to the tea, 'I hope you're done
with distracting me. Zane, please bring in Jessie.'

Going outside, he calls to her. No answer.
He widens his sight and sees a dim form
sitting at the base of a cypress tree.

He walks over and sits beside her. 'Nothing's
the same here,' she says. 'This tree is not like
those I climbed or hugged when I was upset,

'not like the ones I saved against the merchants
who did not care that the forest took decades
to recover, who only cared for money.

'I hugged this tree and felt nothing. No judder
of recognition. No aura of life
flowing from crown to tap-root, back again.'

She knocks her head against the wood. 'This tree
is dead, even though there are leaves and catkins.
I want to return to my world. I want

'to feel living bark against my cheek, see
a caterpillar make its certain way
to a kink in the wood where it can weave

'its ribbed cocoon and wait its change to wings.
This place has no soul. I...I have no soul.'
She drops her head to her clasped bony knees.

Zane rests a hand on her back, strokes her lightly
in clockwise spirals, more for the distraction
than giving comfort. He doesn't know how.

'I don't understand this place,' Jessie says,
still bent over. 'Maybe we're not meant to,'
Zane replies, then wonders if his words are

a commentary on his own ambitions.
For an instant, he thinks the sword vibrates
in response to his words, to his own doubts,

but when he concentrates on the sensation,
which is more like a tremor in the blood
than the din of imminent storm, it withers.

Though her muscles are still tense, he stops rubbing.
'Let's go inside. Apparently, Remesh
has a story for us.' Her head droops more.

'I'm tired of these stories. They don't lead
us anywhere. I want answers.' Zane finds
himself nodding to her words. 'I agree.

'Yet maybe each tale holds a hint for each
of us, especially if we believe
its own truth.' He stands up, offers a hand.

'Besides '—he laughs—'what else is there to do?'
She wriggles her back a little, ignores
his hand and stands. 'I suppose you're right. Thanks.'

They wander back inside. Azra hands each
an engraved china cup of steaming broth.
Everyone sits down and waits for Remesh.

18

The Ice Temple

'When quite young, I had a recurring dream
of long wood-nails spewing out of my mouth.
There was no pain. I opened my mouth further,

'spat-pulled them, anything to help the flow,
for I felt a desperation to speak.
By the time the nails made a pile as big

'as I was, my mouth empty, I'd forgotten
the grand truth that needed to be revealed.
So then, I pushed a nail into my arm,

'watched my flesh swallow it like a rock dropped
into a pool. Then another. Each nail
left behind a bruise, and I found myself

'making patterns on my skin, knowing that
one day the nails would once more fill my mouth,
and I was bound to do it all again,

'until my body was all bruise, all nail.
I would wake with the urge to make those patterns
come alive, hoping the dream would then vanish.

'I was an orphan sent to a new home
in a small country town where prejudice
was a blood transfusion given at birth.

'My olive skin, shape of my eyes, my status,
worked against me, through my schooling and after.
I was always in trouble. Then I met

'Balis, the town's artist-savant, of sorts.
I followed him around and pestered him
till he began to teach me all he knew,

'most of it laborious but essential:
how to draw from life, with life, how to shade,
how to size a raw canvas with at least

'four layers of gesso, then stretch it well,
what oils and acrylics have what effects,
varnish depth, colour illusions and mix.

'Finally, he gave me a brush, told me
to paint what it was I felt the whole world
should know, the one thing that was mine to say,

'the one thing I would shout from a high rooftop
with the whole world waiting below to hear.
The picture took me days, was raw, yet honest

'a corpse with hundreds of nails sticking out,
point first, drenched in blood and gore, garish colours,
anatomy wrong, perspective askew,

'but I was proud of the open eyes glazed,
not with death, but with some sort of dark longing
I felt deep within me. Balis was sickened.

'Couldn't bear to look at me. Stopped my lessons.
Claimed those eyes were his. And maybe they were.
Maybe I had been studying his eyes,

'as well as his brush work, all through my training,
brief though it was, for some clue to how one
conveys that insistent churning within.

'I packed my gear and left. A few days later
he hanged himself. A queer delight filled me,
glee of irony, when I was informed

'he hammered nails into his wrists to let
blood drain on a canvas spread on the floor
as he swung from the roof. That painting sold

'to a collector who hung it beside
the preserved eviscerated remains
of a musician who had knifed herself.

'For some reason I never found out, Balis
made me his heir, so that painting gave me
enough money to buy a city home.

'I painted all day, partied all night, sought
inspiration in all illicit pleasures,
whatever could trigger that hidden dark.

'The best place for parties was The Ice Temple,
owned by Nikolina. We became lovers
after I first went there, but never once

'did I unearth what I was searching for,
for I didn't realise I was searching,
until too late. All I wanted to do

'was shock my peers and my buyers with more
and more depravity, debauchery.
My exploits fuelled my excesses on canvas,

'bought by those in neat homes, who sought confinement
of their own murky chasms in a style
they thought a trophy-cure of pain and craving.

'My taste was much purer. The only painting
I could allow into my living space
was a splurge of colour that formed a flower

'from one angle, simple, delicate brushstrokes,
hidden heart in its corolla, a thing
with wings from another angle, mere clouds

'when you looked at it from the front. I always
wanted to know who Balis bought it from—
He was much too rigid to paint so well.'

As Remesh rubs his forehead, his sleeves fall
from his arms. Jessie notes again the network
of pale scars she'd seen when massaging him.

Rynobar too notices the scar tissue,
wonders why man and society could
inflict such self-disfigurement, and doubts

that such a world could ever survive long
under rampant elevation of self
that is in truth a denial of self.

Zane is too busy stirring his cup while
striving to judge the truth of the man's tale,
to notice the scars, or care if he did.

A crack of thunder overhead, and they
realise the roof is not made of glass,
but wooden shingles, from flotsam and jetsam.

Zane can sense the cloud turbulence above,
and squirms a moment, distant intuition,
as if the coming storm and he were one,

as if he and the storm's focus were one,
as if the roiling in his belly were
always smouldering there, so deep, so patient.

His being seeks some still point above him,
within him, two savage eddies, one link,
one pinpoint of rest that contains another

much deeper yet much wider, as if looking
at the surface of a lake from its bottom,
watching a bubble rise, widen, then burst

as it reaches the surface. Zane's absorption
bursts at the same time and he finds himself
watching Remesh drop his hands and continue.

'Nikolina was dark, lissom, petite,
yet so strong a presence that none who entered
The Ice Temple dared stray outside her guidelines.

'Not that she left much. All manner of vice
was allowed in the back, except the use
of children. She even had her own brood,

'those belonging to clients who had died,
their own hands or others', deliberate
or accidental, didn't really matter,

'with authorities too corrupt themselves
to worry. She lavished gifts and attention
on them far more than any doting mother.

'All else was freely given, freely taken.
The stale public danced and whispered amongst
themselves about what they imagined happened

'behind the salon mirrors, all the time
never seeing their true images in
those mirrors. What went on was always worse

'than they imagined. Nikolina, dressed
in shimmering white every night, her black
hair flowing like an outpouring of grief,

'a long cigarette holder in her hand,
which the audience never saw her use
but imagined uses for anything

'but smoking. It was a prop, a prompt only.
She knew how to play her public. The dancing
never stopped, the intoxicating potions

'never stopped, the whispering never stopped.
Now and then a lucky reveller saw
what went on behind the glass. Now and then

'one would never return and no one asked
about them again. Now and then we moved
amongst our patrons and they touched our hems.

'I loved her. The more I loved her, the less
I painted. The more I loved her, the less
she saw me. The less I painted, the more

'degenerate my acts inside the club,
the mutilations, humiliations,
multiple partners, the licking of lesions

'caused by lash, cane and rack, the proud decline
to less than beast, the succour of submersion
into blind thrust and scream. Yet, always part

'of me wanted to know why she cared only
for her brood of children. I didn't need
to know her reasons for depravity.

'They were mine also. The longing to say
to life there are no rules for happiness,
no punishments in an age where the ruling

'gods were money and power. Death was always
an ending of all amusements, so make
fun while breath lasted. Yet I could not fathom

'her concern for these children. The more questions
I put to her, the more she turned away.
With flesh and drugs I brought her back, for both

'of us were addicted to that denial
of self-care the world enflamed in itself,
all the better for material greed.

'But always, though with increased subtlety,
I came back to my questions, of her childhood,
of her needs, of those children, of our needs.

'Not one thing would she tell me, except that
The Ice Temple was so called for her heart.
Cold. Dead. Finally she discarded me.

'I retreated to my loft and lost months
in stupor. I saw no one, barely ate,
did not paint. One day I pulled a nail out

'of a wall and began to scrape my flesh.
The pain distracted me, yet also showed
how despair feeds itself, a rabid dog

'chewing its own leg. The more I gouged flesh,
the more guilty I felt, yet could not stop.
Focus and release. Distraction and blame.'

He reaches into his pocket, then others,
becomes frantic. Zane walks over to him,
shows him the gift he received from the monk.

'Is this what you're looking for?' Remesh nods.
'Where did you find it?' Zane shrugs and sits down.
'On my travels. Thexlan has many wonders.'

As Remesh turns the nail over and over,
he wonders how he could have carried it
through death anyway. He looks up again.

'Then one day I saw my brushes, decided
on a self-portrait. I thought of that first
surreal corpse, shuddered. I painted a tulip

'in a halo of smoky dusk, called it
Nikolina. Then a chrysanthemum,
also suffused with smoky light. And others,

'all titled *Nikolina*. Nine days later
I heard The Ice Temple had been burnt down,
with Nikolina and her children killed.

'The fire happened the day I started painting.
There were rumours she lit the flames herself.
I'm certain she would not have harmed her children,

'unless to save them from the world. Each painting
after I called *Nikolina and Child*.
No one bought any, but I didn't care.'

He looks at the nail one last time, puts it
in his pocket, then gives a hearty laugh
that draws a thunder-echo from above.

19

Above the Abyss

Remesh sees Azra staring back at him.
'So how can Nikolina be your daughter
when I invented her for this performance?'

The old wizard waves his hand in dismissal.
'We both know the answer to that, my friend.
You have the story you must tell yourself.'

The painter leans towards him. 'And your story?
Why this house of bottles? What is the real
reason you wander through this bizarre world?'

Azra gives a wry grin. 'Another time.'
He turns to Zane. 'This would be a good chance
to hear the story of the broken sword.'

The Dremaan smiles. 'Maybe another time,
after I tell of my apprenticeship
to Shultar.' Jessie stares in disbelief.

'The sorceress who had your sister killed?'
He nods, gathers his breath, then looks around.
'After my brothers let me go, the stench

'of roasted flesh settling over the village
like mud and detritus after lake flood,
I gathered my fisher's tools: knife, spear, rope,

'the net that tangles gills, and sailed across
the lake, not caring that the night was bright,
that star-demons exist, that my wake was

'phosphorescence arrowing shore to shore.
I reached the landing of her keep. No one
was there, no person, no spirit, no shadow.

'I kicked open the door, announced my presence.
Laughter greeted me. Unseen hands threw me
against a wall, stretched me as on a rack,

'disarmed me. Then she came into the room.
"You have the stupidity of your kinsmen,
yet I have sensed in you a rage that can

' "be channelled." She put her face up to mine.
"What is it you wish?" Though her breath was sweet,
something underneath it reminded me

'of the stench at the village, or the smell
of rank decay within an ancient grave.
"Your death," I answered. She sighed. "As I said,

' "just like the others. So predictable."
She peered into my eyes. "We all die someday.
You will have it then. What else?" I stared back.

' "My sister. She did not deserve to die."
"We all deserve death, for why are we living?
You have much to learn." She stood back and cocked

'her head as she surveyed me for some time.
I was certain she could see my deep thoughts,
including those that only come in dreams.

' "Yes," she whispered, like a priestess who sways
before the swaying snake, then kisses it.
She slid beside me, leg entwining mine.

'She placed her head on my chest and looked up,
eyes full of mischief I could barely fathom,
though my body knew much more than I did.

'This seemed to please her as she trailed her fingers
up my inner thigh. So began my training.
Each day I would seek ways to murder her.

'Each day unseen servants would hinder me.
Weeks later I realised each defence
was handled with restraint—it seemed the spirits

'had been ordered not to harm me, though some
were gentle no matter how much I fought.
Not long after, I could tell each one by

'their touch, though none could ever speak to me.
Each day, when I wasn't planning my next
attack, or executing it, or bearing

'her punishments, Shultar was showing me
how to use imagination to harness
the energies of Es Xayim, the tree

'of power that connects Ghajat to Thexlan
and forms the underbelly of Ghajat.
Each night she would visit me, restrain me,

'show me the moist secrets woman entrusts
to man, which ennoble him to the point
he wishes no injury to his pleasure

'except when it is her pleasure. Each day
I strove to kill her, each night, pleasure her.
Then came the day I tried to kill myself.

'Shultar's castle was suspended above
the world's edge. Upon the outer rear wall
was a dead yew tree whose branches stretched over

'the mist swirling from the abyss. I tied
a rope to a branch, climbed the battlements,
looked down through mist, shifting segments of black.

'I thought of Kerrilea, failed revenge,
wondered if Shultar's servants would warn her,
would stop me. As I adjusted the noose

'and stepped into space, softness brushed my face,
gentle like the caress a mother makes
when a child leaves home for renown and fortune.

'I swung for timeless moments. More than once,
I choked as weight dragged me into the heaving
dark. But other times there was no sensation,

'as though the abyss were light lifting me
to light, like a note of music ascending
from a bird's throat and joining every note

'sung or played or imagined within speech.
Soon these moments wove in-out of each other
and I began to fade, as if the world

'were a sand painting I was brushing clear.
Suddenly through the mist I saw a face—'
Zane gapes at Jessie, pupils wide with shock.

'Your face. Scarlet-puffy from tears and effort.
Eyes that flashed happiness and hidden grief
as you looked at your swaddled newborn child.

'Then you turned to me and said, "Only you
can save our daughter. Follow your song-spark
to the core of its fate and save us all."

'Somehow I swung back to the battlements,
found myself lying on the ground, the rope
loose around my neck. I was lifted up

'by unseen hands, whose voices I could hear
for the first time, and carried to my room.
As I lay there, the vision fading quickly,

'I vowed I would no longer be a slave
to anyone, would be master of all.
And now I had a plan for my revenge.'

Remesh starts clapping. 'Splendid tale. Nice touch
with the vision, though easy to refute.
Jessie, have you ever seen Zane before?'

She paces the other side of the room
and throws her hands about, like one debating
with herself. 'I can't remember. I feel

'there is subtle life in his words, a trace
of truth, but I can hardly grasp its end.
How can I know him? My world is not his.'

'Yes, but every world is a part of Thexlan,'
Zane says. 'And links can be forged between them.
To you, my dying may have been a dream,

'just as your face and your words were a vision
to me. You saved my life, you set me on
my true path. Never again would I let

'any world determine my fate. Suspended
above that void I saw nothing and knew
the only thing was what I made myself.'

Jessie gives a blank look. 'But I have never
been pregnant. You've imagined the whole thing.'
Zane shakes his head. 'I saw you and the child.

'Maybe the scene was a dream you were having.'
Rynobar laughs. 'Or an event that will
happen.' They turn to her. 'What do you mean?'

The *hoya* rustles her wings. 'If time does
not really exist, both tales can be true.
For Zane, his death attempt is in his past.

'For Jessie, that cherished child is her future.'
The pale woman's gestures of puzzlement
grow more frantic. 'I can't avoid the view

'there is truth in Zane's depiction.' The *hoya*
nods several times. 'Your intuition, then,
that sense of patterns underlying all.'

But Jessie isn't listening. She hunches
in her chair and stares at the fire. Zane takes
a step towards her and she huddles further

into herself. He stands back and stares also
at the flames, which, in their constant sway-flicker,
their flare and furrow, their sliding fuse-colours,

like storm clouds erupting through one another,
remind him of the billowing effusions
in the shapeless void beneath Shultar's castle.

A rattle of windows and Azra's ravens
appear. Their cawing is so loud, each bottle
begins vibrating in response, the pieces

of paper within them contorting wildly.
Azra leaps from his chair, listens intently,
then urges everyone to race outside.

'The storm has become a much darker thing,
a peril we're not yet ready to meet.'
Soon Phaox is taking them down a lane

as Azra directs the creature to follow
the direction of the ravens, which is
away from their path earlier that day.

Jessie looks back, is stunned to see a dark
swirling mass near the distant road—the thing
widens as it moves, and slows as it widens.

Its smoky tentacles search every hollow
of the landscape, and then the roiling darkness
reaches Azra's house. It heaves itself into

a towering mass of flickering lightning.
It stiffens, and Jessie holds her breath as
a tendril pokes the grounds about the house.

Then the dark mass hunches briefly before
launching itself along their trail. Its speed
increases as its bulk contracts and surges.

Hearing Azra's calm commands to their steed,
Jessie squints against the wind of their flight
and glimpses a change in the landscape colour.

She sniffs and realises they are heading
towards the sea. As Phaox charges round
a large hill, she makes out a ragged island

a little offshore. Azra nods to her.
'If we reach that island we should be safe.'
His voice falters. 'Though I would not go there

'by choice. The endless Scylarii dwell there.
Let's trust they are still sleeping, which they have
since before they fashioned time, so some say.'

Jessie wants to say she had thought no one
slept in Thexlan, but is distracted by
a sound behind her. She thinks for a moment

the beast is baying as it gains on them,
sees Zane standing near Phaox's hindquarters.
He is swinging the crystal sword in circles,

broken blade roaring like an angry bull
and flare-pulsing with vivid energies.
She wonders if the Dremaan's exaltation

is feeding his sword, with it goading him
in turn. She hears him chanting the same phrase
over and over: 'Time to fight for death.'

Phaox lurches abruptly and tilts forward.
Grabbing the back of a seat, Jessie fears
for Zane, but quickly notes how steady is

his battle stance, legs astride, knees and hips
fluid poise to each lurch, tilt, heave and roll.
She glances to the side and realises

they are scrambling down a long, loose sand dune.
Then Phaox stagger-slows. The shadow's tendril
has snaked ahead of the body and latched

onto Phaox's tail. Zane chops at it
with his sword, while chanting another song.
His left hand is shaped like a tiger's claw

and it begins to glow with dazzling spikes
of scarlet energy. He casts his hand
forward and a ball of light speeds to where

the tendril joins the body. The same time
the energy ball strikes, he hacks the limb
with all his strength and the tendril breaks off.

Phaox lurches forward, front legs already
in the ocean. A second tendril slithers
towards them, but Zane is ready this time.

The tendril dodges his lightning spell, but
the delay gives Azra time to urge Phaox
across the channel and up a rock slope

to where it can settle on a wide ledge.
Then a huge wave slides sideways from the sea
and mounts the beach towards the pulsing shadow,

which shrieks, shrinks away, slithers to the base
of the dunes, settles like a massive watchdog,
with its heaving-pulsations, steady panting,

its crimson flickerings, hypnotic gaze.
Though the creature makes no sound, a fierce howling
sounds inside their heads, fades to rasping whispers.

20

To Meddle

Jessie turns to Azra. 'What is that thing?'
The wizard climbs down from the pannier
to inspect Phaox's wounds. He is worried.

The mount is panting and shivering wildly.
Its skin colour, too, has faded, the tendril
having drained some spirit as well as blood.

He strokes Phaox between its eyes and whispers
a spell of healing. The mount's eyelids droop
and the body sags into a deep sleep.

'We must remain here till Phaox recovers.'
Zane pokes his shoulder. 'What about that creature?'
Azra shrugs. 'I have seen nothing like it

'during all my travels, though I have heard
of a thing called Abzzu, which is the shadow
of all shadows, if that is possible,

'which I suppose it is, given that Thexlan
is the place where anything can exist.
Maybe pain summoned it to change through pain.'

Seconds later his ravens land near him.
He bends towards them, nods, looks at the others,
takes out a small parcel tied with silk scarf.

He unwraps a deck of cards, shuffles it,
turns over the top card, which shows a dragon
fanning its wings of flame into a cave.

He grimaces, returns it to the deck.
'So, you know what thing has been hounding you.'
He puts the rewrapped cards in his coat pocket.

Zane surveys the faces of his companions
and takes charge. 'We have had hints, vague encounters,
but nothing certain. We don't know as yet

'if that thing is what we saw in our visions,
nor why anything would be chasing us.'
He pats his sword. 'But we can handle it.'

Azra sighs and points at the pulsing mass.
'That thing is both more than can ever be
known and as simple as false memories.'

For the first time since they began their flight,
Rynobar makes her presence known. 'So why
flee a shadow we never knew we had?'

Jessie studies the patterns on her skin,
remembers darkness engulfing her near
the cemetery gate. 'We can know only

'what we dare embrace and suffer. We flee
because we fear.' Remesh looks to where Zane
is now crouching on the rock ledge, gaze locked

with the flame-torn creature. 'Maybe because
we only find bliss in conflict, the quest
for mastery of everything that is.'

Jessie follows the painter's look and has
to admit Zane's aura is glowing more
than it has since the clash within the maze.

Who else is impulsive enough to summon
such a monster? Then she recalls what Azra
had said earlier. 'Who are the Scylarii?'

His face pales. 'Their progeny are what our
nightmares experience when they have nightmares.
They were, will be, before us, after us.

'Thexlan is home to other destinies
than the human. The Scylarii are best
met in sleep, for we can always awaken.'

Jessie sits down. 'Why do they sleep? I thought
nothing slept here.' The old man pats his steed.
'Because it's not their time.' He checks its wounds.

'Some say their dreams are what we live in Thexlan.
Should they awaken, we may disappear.
Not something I would like to test.' She nods.

'We can't stay here forever,' says Remesh.
'I know,' Azra answers, 'but I can't see
a way to escape.' The painter slaps Phaox,

lifts an eyebrow. Azra replies: 'The ocean
is too deep for it to swim. Maybe one
or all of us will have to face that shadow.'

No one hears Zane climb back on board. 'There is
another way. I know of the Scylarii.
They have wings.' Azra stares in disbelief:

'We'd be mad to wake even one of them.'
Zane turns his palms. 'I don't intend to wake
anything. All creatures move during sleep:

'the dog, with its twitching legs, chases cats.
We need only feed the beast the right dream
and it will fly us far away from Abzzu.'

'That thing needs to be faced,' Azra declares.
'Instead, you meddle in matters with cosmic
consequences.' Zane shrugs. 'Not the first time.'

All through their argument, and after, Jessie
is studying the shadow mass. She notes
how a ripple travels from end to end

with steady pace and force, how ligatures
of lightning play about it in a rhythm
faster than each ripple, yet tuned to it,

the one feeding the other, and its colours
varying with each pulse, much like a fish
changing colour when it fins along or

when wavelets change angle and depth of viewing.
The creature seems a huge, smoky snake crackling
with hidden energies and blazing skin.

Jessie remembers sitting in the crook
of her tree and glimpsing a black snake settle
in a coil where she climbed the trunk each day.

She watched it closely, as sun dropped behind
cloudbank and surrounding peaks. Soon she started
to shake with cold as well as fear, but knew

the cold would affect the snake even more
than it would her. When it was almost dark
she inched down the trunk towards it. She held

a cluster of seed-pods she meant to use
for distraction if the creature should stir.
When only a few feet away, she saw

the snake turn its glistening head and stare.
There was no malevolence in those slits,
just curiosity. She threw some pods.

The creature raised its pale brown snout, hissed loudly
in short bursts, flattened its neck and forebody
towards the ground in slow, sinuous waves,

then settled back. She waited a few minutes
then threw the rest of her pods. This time, nothing.
She scrambled along a branch opposite

the snake. She swung herself down, almost screeched
when the branch dipped, held, dipped more. As she swayed,
the snake uncoiled itself and rippled through

the grass, its path directly beneath her.
The branch creaked again and dropped a few inches.
There was a crack. The branch dropped even more.

Then her hands could hold no longer. She couldn't
see if the snake had gone or not. She let
go and jumped sideways once her bare feet touched

the uneven ground. Landing on her belly,
she looked up to see the tail of the snake
twitch once and disappear into the bush.

She hears Azra shout: 'You will destroy us
if you continue.' With an urge to see
those who dream her life, she runs after Zane.

21

The Cave of the Scylarii

They walk in silence. Zane has learnt from Azra
the Scylarii sleep in a cavern somewhere
on the seaward side of the isle. As far

as he knows, no one has ever seen them.
He has been told there are immortal guards
who have kept the curious away, knowing

what will pass if the Scylarii should wake.
Azra and the others will care for Phaox
and keep watch in case Abzzu summons allies.

The ledge extends around most of the island,
a flat causeway for its inhabitants
or their servants. As Zane and Jessie reach

the seaward side, they are greeted by wind
that is bitterly cold and whips salt spray
into their eyes. Before them is a mass

of boulders and shifting layers of pebbles,
which forces them to scramble slowly over
the sea-drenched surfaces. Zane first considers

the mounds of debris a ploy to discourage
carefree explorers, but Jessie points out
the fractured cliff face and its sliding scree.

Seconds before pointing out the rock fall,
movement had drawn her gaze to the cliff top
and the sight of a person standing near

an outspread tree with white globular blossoms,
which reminded her of the jewel she carried,
but when she blinked, person and tree were gone.

Not long after they pass around the edge
of the island, Abzzu's whispers recede
from Jessie's mind. She finds it easier

to concentrate on the climbing and needs
Zane's aid less. The wind shrieks into their faces,
while thronging waves smash against the isle's bulk.

Zane points out an opening in the cliff.
The closer they come, the stronger the stench
of rotting seaweed and decaying flesh.

Zane tears two long strips from inside his cloak,
dips them in a rock pool, hands one to her.
Once protected, they traverse the last rocks

in front of the sea cave, then pause outside.
Zane unsheathes his sword, points it to the four
quarters, then above him, all the while chanting

words in a sibilant tongue that makes Jessie's
skin seem infested with ravening insects.
She feels the air still-thicken about them,

knows he has built a wall of energy
that dampens sound and light, to hide their presence
and protect. They step into the warm darkness,

and Jessie is surprised she can still see
with the clarity of the daylight world.
Again she wonders where Zane has acquired

his powers, and why he is travelling
the sacred road if he is such an adept.
And why is she here, who is not so strong?

He halts. The pebble pathway turns right angles.
The rock ahead is deeply etched with profiles
of figures more than twice his height, some human,

some with animal heads, though Jessie knows
none of them, even given her wide reading,
all portrayed with incised markings for garments

and jewellery and weapons, their eyes hollow,
the fluctuations of light from outside
giving the appearance of subtle movement

in limb or eye. Zane sends a tenuous
trickle of pale energy at the wall,
and she thinks the first figure—human body,

head of raptor—flickers around its edges
briefly, before turning its face to them.
She blinks, but the figure is again profile.

Zane leans towards her and whispers: 'The guards,
like their charges, are hovering in dreams.
We must be wary.' Jessie follows him

down the passageway and perceives their shield
thicken further. As they pass the first figure
the head becomes more beast than bird and Jessie

wonders if the gloom is the only guard,
which assumes the shape of whatever image
of authority or punishment lurks

guilt-deep in the mind of each interloper.
Would she meet her father in some new guise?
Could she trace whatever guilt was not hers?

At each turning the sense of being watched
from the rock persists, though Jessie can't see
any other etchings, is seeing less

the farther along the passage they travel,
as if a thing much greater than mere darkness
were dampening Zane's spell. Then she detects

a change in the texture of air, a numbing
of their faint sounds of passage, like dead echoes,
knows they have entered an enormous cavern.

She shudders with the thought that maybe Zane
suggested this mission purely for power
and knowledge. She hopes he is skilled enough.

Instantly, her eyes are seared by tense light
and she fears the Scylarii have detected
their presence. A shadow eases the pain

such light always drives through her fragile vision,
which she quickly sees is cast by Zane's hand.
'I'm sorry. I forgot about your eyes.'

When her sight recovers, the flare becomes
a dull glow emanating from Zane's sword,
a risk of radiance in shifting darkness.

She looks past him, gasps, then clamps a hand over
her mouth as Zane glares at her. For an instant
she totters, and thrusts out her other hand

for support from a nearby stalactite.
She recoils from a touch not of rock, more
like flat toughened hide with serrated edges.

Her knees crumple as she stares all around.
Mounds and coils, trailing limbs and bulges rise
and settle, recumbent leviathan

of scaled flesh, no cave surface that is not
transfigured by multiple flesh and wing,
twitching claws longer than Phaox's legs.

Each scale shimmers with rainbow colours, even
when Zane moves his sword and the scale is shadowed.
As she peers at the nearest one, the colours

resolve into a scene of champions
on horseback parading through cheering crowds.
A second shows *hoya* absorbing victims,

while in another she is stunned to see
Remesh and Rynobar searching for plants
for Phaox's wounds, clashing constantly.

As she turns, another scale catches her:
Rynobar landing near the tree of lights,
enfolding the trunk with her wings, which blaze.

Jessie judges Zane mad to even think
he can control such a mysterious
and powerful creature. Surely his venture

is already displayed, past-present-future,
on one of the pulsating scales, with others
showing her peering into them and out.

She rouses with urgency for retreat,
starts to pull his arm, is abruptly gripped
by screaming pain inside her head. She sinks

to knees, fists squeezing her temples as fire
splinter-surges through her mind. She rolls into
a ball, feels her screams shatter all her senses.

Then she is gasping, all pain gone, as though
the inferno had burnt it away, but
for the bile splattered on the granite floor.

22

Serpent Song

After sitting up and wiping her mouth,
Jessie is stunned to see Enheduanna
leaning on her skull staff and watching her.

The intensity of gaze and its gleam
remind Jessie of the meeting with Dukor.
With a shock she knows the woman is also

Neshxi, the *Turma* maker's mother-wife.
Enheduanna bows at Jessie's insight,
and Jessie bows back. 'You guard the Scylarii?'

'In a manner of speaking. We all do.'
Her eyes glitter in the dark. Jessie looks
for Zane, but finds no sign of him, no sign

of the Scylarii. The cavern is empty,
except for a halo of shining motes
that dance in shafts of light that also move

in the rhythm of breath, hers or another's.
'Where are the Scylarii?' The goddess smiles,
and the answer forms inside Jessie's mind:

'Who says they are not here still, your awareness
closed to them, because of fears and deep yearnings?'
Then she thinks of Zane. The reply comes fast.

'He is dealing with his presumption elsewhere.'
Jessie says in her head: 'So, where are we?'
'This moment is a Scylarii breath-scale,

'as all things are, will be, once were, including
themselves.' Neshxi's gaze fills Jessie, amusement
replaced by a glistening gulf: 'Tell me

'why you are here.' Jessie sends images
of the pursuit by Abzzu. She shows Zane
discussing dream control of the Scylarii.

'Yes, that one has always been impudent.'
For a second Jessie thinks Neshxi said
my son, not *that one*, but cannot be certain.

'Let me tell you a story,' she continues.
Jessie finds the mental voice and its pictures
comforting, the kindness-scent of compassion

that can abide any fault. Yet a part
of her knows the guardian can inflict
great pain, even for those already dead,

that Neshxi can sudden-spin any soul
to the start of its task, with full distress
of all it once had faced and would again.

She listens: 'Before any world began,
there was a sea without a sky. Before
any sea began, there was a keen whisper

'without a voice. And before any whisper,
there was nothing. When a silver bird flew
out of the sea, feathers of foam, and sang

'its song, for us, to us, through us, a fish
had already begun seeking its mate.
For every bird, a fish, for every song,

'another sea. Soon the kosmos was filled
with seas, so that between them land emerged
and around this a blind serpent appeared,

'dense with glitter and breath, to prevent all
vanishing back into nothing. Each sea
is reflected in its scales, each song is

'the hum and ring of rubbing scales as body
swells with breath. Whenever the serpent sheds
its skin, seas drain, skies vanish, but the song

'of the dead skin becomes the new skin's dreams
and each land remembers itself, while blazing
with the urgency of new dreams, new lives.

'But if the serpent were somehow to waken,
slither away into undergrowth, nothing
would remain for memory or for dream.'

Jessie squeezes at tears swelling her eyes
and hopes the guardian can forgive her
invasion of the Scylarii's repose.

As she sniffles, Jessie hears Neshxi whisper—
as though the story had never been told—
'But why are *you* here?' The answer seems clear:

she did not choose to visit Thexlan, but
when she starts to speak, the cavern is dark.
She hears a slow creaking, as of bed springs.

Smells sweat-musk. Lifts her head. The full moon shines
through her open apartment window, glazes
the arms of her lover reaching for her.

She jerks as he tweaks, sucks, each erect nipple.
Moans when he blows breath over her breasts, down
her belly, such shiver of delayed touch.

His teeth nip at the insides of her thighs
and she arches. Hands clench her buttocks, lift
moist ridges of skin to his tongue, which flicks

and sucks, the reverberations of flinch
and groan nipping at throat and sprinting heart,
wave on wave of glitter-burst, deeper, deeper

till her body quivers, shrieks, and she craves
his deeper presence. She pulls at his hair,
his shoulders, hauls him above her, in her,

the rocking pulse of clench and pause, the rapt
reunion with single rhythm, no self
to lose, to find, only the shiver-bliss

from touch to leap, breath shattering, to tremor
of opening, tingling skin, heave and sigh,
long blossom of moonlight as fingers spark.

23

The Design in Stars

Jessie opens her eyes to find Zane standing
above her. He hauls her to her feet, says
in a strained voice, 'There's nothing here for us.'

He does not tell how the goddess confronted
him: 'Again you challenge Thexlan, ignoring
your role in All and All in you.' She gestured—

He saw himself falling through darkness, screamed
as it enveloped him, sliced him apart,
choked him, then shrank itself to nothing but

a mote flickering between presence, absence.
Great leather wings battered it, tossed it high,
and it disappeared into rippling blackness…

Their journey back from the now-empty cavern
is shorter than the outward trip; and as
neither of them is keen to explore further

their encounters with Neshxi, their report
is much shorter still. Azra tells them that,
when they left, the creature shifted its bulk,

in anticipation of an escape,
but then settled back, not moving except
for the cyclic ripples along its flanks.

Jessie takes up her surveillance of Abzzu
and replays in her mind the last few hours,
a sense that something seen or something dreamed

can offer a solution to their problem.
Soon she stops thinking on these events, lets
the rhythms about her weave a deep hush

into her mind—the constant, shifting glints
on water, like a speckled, surging creature,
waves fringing and fingering the sand, breeze

lifting the pale hairs on her limbs. She looks
at a vein pattern like a coiled snake, shivers
a moment, then delight quickens her breath.

She tells the others her idea: the use
of cold and guile to shock Abzzu. Believing
he has power enough, Zane agrees, but

not the others, who worry what might happen
if Abzzu reads the signs of their attack.
Zane lifts his sword: 'I'm not waiting for death.'

Jessie scrambles to a new vantage point,
where she can watch both the creature and Zane.
She hears him begin a low chant and knows

the preparation for the task will need
all his skill. On a higher ledge she sees
the strange, white tree, thin branches wavering,

no sign of guardian or shining globes.
She removes her pouch, examines the sphere,
knows the tree etched upon it is the same.

She imagines that the ten tiny suns
may represent those people she will meet,
those important in Thexlan and back home.

The chant-rhythm falters once, twice, then steadies,
quickens. As wide, dark clouds gather above
Abzzu, its undulations start to slow,

the flickers and crackle of lightning fade,
proof of her insight: that here, more than elsewhere,
all living things, even shadows, need light.

Jessie turns to the channel, sees the water
receding, hopes the creature is too numb
to notice or probe. Her skin starts to tingle,

the earth underfoot quivering. Zane stands
legs apart, arms raised, voice deep, sonorous,
the air cracking with the pulse of his chant.

She trusts the goddess will be vigilant
and understanding enough to not let
Zane's magic disrupt the Scylarii's sleep.

She glances at the channel's narrow entrance.
Zane has built a high invisible wall
against which waves crash with greater and greater

frenzy. He pours energy into each
as it passes him and feeds off their frantic
clawing at the barrier and their fall,

pumping this into the next wave, the next,
until a coruscating wheel of magic,
with him at the centre, grows brighter, spins

faster, screeches higher. Waves beat the wall
in rapid succession, till suddenly
the water recedes and gathers itself

into one enormous wave-bulge. Zane drops
his arms, voice silent. As the wave draws near
the shallows, it thickens and rears, bursts through

the place where the wall was, looms higher yet
as it climbs the sloping, exposed sea floor
towards the beach, upraised hammer of green.

The shadow monster, distracted by Azra
and Remesh guiding Phaox to the end
of the causeway, turns too late. The wave-hammer

falls, tons of compounded ferocity.
The engulfed landscape explodes with the sound
of giant shields clashing. Clouds of steam billow

across the isle, buffet whatever is
standing. When they clear and the sea returns
to its set rhythms, the creature is gone.

Jessie struggles with an exhausted Zane
along the path to where the others are
grinning wildly as they climb aboard Phaox.

They strap him in, cover him with a blanket.
Soon their mount is climbing the dunes and racing
across the unusually quiet land.

Zane leans back and cycles four-by-four breath
through his fatigued body. The summoning
of the sea-wave had drained all his resources,

had drawn on nearly every magic skill
he possessed, but to what end? Though he longed
to preen and strut, to remind his companions

without him Jessie's plan was only words,
Zane couldn't indulge himself anymore.
Abzzu will recombine, renew the chase.

Maybe it has minions who will track them.
Maybe one of the party is aligned
with it, had summoned it the night before.

He gazes skyward, notes the clouds he roused
have thinned to a dark membrane that lets through
a view of the slowly moving star clusters.

If, as some say, their patterns exert power
over the journeys of men, if these patterns
are fixed, then those of men are pre-determined.

And what of Rynobar? *Hoya* who sways
the lives of others, or itself a being
governed by an unseen pattern, or both?

Maybe everything connects in fixed ways,
their encounters with the monster already
set down in the design and fire of stars.

By fathoming such patterns, they could be
ready for those conflicts awaiting them.
He shivers, groans. Someone tightens the blanket.

Zane sees that any flair at reading stars
would also be fixed in their wheeling movements,
every thought, every dream too. His mind teeters,

ice mass at edge of fracture. As he seeks
to regain rule, a voice whispers, 'Why bother?
Your failure or success in any task

is already fixed by the past. Let go.'
And he knows this message is also set.
He squirms around, feels those hands steady him.

Breaking away from this spiral of thought,
he abandons himself to a grave sleep
of stars plunge-wheeling into maws of laughter.

'He has a fever,' Jessie tells the others.
'Do you think we can get some help from where
we are going? Rest may not be enough.'

After showing Remesh the reins, explaining
the voice commands, and slowing Phaox so
the painter can safely take over, Azra

checks Zane's pulse, pads of three fingers on wrist.
'I understand your concern, Jessie, but
he breathes easily and there is no pain.

'Still, it is wise to be careful. We are
close to a friend of mine, who has a well
with healing properties. Then we'll continue.'

'To where?' Jessie says. 'Are we just evading
that thing or is there a specific goal?
Before you met us we were travelling

'to Mt Alkerii. Now we're being chased.'
She waves her arms. 'I don't understand this.
I don't understand my place in this quest.'

Azra's face is solemn. 'And have you ever
understood your life?' She lifts a pale arm.
'Not this. I couldn't go out in the sun.

'I made no friends at school because they thought
me a freak. My father claimed I was tainted
by my mother's sins, yet would not explain.

'No one dared touch me, a terror they would
become like me.' Azra glances at Zane
and Jessie realises she is shrieking.

After a pause she says, 'Nothing made sense.'
Azra nods. 'Yet you succeeded.' 'At what?'
'Your studies.' 'Because there was nothing else.

'I found I had a gift for ancient tongues,
became a researcher of the far past,
because the present was always too painful.'

'At least you understand the past, which must
help your present and future.' She objects.
'I became more puzzled the more I studied.

There is so much there that has never changed.
Human beings still wreak pain on each other,
still treat the world as possession, not duty.

'Existence has puzzled them, wearied them.'
Azra tugs at his ear. 'And they have always
loved others and accepted their existence

'with humour and wise counsel. For each anguish
there has been exhilaration. For each
evil there has been love. For each confusion

'there has been a wisdom. If it were easy,
there would be no accomplishment. If it
were impossible, there would be no meaning.

'Those things we do not understand draw us
to wisdom. Those things we do understand,
we share. Whenever we share, we love more

'than ourselves.' He sweeps his hand past the view
before them. 'All of wisdom is out there.'
He points to a vein in her arm. 'And here.'

Out There. Remesh shakes his head as he listens.
Looking out over the horns of their mount
he sees nothing but stunted trees, cracked earth,

dust devils, wisps of withered spinifex.
Like looking at one of his paintings, though
he has never done an unpeopled landscape.

The vast desolation mirrors the depth
and burden of his feelings before meeting
Nikolina. He still can't understand

why his style had suddenly changed. The darkness
still had him in its grip. Maybe the change
had been a response to hope. Yet she had

killed her charges and herself. Where was hope
in that? Is she elsewhere on Thexlan now,
doing penance for her sins? Is he also?

Thexlan is every land, Azra had said,
so somewhere Remesh might find himself painting
the lurid description of his soul. Maybe

this landscape is a painting done by him
in another world. Every story is
in Thexlan, every scene imagined or

painted. Every sculpture. His knuckles whiten
as he grips the reins and he wonders if
Phaox is somebody's imagination.

Which comes first, the image or its enduring
manifestation in Thexlan? Like Jessie,
he does not understand how everything,

how anything, works, and what he is meant
to be learning now. After Nikolina
died he painted flowers until no one

bought his work anymore. When he ran out
of money he did anything he could
to survive, including selling himself

to many he recognised as past patrons
of the club, though they never recognised
him. They had forgotten him, so enamoured

were they with the newest painter of fashion,
an Abstract Conceptualist Remesh had
once dismissed as a poseur. Maybe he

himself was the poseur. Maybe he had
no original painting in his veins.
Maybe he was just as lost as his teacher.

He looks at his hands, sees nails piercing them.
He feels no pain. He wonders why the others
don't see them. He blinks, and they disappear,

leaving the pounding of arterial
walls in his wrists. Is he alive or dead?
If dead, why can't he recall how it happened?

And why worry about the brooding creature
chasing them? There is no purpose. They live,
they die, live again in some realm where fears

still plague them. What use is Thexlan at all?
What can he learn but how lost he is now,
has always been, how despairing life is?

Azra taps him on the shoulder and points
to the right. Remesh nods, slowly turns Phaox
towards a dark smudge on a distant hillside.

Azra spoke of a friend. Maybe this person
can answer without resorting to riddles.
He isn't a child anymore. Give me

a clear answer, he has wanted to scream.
Why did she reject what he could give her?
His shoulders slump. Yet he could offer nothing.

He was as mired in corruption as she,
without the benefit of children's arms
to plea for love and help, the wrench of care.

Phaox lurches, bringing him to the present.
With a shake of the reins he guides the creature
to a clearing near an old country mansion

overshadowed by a giant tree gleaming
with silver leaves and wind-chimes of bamboo,
glass, strips of polished metal, but no sound,

no movement. He hopes to meet Nikolina
in Thexlan, give her hope other than fire,
if there is to be a next time for them.

Remesh notices Azra's puzzled look
as they slow to a stop and nothing happens:
no face at window, no door opening.

24

The Sentinel Tree

Though Zane's thin clouds partly obscure the sky,
there is no light inside the house, except
what the silver leaves reflect through the curtains.

Azra walks towards the front porch. He stops
without mounting the steps. No one appears.
A single bird cry, then all is dense silence.

While the rest wait, he peers around both corners
of the house, then cocks his head and calls out,
'Devina.' The sound echoes, fades abruptly.

He calls out again. Nothing. He walks back
to where Remesh and Jessie support Zane,
Rynobar behind, face filled with concern.

'I don't like this, not at all,' Azra says
as he rummages through his inner pockets.
'She would leave a message if going far.

'Maybe someone nearby needed her help,
which has taken longer than she expected.'
He pulls out a small, ivory bird-whistle,

blows a short trill. The tree's leaves shimmer-swirl,
focus reflected light on the front door,
which opens noiselessly. He gestures them

to go inside. 'Make yourselves comfortable.
I'll get some tonic for Zane's weariness.'
As Azra steps towards the old well hidden

by a hawthorn hedge, all the wind-chimes start
clattering madly, just like violent winds
battering the branches. Both Rynobar

and Remesh had just mounted the first step.
Azra's face is pale. 'The tree is Devina's
sentinel. I fear some evil has happened.'

Remesh raises both hands in innocence.
'I don't know Devina. Never been here.
I bet it's her.' He points to Rynobar,

who says, 'I have been here before, to talk
about my search, but not for a long time.
I don't know why the tree would react so.'

She glares at Remesh. 'Maybe because he
is the only one here who is dead, who
does not yet believe this journey is real.'

Remesh glares back. 'All of us have our doubts.'
He jabs a finger. 'Maybe you were spying
for your fellow *hoya* to kidnap her.'

'Stop fighting,' Jessie shouts. 'Whatever caused
the tree's reaction, we need to remember
why we're here.' The others nod and help her

move Zane, who is still only half-awake,
to a wooden bench away from the tree.
The wind-chimes settle to an angry chatter.

Azra returns with a pitcher of water.
Its sweet fragrance, honey, rose bloom, refreshes
them all. Zane lapses into dreamless rest.

Remesh and Rynobar stand yards apart
from each other, exchange defiant stares,
and frown as they ponder the situation.

Jessie and Azra move away from Zane.
'Who is this Devina?' she says. 'What makes
you think the tree is responding to danger?

'Maybe it and Devina are the danger.'
The wizard waves his hands vigorously.
'Her path leads her to be one who preserves.'

They watch Remesh take a step, then stop when
the tree begins to jangle again. 'Maybe
she's been subdued by Abzzu, with the tree

'bewitched to trigger conflict.' Azra nods,
then stares intently at the others. 'Yet
we know darkness exists within this group.

'Maybe those two called Abzzu for their own
reasons and are not really enemies.'
Remesh overhears him and laughs. 'And why?

'I know nothing of Thexlan and its beings.
I travel with these others to learn why
I'm here. What would I gain from such a pact?'

Azra moves to the guard tree. 'Maybe Abzzu
is some repercussion of your past sins.'
The tree shudders with his touch. He takes out

his whistle, and scratches more runes on it
with a small knife. Zane, who has just awoken,
gets up on one elbow. 'Remesh is not

'the only one who has sinned. What of you?'
Azra ignores the question and continues
to mark the whistle. 'That's right,' Jessie adds,

'no one is without sin. Maybe that thing
was called by us and since we fear to face
the consequences of our sins, it grows.

'Have you always been in Thexlan? Have you
not lived the human life like we have? Who
are you really?' Azra frowns, shakes his head.

'Haven't you listened to what I've been saying?
Thexlan is, as you put it, human life.
It is all life. It is All, and the nothing

'beneath the All. I am human and also
an archetype that draws the human forward.
And so are you.' Remesh begins to shout:

'I'm sick of these paradoxes. Are we
dead or not? Human or not? Tell us what
we need to know. This place is not the world

'I once lived in. There's nothing human here.
No wine, no sleep— Jessie touches him gently.
'There is fear and there is love. We are still

'human and still live, whatever the fashion.
We do what we always do, muddle through,
hope we'll find answers at the other end.'

He pulls away from her. 'What if there is
no other end, no answers either way?'
She scrunches her face, then relaxes, smiles.

'That too is an answer, and a decree:
to live with what we know, what we assume,
can guess, accept, can tolerate.' She points

to Azra, who is cleaning the new runes.
'He is probably as puzzled as we.'
Remesh nods, and joins Zane, now sitting up.

Jessie strides to the tree, which shivers once.
'What are you doing now?' she asks the wizard.
'Trying to track down Devina's last movements.

'That should do it.' Azra plays a shrill tune,
and the tree's leaves swivel in unison
to focus light into a narrow beam

that plays around the hill. After completing
one circuit, it moves down the slope, then sideways,
a spiral path. The wind-chimes hum like bees.

All at once the beam retreats a few feet
and begins to circle a small, dark hollow
in the side of the hill, then becomes still.

After motioning the others to stay,
Jessie follows Azra, who races down,
skirts past the spot, then edges towards it

from below. The reflection from the beam
shows the alarm in his face. By the time
she reaches him he is kneeling beside

a small form. After examining it
for a few seconds, fingers deftly probing,
he lifts it with both hands and nurses it

to his chest. He says nothing as he walks
past her, but she sees tears scalding his eyes.
When he reaches the tree he sets the bundle

gently on his lap. Making cooing noises,
he starts to stroke it, though the barely-breathing
creature isn't responding. With a shock

Jessie realises that what she took
as coloured patterns on animal fur
are tracts of scarred skin, where something has stripped

the fur, and cut crude markings in the flesh.
Her gullet fills with bile, and she turns slightly
away, forces her body to ignore

the surge-trembling of shock, rage and disgust.
Recovering, she removes her coat, places
it around the still form. Azra thanks her.

She wants to do more, but can only watch
his healing care. The old man perceives this,
gives her a frail smile. 'In another time,

'Devina and I were lovers. Still other
times, both mother and child, father and child,
brother and sister, friend and foe. This is

'the way of souls, until soul is not needed.
Always travelling with us is a third,
a cat or some other domestic creature,

'to keep reminding ourselves of the part
nature plays in the pilgrimage of soul
through nature to God. This is Siraporn,

'our new companion.' The chocolate-eared cat
is purring now. 'She is battle-bred. Sitting
on her warrior's shoulder she would launch

'a claw attack at the enemy's eyes.
Savage to all foes, tender with her owner.
Clearly she defended as best she could

'and was punished.' Jessie goes to the well
and brings back a bowl of the healing liquid,
some of which she dabs on the wounds, the rest

she allows the purring feline to lap.
The wizard smiles his thanks. 'She will recover,
but much faster if Devina were present.

'We must find her.' He looks up to see Zane,
supported by Remesh and Rynobar,
standing before him: 'All of us will help.'

He thanks them, then they all notice the tree
has not reacted to the newcomers.
Azra scratches the cat's ears, shrugs and sighs.

'This is beyond my ken. Maybe the tree
wasn't responding to them at all, but
was still in fear and shock from the attack.'

Remesh offers the animal the back
of his hand. Siraporn sniffs, hisses sharply.
He does not move. The cat bares its teeth, growls,

hisses again. Remesh moves his hand closer
and coos its name. Siraporn sniffs again,
licks the skin once, settles in Azra's lap.

closes its eyes. 'What was all that about?'
Zane says as the painter props him beside
the now-silent tree, settles down with him.

'The Ice Temple had many rituals.
Some involved blood-letting and sacrifice.
But not of people. As I said before,

'Nikolina did have a few strict rules,
though animals were another thing. Maybe
the tree detected some of this in me.

'Clearly Siraporn did.' He rests his head
on the top of his knees, takes a deep breath.
Seconds later, he feels Azra's firm gaze,

its warm glow of compassion. He looks up.
'How do we find Devina?' Azra gives
Siraporn to Jessie, takes out his whistle.

The tree focuses the beam, which returns
to the hollow and continues its spiral
search. Minutes later, it reaches the bottom

of the hill and begins sweeping across
the plain in large arcs. Abruptly it pauses,
then begins tracking a faint path that leads

directly from the hill. Azra calls Phaox.
'She's been taken that way.' He plays the whistle
and the beam vanishes. Jessie looks up

from her charge. 'And Siraporn?' 'We'll take her,
of course. She should be able to detect
Devina's presence when she's close enough.'

'And Zane?' Remesh says as he hoists the man
to his feet. 'I'm fine,' Zane says. 'The exhaustion
is leaving me. And nothing else is damaged.'

While they climb aboard, the sentinel tree
sounds a joyous peal, which follows them down
the hill and onto the widening plain.

25

Shultar's Secrets

Once Phaox settles into a fast rhythm,
Zane swivels in his seat and faces Jessie.
'What do you think really happened back there?'

He quickly glances at Azra's stern face
gazing in the direction of their travel.
Jessie tightens her coat around the cat.

'What do you mean?' 'It's all quite obvious.
The only person who knew we were coming
to see Devina was Azra. If Abzzu

'took her, how did it know we would need her?
If someone else, who, why? I think we should
make ready for a trap during this rescue.'

Jessie pats Siraporn and is rewarded
with a lick of her hand. 'Such distrust will
surely send us crazy. The only thing

'to fear here obviously is stagnation,
is not allowing ourselves to learn, change.
So, let's open ourselves to trust,'—she smiles—

'but with weapons ready.' She indicates
his sword. 'I'd feel safer if that were whole.'
Zane adjusts its harness. 'My thought as well.'

Remesh turns around. 'Can you tell us now
how it was broken?' Zane studies the road.
'I challenged the gods in my world. They lost,

'but then, so did I. Another long story.'
Jessie notes the featureless terrain stretching
towards the horizon. 'I'm sure there's time.'

Zane shuts his eyes, drops his shoulders, relaxes,
takes a deep breath, begins: 'After I tried
to kill myself, Shultar softened a little.

'One morning she showed me into a room
I had never seen before, which held trophies
and artefacts from her travels throughout

'Ghajat and beyond. It was here I saw
my first *Turma*, a living land of snow
that reflected the colours of a glowing

'sphere above it, brighter than anything
I could imagine, light like all the skies
I had ever seen combined into one.'

He gestures to the horizon. 'Ghajat
has always been like this too, the sky changing
colour day by day, but not wholly open

'to every colour, like that *Turma*, though
the swirls around that sphere were not like life.
In fact, I'm not sure how much in that room

'was concerned with life. On a shelf I found
a highly polished silver ball the size
of a baby's fist. I sensed a strange kinship,

'but Shultar wouldn't let me near it, said
only great power could unlock its secrets.'
He strokes his jaw. 'Afterwards she announced

'she was training me to be a Dremaan,
though she didn't mention the other schooling.
Maybe she did love me in some warped way,

'but all I could remember was the look
Kerrilea gave me before the flames
consumed her life. I resolved to learn all

'I could from Shultar. She must have a weakness.
A while later we paused before an alcove.
Set on a pedestal was the bronze statue

'of a goddess beckoning with bare flesh.
There was nothing wanton about that pose.
Half-lidded gaze. Smile like one who is privy

'to the secrets of Chos. Her right forefinger
pointing to the ceiling. Left palm face up.
Shultar said she was the reincarnation

'of this goddess and someplace in Ghajat
was a statue of the goddess's lover.
I knew it would resemble me, and shuddered.

' "Why are they apart?" I said. "Their sects are
at war." "Why?" She didn't answer. I had
a strong vision of shadows stalking me,

'plunging a knife between my shoulder blades
while she watched from a doorway. And this vision,
like all my thoughts, she could read, and control.

' "I have also saved your life," she said. "Twice.
I saved you when you first tried to kill me,
because I had saved you once before. Water."

'She said nothing else and I was appalled
by her presumption. She may have saved me,
but the brutal murder of Kerrilea,

'death those other times, reasons to kill her.
Our twin incarnations repeating murder
with variation until…' He looks skyward.

'Maybe there is no *until*. Like the stars,
our patterns repeat forever, through lives
and mirror-lives, same actions, same results.'

Jessie traces a pattern on her arm.
'I can't believe that. To repeat life till
the kosmos disappears is ludicrous.

'What about free will? Even if we go
into other lives, surely we can break
such patterns, choose better paths, always learn.'

Zane rubs his forehead. 'There is nothing *better*,
nothing to learn but to accept one's fate.
And mine was to punish my sister's killer.'

Remesh leans back in his seat. 'Because Shultar
took Kerrilea away from you, or
because she disobeyed eternal law?'

Zane scowls. 'Both. I was Shultar's nemesis,
natural and divine judgement, a role
I gladly took.' Jessie's eyes fill with pity.

'To take a life is not a time for joy.
You glorified in your role, which is maybe
why you are still here.' Zane's dark eyes are shining

with righteousness. 'She deserved her death. More.
Though I did not fulfil that task.' He slumps.
'I am ahead of myself. Two more years

'I studied gestures, symbols, chants, rites, all
levels of trance and vision. Soon I could
see the blurry outlines of Shultar's guards,

'and found another reason to hate her.
They were the souls of those drowned in the lake,
including my parents. Shultar had drained

'their minds of all that could lead to compassion.
They obeyed every order, no awareness
of their state or what they did. So I thought.

'Then I discovered the weakness I needed.
Whenever the *sorra* tribute arrived
Shultar would banish me from her earth temple,

'but I always noticed a sickly-sweet
perfume, like rotten flesh cooking in cider,
suffusing the castle for many days.

'Every time I tried to spy on her work
the spirits would whisk me away. No matter
how much stronger I became in the art

'of changing the world to suit my designs,
I could not evade their exact attentions.
One month, just before the tribute was due,

'I decided to evoke my own helper.
I spilt blood around my circle and chanted.
Shultar's spirits must have thought, as I hoped,

'I was training, and did not interfere.
After the third spell, the air about me
grew chill, while outside the circle, a pillar

'of swirling mist assumed the shape and substance
of a person caught in a ruddy nimbus.
My Kerrilea. I was overjoyed

'to see her again, thought her tears the same.
But she didn't know me. I had snatched her
from whatever Paradise she had earned

'and when her tears faded she became angry.
The nimbus flared with crackling energies.
It took all my knowledge to control her.

'She begged me for release. I refused, and
nothing I said could convince her the vengeance
I was seeking was for her, all for her.

'At one point her eyes cleared and she called me
Bibble, her play word for brother when learning
to speak. "Why do you mess things up, again?"

'I didn't know what she meant and assumed
she, like all summoned spirits, was resorting
to deception to unravel the magic.

'I did not look into those eyes. I shut
my senses to screams, the smell of burnt flesh,
forced her to spy on Shultar and the *sorra*.

'I spent the night pacing in my small circle.
When Kerrilea returned, I spelled her
into a mirror. I saw Shultar take

'the tribute and distil the plants for hours.
Skin pasty and blotched, she was hollow-eyed,
her movements jerky, her breath in hack-spasms.

'Here was the reason she would disappear
for days before the *sorra* was delivered:
each month, death was as close to her as breath.

'At last she had a vial of purple liquid
which she exposed to starlight while intoning
the same sibilant words over and over.

'Her voice became weak and her body withered
as she chanted and swayed and the cold stars
danced themselves senseless above her dark castle.

'By the time the vial was a dazzling hue,
she was almost too feeble to lift it.
The instant she drank the fluid, she fell

'unconscious to the floor and did not move.
If I were ever able to gain entrance
at that point and defend myself against

'her guardians, I would have my revenge.
I watched as her body grew younger, firmer,
her features filled again with arrogance.

'The mirror became blank. After returning
my sister to her former shape, I gazed
at her one last time. We both shed tears, though

'hers were of delight at being returned
to that Paradise I could never claim.
Once she left, I began to plan my vengeance.'

Suddenly, they are thrown around as Phaox
jerks to a stop and trembles violently.
It takes Azra some time to calm the creature,

soft voice and gentle stroking of its neck.
'We must find some shelter,' the old man says.
'Phaox's wounds are plaguing it again.'

Jessie leans over and pats its flank. 'Why?'
Azra points to the far edge of the field
of stars. Barely visible in the distance

is a pinprick of darkness, hardly moving,
with a short, thin tail. All the dancing stars
in front of it are fanning to the side.

As they watch, they see a small burst of lightning
far below the new celestial body,
realise Abzzu has reformed again.

Azra urges Phaox into a trot
as the others watch the strange sight above,
with occasional glances behind them.

Zane points to what looks like a ruined fort
set atop a hill far off to their left.
No one speaks until they have to dismount.

'It's not a fort at all,' Remesh observes,
'but a jumble of boulders like…the marbles
of giants. Plenty of places to hide.'

They climb the sandy slope, quickly discover
a hollow between three of the rocks, large
enough for Rynobar to spread her wings

without disturbing Phaox at the side.
After casting healing spells for their mount,
and building shields of protection against

the approaching night, they gather some wood
for a fire, though Remesh thinks this is foolish.
After starting the blaze, Zane turns to him:

'Abzzu knows our path, will find us when it
wants to. Besides, it's some distance away.'
'Maybe that's because we're not ready yet,'

Azra observes when he returns from Phaox.
'Some of you seem to know about that thing
above us. Is it connected to Abzzu?'

Zane looks up, gives a half-smile. 'It appeared
in a *murga*, but we know nothing else.'
Azra looks skyward. 'I sense things in motion

'started long before this cycle of Thexlan,
long before any cycle, a hard fate
for all of you, whatever you may choose.'

'If Thexlan is everything possible,'
Remesh says, 'how can it exist in cycles?'
'Thexlan is Mystery, too,' Azra answers.

Jessie raps Azra with a piece of kindling.
'I don't think we'll get far with this discussion.
Some more stories should help us through the night.'

Azra nods, leans back. 'Who's first?' Remesh says.
Jessie and Zane exchange looks. 'Since you asked,
how about you?' they both answer with smiles.

26

The Next Breath

'Actually,' Rynobar says, 'I think
it is my turn to play your story game.'
The star-demon stands before a large boulder

and fans her wings. Colours and contours shift,
combine, flow, settle. 'Though usually, *hoya*
prefer to dance in silence than converse.'

Folding her wings, Rynobar looks at each
traveller in turn.' We *hoya* know nothing
of our origins. The first recollection

'for each of us is an intensity
of heat and light, followed by unrelenting
music we quickly realise not only

'surrounds us, but also comes from within us,
is made by us as we breath, as we move,
and, above all else, as we dance. We wish

'nothing more but to dance in the night sky
and be the patterns of fate for Ghajat,
be the music others hear when they still

'their minds and listen for the source of All,
or so they hope, and so I have been told
when I first spoke with those I had once hunted.'

Sharp intakes of breath by Remesh and Jessie
cause Rynobar to pause. She nods to them.
'We *hoya* know nothing of human morals.

'Our only concern is that bliss we gain
when we sway and soar, always listening
to the music in us, around us, songs

'that weave and pulse with every other song
until the dark is a vast humming sphere.
Night after night we dance our songs and patterns,

'yet bliss fades and a hunger we cannot
recognise draws us to the world below.
And so we hunt souls, not knowing what else

'will ease the hunger, return us to bliss.
For a time the dance resumes, even though
some of the stars have not returned. But soon,

'the hunger forces us again to hunt.
Once, when I found a lonely traveller
and tasted her soul, my whole being shuddered.

'Unlike others, this soul contained the trace
of a *hoya* I once knew. I stopped hunting
that night and resolved to discover where

'the missing *hoya* went and if we now
were the ones being hunted. I have searched
many lands, but have not found fitting answers.

'I hope Thexlan will help me solve these puzzles
before the hunger overpowers me.'
Rynobar floats to a low rock and sits.

Remesh shakes his head and glares at her. 'See.
She's a murderer, just like all the other
star-demons. I told you we can't trust her.'

Zane laughs. 'So I assume you will vote *Life*.'
Remesh jumps up. 'Yes, her story is true.
Remember what the other *hoya* did.

'She's the same.' Jessie walks over to her
and touches one of the star-demon's wings.
She senses the whole body quivering.

'Whatever happened in the past was done
in ignorance, by someone now changed, who
suffers still and is trying to atone.'

She glances at Zane and Remesh. 'Besides,
can anyone here say they haven't sinned.'
She walks back to her seat. 'And I vote *Fable*.'

Zane thumps his thigh. 'Well said. As for my vote,
because Rynobar and I have discussed
her search many times, I also say *Fable*.'

Azra votes for *Life*, but does not pass judgement
on what had been said. The game is a tie,
and they look to Remesh for the next story.

The artist closes his eyes for so long
the rest think he has snubbed the game. Just as
Jessie leans forward to prod him, he speaks.

'Don't worry. I have a story for you.
It's about a man I met in a bar.'
Jessie sniggers. 'Sounds like a joke I heard.'

'No joke, this,' Remesh says. The wind wails briefly.
The smoke from their fire leans in the direction
of the meteor. No stars can be seen.

'When Nikolina died, I was already
wavering between self-pity and rage.
My work was the only thing that made sense,

'though the public didn't think it had any.
My money gone, and other ways of living
too degrading after a while, I managed

'to find a job serving drinks late at night
to those better than me, or so they thought,
some for a quick drink before heading home,

'some to meet friends, seek lovers, some to scrounge
a deal, some to stare at the rim of life
or lose their gaze in the froth, some to talk.

'One night, I spotted a well-dressed man sitting
in a corner booth on his own. He sipped
a whiskey and dealt himself cards laid out

'in various patterns. He would read them
for a few minutes, make some notes, then gather
the deck, breath on it, lay out a new spread.

'He continued this for hours, but each time
I arrived with his next glass, the cards were
turned onto their faces, their backs designed

'with a moon-tangled tree on a black background,
their size bigger than normal playing cards.
Almost a week it was the same routine.

'Then one night, after all the dreamers, drunks,
schemers, false lovers, those lonely and lost,
and those with dead hope ready for their last

'look at the world before knife, poison, leap
rolled back their eyes, after these had gone home
to fate or duty, he beckoned me over.

'Tall, thin, he had red-black snake tattoos on
the back of both hands. He shuffled the deck
and sat me opposite him. He laid out

'nine cards in a spiral pattern and turned
over the outer one. My skin felt like
it had been dipped in prickly slime. The picture

'was of my first painting. Only my mentor
had ever seen it. Before I could ask,
he held up a bony hand, while the other

'drummed the central card. "All answers are here.
Do you want to know?" I nodded. "Then silence
is required." He did nothing for seconds

'but stare at the upturned card, and I felt
a slanting-shiver in my mind—for somehow
he was viewing it with and through my eyes.

'Suddenly I knew that card represented
my first instance of decision in life.
The next card was the first painting I sold.

'Not the one from my mentor's dripping blood,
but the first I painted in my rooms: naked,
horned angels cheering the slaughter of children—

'which I later discovered in an alcove
deep in the recesses of The Ice Temple.
Nikolina had purchased it by proxy.

'The opening gambit in our affair.
Given her protectiveness of her children
I always wondered what made her buy it,

'some sort of censorship, or recognition
of her own hidden desires, the self-murder
of innocence. Did she hate me for it

'or respect me? Then, the first one I painted
for her after we became lovers, two
ruby demons disembowelling each other.

'The first when I met her children, a corpse
devoured by crow-headed maggots. The first
painting ordered by a private collector.

'The last I painted before she left me.
The first I painted after she left me.
The first after I heard about the fire.

'He tapped the last card. I had only painted
flowers since, so I couldn't figure out
what it could be. The more I stared at it,

'with something like his gaze, the more I felt
the card showed my first painting after death.
I don't know what gave me that absurd thought.

'Maybe it was his open smile, so guileless
yet so arcane, like the scudding of clouds
on a windless, full moon night, desert silence,

'long fingernail of his left index finger
drawing circles on the cardboard. I knew
if I turned over that card I would die

'soon after, then would paint that picture, whether
in hell or heaven, image of my soul,
a judgement that would seal my afterlife.

'When I was found hours later, hiding under
a bridge during a wild storm, river water
lapping my ankles, my clothes torn, blood-spattered,

'they thought my bizarre babbling was from guilt,
because a badly-burned body had been
found in the blackened ruins of the tavern.

'The blood was mine. The fire was caused by lightning.
I never painted again. Was afraid
I would die before finishing it, then

'find myself in the afterlife condemned
to re-painting it again and again
but never completing it. Just like us.'

Somewhere an owl hoots and wind brushes cheeks
with the touch of feathers. Everyone shifts
uneasily in place. The fire sheer-sizzles,

sends up a plume of sparks as a log settles.
Remesh has closed his eyes again. The others
study the writhe-smoke or the shapes of boulders.

No one votes, no different from the first time
Remesh told his story of Nikolina,
Azra's daughter, and thus more Truth than Lie.

Siraporn cries out in her sleep, and Jessie
strokes the cat, who had settled in her lap
after she had gone to check Rynobar.

Jessie then realises it's her turn
to tell a story, but can't think of any
worth telling. Her own life is uneventful

compared to the adventures of the others.
And to repeat what she'd read in her studies
would be cheating, unless it was improved,

though she didn't have their inventiveness.
Her best story might be this present life,
but are lived stories better than told ones?

She stares into the fire. Always she hated
such strutting of colour as an affront
to her condition, but here she can marvel,

can sink herself into the convolutions
of flame and curve, the clamour of consumption
and shifting weight, can track a spark propelled

from the furnace like a bequest to darkness.
She understands now how imagination
can unravel dream and fate in contortions

of flame, and for a second thinks she sees
the face of her mother resolve itself
into a tree of sparks, then a bright fissure,

then another face, her own oval shape,
small ears, but dark skin, hair and eyes, a twin
of younger age with someone else's poise.

The only thing she cannot see is pallor,
recalls that some fuels burn white-hot before
they become ash. The dark twin smiles, then speaks:

'Imagine absolute nothing. No presence.
No potential. Nothing with opposite.
Not time. No absence of time. Nothing but

'your capacity to imagine nothing.'
The wind has faded. There are no night sounds.
The flames are tethered in firm radiance.

No one had seen the image in the flames,
but all had seen Rynobar behind Jessie,
a wingtip on each shoulder, their two forms

flowing into each other as the flames
flickered wildly, and they all thought her voice
of higher pitch, though with a younger tone.

'Imagine this nothing spitting out two
strange realms, which together add up to nothing.
See how they part ways, outside and in nothing,

'how they vibrate with reverse rhythms, how
they ripple with contrary colours, how
they interact without touching, both halves

'of being laughing and chasing each other.
See how each begins to split, always into
opposites, and how the network of movements

'begins to intersect, recombine, split
again, a dance of universes spinning
about the common ground of nothing. See

'how each universe evolves thought and action,
reason and contemplation, inspiration
and construction, here more light, there more dark,

'here the chaos of swirling particles
in a shaft of light, there the balance beam
tilted with unequal weight but unmoving.'

Zane has a vision of Rynobar's wings
overlapped with others, like multiple
dragonfly wings of different size and contour,

each set a double universe, each set
sliding, twisting, spreading, folding, through, out—
shimmering petal-feathers blossoming.

'Now imagine the pattern of this dance
outside time, which only exists within
each universe, their beginning, their end.

'Etch the pattern into skin, into blood,
into sinew, into the honeycomb
texture of bone, just before breath, and know

'you are nothing till that breath kindles nerve
and movement, as those universes dance
and split and merge again, until that moment

'they form two then none, then comes the next breath,
the next dance, and we are both inside breath,
inside dance, and outside all, which is nothing.'

A log shifts, sending up spark-constellations,
and presence recovers motion again.
Jessie blinks, blinks twice more, as from a daze,

the tale's last words echoing in her ears
with the sensation of a voice like hers,
yet different enough not to be an echo.

Once the voice ceases its inflections, Zane
does not see Jessie's confusion, because
he's caught in his own musing. Finally

here is a clue to that secret long sought:
how worlds are linked, are braids of the one kosmos
that emerges from nothing and are fated

to fade to nothing once their energies
are duly spent, or they collide to nothing
if brought violently together much sooner.

After the tale, both Rynobar and Jessie
are unable to account for what happened,
though they do perceive it may be related

to the *hoya's* mission. During this talk,
Remesh says nothing, being so confused
by what he saw while their two forms were merged.

Azra cocks his head, turns to Zane. 'Feel it?'
Zane nods, takes out his song bag. Jessie peers
at him. 'What are you doing?' He bends down.

'*Glymsen* is coming, and there's time enough
to complete a *murga*, to rid ourselves
of Abzzu.' They all protest the idea,

especially as his last *murga* failed.
'But I didn't have this.' Zane takes his sword
from its sheath and plunges it in the soil.

'This is the blade of those who serve Ghajat.
If anything can stop Abzzu, this can.'
He refuses to reconsider, so

the others move to the edge of the hollow,
watch him cast a circle around the sword,
watch him place the *Turma* fragment inside.

As Zane chants, the air in the hollow chills,
the Thulsword flashes with indigo light,
rushing rhythms that pause sporadically.

Then a picture of Abzzu, with its lightnings
rippling through and around it, forms above
the *murga*, and slowly turns as Zane gestures.

The first tremor of *Glymsen* reaches them.
Zane claps three times and a solid white ball
with a silver halo appears above

the Abzzu image and fine traceries
jump between them. The second tremor rocks
the landscape, but the *murga* doesn't move

until Zane drops his arms and the two parts
move slowly towards each other. The lines
of power between them thicken and tighten

as Mt Alkerii discharges its ring,
which ripples through the landscape towards them.
Abzzu and the white ball touch the same instant

the Keth ring reaches the hollow. The flash
of a thousand *Glymsens* stun-pulses through
everything. The world tilts madly and shatters.

When the land stops heaving and their eyes open,
the *murga* is gone, the hollow is filled
with rubble, a band of cobalt light streaked

with indigo rises from the horizon,
and Azra is looking in horror at
Zane's crystal sword sticking through Jessie's stomach.

27

Only Chance

They crowd around her. Though there is no blood,
Jessie is shaking wildly and the *hoya*
holds her while Azra probes around the wound.

'Are you in pain?' 'No,' she mumbles. Zane sits
beside her. 'Forgive me. I can fix this.'
She looks at him through dazed eyes, but still nods.

Zane takes hold of the hilt. Azra grabs him.
'What are you doing?' Zane shakes him off, says
'Only a Kenri can deal with the Thulsword.

'And I can heal the wound.' He puts his hand
on her stomach and chants a spell of stasis.
Then, before the rest can react, he yanks

the blade from her flesh. She jerks with the action,
eyes wide open in shock, but does not utter
a sound. Rynobar starts to fold her wings

around Jessie for a healing, when Azra
points out the skin closing without a wound,
as if the sword had never impaled her.

Zane mutters, 'That's impossible. Unless...'
'Unless what?' Azra demands as he shifts
Jessie, who is still staring at her stomach,

to a sitting position. Zane steps back.
'I'm not sure. I need to think about this.'
He points skyward, where the meteor is

still moving slowly across, its black tail
starting to open up, like a ship's wake.
'Maybe what happened is linked with that object.'

Remesh confronts him. 'Or maybe your *murga*
failed us yet again, and almost killed Jessie.'
He pokes him in the chest. 'You're not as clever

'as you think you are.' Zane raises his fist,
covered in flickering tongues of blue flame,
but Rynobar holds him back. He checks Jessie

one more time, glares at the others in turn,
stomps away, puzzlement, anger, concern
thrashing the composure of blood and breath.

He walks over the peak, sits on a rock.
Maybe he should leave. It was only chance
that had brought them together. Or was it?

While Zane muses on this, the *Forii* come,
voices that were his father's, his grandfather's,
all the generations of Tarlkar headmen,

voices that now echo Remesh's charge:
'You are evil if what you desire is
not as vital as what the village needs.

'Leave, if you cannot live as the group lives.'
He admits the logic, but will not leave,
for a nagging intuition tells him

they are necessary for his own task,
especially with the marvel of Jessie
surviving the Thulsword wound without damage.

He rubs the spot where the artist poked him.
Zane's annoyance craves release. He strips down
to the waist, warms his body with arm swings,

leg raises, muscle stretches, starts a set
of martial exercises. He kicks, punches,
multiple blows, tosses his body high,

drops low, spins, tumbles, graceful arch of limb
and body, swift thrusts and blur-rapid changes
of stance, till sweat soaks his pants, and he is

not thinking of his movements, nor of Jessie
and the Thulsword, nothing at all but reflex
and response, mind resting at the still centre

of the whirling body, no mind, no presence
but the world itself in the dance of contest
with itself, time outside time, within time…

The sound of gravel under foot—he stops
a flurry of punches, and crouches low,
all senses tuned to flutters in perception:

behind him he knows from footstep and breath
that Jessie is watching, that she is anxious
for resolution, that he must appease.

Turning, he notes folded arms, unsure gaze.
He dresses quickly, then moves towards her.
An arm's length away he says, 'I was wrong.'

His voice has a thin quaver of contrition
that astounds him as much as it does her.
'I don't know.' Jessie's voice is hesitant.

'We need to be more careful, even when
we have good intentions.' She rubs her stomach.
'I don't know what happened, but I don't want

'to go through that again.' Jessie looks straight
into his eyes and Zane fidgets, as when
his mother chided him for needless *murgas*.

She touches his arm. 'The ravens told Azra
we need to go. Are you coming with us?'
He smiles and follows her back to the others.

Soon Phaox is taking the same direction
as the night before and the meteor
is growing larger and picking up speed.

28

The Garden of Play

They travel through undulating terrain,
the valleys so filled with damp morning mist
progress is slow, their conversation stilled.

At one point, Phaox is creeping along
a dry ravine when all at once a break
in the mist reveals a massive stone wall

that extends left and right and is much higher
than the tree on the isle of the Scylarii.
'Where are we?' Jessie says, as Siraporn

stirs in her sleep. Zane cranes his head towards
the wall, then thins his eyes, closely confirming
what he knows of the stonework and its carvings.

'A wall like this was built around Adiska,
the jewel city of Ghajat, to keep out
the drifting sands some said emerge from Chos.'

He points to picture-graphs of sun-topped towers,
of regal figures palms up to the wind,
of prostrations in bricked up caves. 'It failed.

'If my mother is right, all cities echo
the first and perfect city, all key features,
and there should be a small gate hereabouts.'

Jessie shudders as she recalls what happened
at the graveyard gate. Are all openings
guarded by such shadows we must confront?

'Are you all right?' Azra says as he gently
places Siraporn in a shoulder pouch
slung across his chest. She shrugs, smiles her thanks.

Once at the wall, they discover the stones
have been fitted together without mortar,
so close no blade could be pushed between them.

'A magnificent feat of engineering,'
Azra says with admiration. 'As is
all else here,' Remesh adds, with a wry grin,

'from a certain point of view.' No one laughs,
so he continues. 'Should we split up now?'
Azra tugs his ear. 'Best we stay together.

We don't know what we are facing.' Zane hitches
his lyre-bag over his shoulder. 'Agreed.'
Jessie ruffles Siraporn's ears. 'Besides,

'she'll let us know if her mistress is close.'
Because it leads downhill, they take the left.
After they walk at least a hundred paces,

Siraporn begins to squirm in the bag
and yowl. Azra soothes her and they continue.
Sometime later, the ground dips and the structure

kinks slightly. The cat yowls again and Jessie
notices a narrow door in the crook
of the wall. Zane draws his sword and waves them

behind him. He tries the handle. No movement.
Remesh sidles up to him. 'Let me try.'
Once on his haunches, he takes his wood-nail

and jiggles the workings of the door's lock
for a minute or so until they click
into place. He chuckles. 'Nothing to it.'

Zane scowls at this conceit, shoves him aside.
Sword at the ready, he opens the door.
They find themselves in a tight, twisting passage.

Zane whispers a short spell and his sword hums
briefly then gives off a low, pulsing glow.
They move quickly, though Jessie perceives someone

watching them, as at the Scylarii isle.
She wonders if any guardian here
would be so forgiving of blatant trespass.

The air is thick and clammy, as though sweaty
beasts of burden had passed through recently
carrying maggot-blown bodies from battle.

Siraporn has become quiet again
and more than once there is a muffled curse—
elbow swinging out, heel trodden upon.

Zane stops abruptly and everyone bumps
into each other. Another door blocks
their way. He gestures silence before trying

the handle. The door opens noiselessly.
Extinguishing its light, he thrusts his sword
before him as he glides through, promptly gasps.

The others bustle after him, are brought
to a standstill, eyes wide with wonderment,
as of a child's first gift, and disbelief.

After the corrosive drab of their journey
so far, here is profusion of bright colours,
multiplicity of perfume and texture,

a thousand species of flowers, some known—
bluebell, pansy, freesia, azalea,
dahlia, chrysanthemum, violet, orchid—

most unknown; filament buds, florets, petals,
shapes of circle to ellipse, small and tapered,
fronds the size of elephant ears, bush-surges,

sunburst and peacock ground cover, haze-shine
just like swarms of tiny metallic insects
flitting from gold nectaries deep within,

spectrum of trees, courtiers, sentinels,
boughs hung with lanterns, streamers, shimmer veils
like webs of pulsing fireflies, syncopations

of stringed instruments, sometimes wild like windstorm,
sometimes lugubrious like blackened tears,
endless accompaniment of reckless laughter.

Jessie blinks, rubs her moist eyes, yet the scene
remains. Her spirit lifts upon this finding
of contentment like that revealed in childhood.

Delight swells within her when a small creature,
vivid tawny fur, lopsided ears, bounds
up to them, sniffs Rynobar's wings, mews once,

then dashes back into a mass of heather.
Azra grapples with his bag as the cat
yowls, tries to claw her way out. Savagery

surprises and she topples out before
he can restrain her. The instant she lands
she sprints, ears flat, after that tawny creature.

'Should we go after her?' Jessie says while
checking Azra's arms for scratches. 'We don't
know if it's a trap,' the old man replies.

Remesh waves his arms around. 'Look at this.
This is too beautiful to be a trap.'
Zane grabs the painter. 'Some of the most deadly

'creatures are also the most beautiful.
What about Nikolina?' But Remesh
wrenches his arms away and starts to dance

around the clearing, short leaps, pirouettes,
as if the garden's perfume held a drug
that only affects him. 'Her beauty was

on the outside.' His voice quavers. 'But here,
it's pure beauty. Can't you feel it?' He grabs
two globules from a bush with scarlet leaves

and shoves them into his mouth. The plum juices
run down his chin as he dances. 'Delicious.
See. There is no danger here. I would know.

'I've touched more corruption than you can ever
imagine. There is nothing like that here.'
He starts to spin on the spot, head right back,

mouth open, as though the air were a spigot
for drinking the garden's heady wine-aura,
twirling faster and faster, till it seems

he will drill himself into the jade earth,
or fly apart, victim of forces challenged.
Startled by his antics, no one dares move.

Suddenly he staggers back, like one struck,
then lurches from side to side, rapid rhythm
of teeter, before toppling to the ground.

Jessie, the first to reach him, finds him giggling.
'What happened?' She wipes his chin, checks his head.
His giggling intensifies till he coughs

and starts to wheeze, his words choked between pants:
'That…was…fun…You…should…try…it.' Then his features
stiffen, body spasm-arches, collapses.

Jessie shakes him, but his eyes remain closed.
She bends to his mouth to ascertain breath.
A child's voice sounds above them: 'He's not dead.

'Only weary.' They look up to see branches
part and a blond-haired boy grinning at them.
'I'm Alyston. Who are you? Do you like

'my garden? Let's play.' The branches swing back
and the canopy rattles as he scrambles
down the tree, then somersaults over them

to land with aplomb. 'I want to play now.'
He is dressed in white tunic with gold braiding.
A small quartz pendant hangs around his neck.

Turquoise blue eyes flash as he surveys them.
'I haven't had friends for such a long time.'
His face brightens. 'Now we'll have lots of fun.'

Azra approaches him. 'Have you not seen
a red-haired woman brought here recently?'
Alyston frowns. 'No one, but I did see

'a small animal chasing one of mine.
Poor thing looked like it had been hurt.' He smiles,
then starts to dance and cartwheel around them.

Azra shifts his cat pouch. 'That's Siraporn.
Will she be safe? Are there any wild creatures?'
Alyston's laughter surprises them, deep

like water tumbling through a hollow cavern.
'Nothing wild here. This is the safest place
you could desire. My mother sees to that.'

Jessie moves beside Azra. 'Has she seen
our friend?' she says in a gentle voice. 'Maybe
you can take us to her.' Alyston scowls.

'She's busy.' He picks up a broken branch
and decapitates a row of sunflowers.
'Too busy now to talk to anyone.'

He tosses the branch against a tree trunk.
Azra smiles at him. 'I'm sure she'll see us.'
The boy looks from face to face and breaks out

into a mischievous grin. 'All right,
but first you have to play a game with me.'
'What are the rules?' Azra says. The boy smiles.

'They're a secret.' He claps his hands, sits down,
closes his eyes. His breathing slows, appears
to stop. The air about the strange boy shimmers,

heat waves from a desert mirage sway-pulsing
with wild colours and spreading rapidly
throughout the clearing. Everything they touch

shimmers too and emanates its own waves,
until the scene fills with colliding, roiling
serpentine colours. The companions back

away until they find themselves against
the stone wall. Zane tries to counter the changeling
light, but is still worn out from his encounter

with Abzzu. The air ripple-tingles them,
and as they breathe, it fills them with a mixture
of dread and excitement, as when first meeting

one's first lover. As the shimmering quickens,
the whole clearing vibrates with scintillations
of light, and a sound like a giant top

spinning out of control. Senses cascade.
Heartbeat and breath pound each other, until
a crack of thunder over bells, and darkness.

29

The Death of Shultar

The hardest thing is learning to speak backwards,
those times I present in another's body.
It's not as if I wake up any morning,

live a normal day as you would, then sleep,
only to wake up the previous morning.
Every moment is previous. My day

runs backwards, as heart beats, breath circulates,
body and mind inside out, twisting past
each other like a spinning barber's pole.

How easy to foretell your future, how
awkward to talk with you when I have said
such words to your future self. How to summon

the truth of our worlds, not trickles of sand
out of hands, but sand on an endless beach,
we each the wind caressing a grain here,

a shell there, believing we are the grain
or shell for the moment of that caress.
Often the wind swirls everything to movement,

and a grain thinks it other grains, or sea,
or the light shining on all, till once more
wind touches a grain and we mould a lifetime.

What is the lifetime of the universe?
The blink of sun above that beach whenever
a cloud passes. How many universes

are there in the kosmos that is forever?
As many grains of sand that could exist,
each one unique as soon as wind or light

or sea touches it. Somehow you and I
have touched the same grain together, or maybe
it is the elements that in their touching

have created this tale of you and me.
One day, past or future, our place will be
flow of air, sea, light, memory of sand.

Zane clears his head of the tumult, half pain,
half delight. He looks about him and nods
to the balding, green-eyed man before him,

who is holding a sword in his one hand.
Zane's is on the floor. 'Pick it up, and start
again. You will never be a Dremaan

'if you can't even control your own body.'
The man settles into a fighting stance.
After retrieving his own wooden sword,

and marvelling at its ease in his hands,
Zane settles into his stance, drops his breathing,
tunes eye, ear, muscle to an open focus.

The rest of the day is filled with feint, thrust,
counter-thrust, parry, block, the clack of wood
on wood, swift changes of stance, swivel, dodge,

his cries of anguish at each sudden strike
to hand, to stomach, though he does evade
more blows to head. He goes to bed with that

contentment of complex physical skills
tried and mastered—muscles ablaze with ache,
mind weary, keen, elation of new vistas.

This training is nothing like Shultar's lessons.
His fists clench at thought of his enemy,
then relax when he remembers her death.

It took him months to realise he could
never bypass her guardians while she
was incapacitated, so each night

he undertook dream journeys and ranged over
the barren countryside in search of allies.
Each time he passed his village he took great

satisfaction in disturbing the sleep
of its inhabitants, who had consented
to Kerrilea's fate and were as guilty

as Shultar. He would punish them all, even
his brothers. One journey, he felt the presence
of an aura as powerful as Shultar's,

with similar flair. Another Dremaan.
Although asleep, the adept was alert
to all pressures of magic. At the instant

he detected the intrusion he caught
Zane's dream self in a web. His mind sought out
the dreamer and Zane knew the mage could read

everything of him at a single touch,
more than he wanted to reveal just then.
He summoned up the images of what

the village had suffered and what he had
endured because of Shultar. 'We do not
interfere in the affairs of our fellows,'

the Dremaan mind-whispered. 'We trust the visions
we each follow. What you see as pain is
no different from any transition. Childbirth.

'The butterfly breaking through its cocoon.
At times we are the means of change for others.'
Certain the man would dismiss him without

further thought, Zane announced Shultar was seeking
to use the Spell of Unknowing. The man
sat up, his aura fierce, demanded more.

Zane had not been idle those days his jailor
was indisposed each month. He studied scrolls,
parchments, mouldy books, and had found some lines

of verse in a drama written as fable.
Both hero and villain sought the spell used
to unravel other spells—the true hero

striving to reverse the curse a witch cast
on his lover, the power-frenzy villain
seeking to destroy the spell beneath all,

so full of self-hate, other-hate, was he.
Then the typical final battle after
three setbacks, the hero winning the clash,

the villain banished to serve as foundation
of the very spell he sought to undo,
hero and lover together once more.

A minor story by a minor poet,
but Zane had seen value in the idea.
He told the old Dremaan, whose name was Elgron,

Shultar was obsessed with finding the spell
that would undo Ghajat. He said she had
a Keth shard that would help her to escape

the destruction she wrought. The shard was real—
he had seen it around her neck and guessed
what it was, while his studies had revealed

how it might be used. Zane also told Elgron
Shultar planned to create a new Ghajat
in which she would never die and all power

would be hers. She would then launch a campaign
to conquer other worlds. These final details
convinced Elgron to join forces with Zane.

Elgron knew of her addiction to *sorra*
and devised a plan to taint the next shipment
with magic poison that would craze her powers.

The next month, after she imbibed the potion,
Shultar was feeble-mad for days on end,
till that moment Zane could summon his ally,

who had been waiting in disguise at Tarlkar,
and they stormed through the Dremaan's barriers
into her chambers. Still, Shultar was able

to summon elemental and demonic
forces and a prodigious battle followed,
clash of typhonic energies, like mountains

tossing boulders at each other, till Zane
focussed all mind and thought—like ocean through
blowhole—to hew a chasm beneath her

and so drop Shultar into the abyss.
She fell, but was briefly saved by a spirit,
who at the same time caught hold of Zane's sleeve.

The three of them swayed above the growl-mist,
cloth tearing, limbs straining for grip or freedom,
foes cursing each other and the world, till

Elgron cast a minor spell of completion,
and the shade, whom Zane was to realise
later was his mother, slowly dissolved

to sighs. As Shultar plummeted through plumes
of mist, paroxysms of rainbows, she screamed,
'They died because of you.' And then she vanished.

Zane stared into the shifting haze and almost
dove after her to make sure she was dead.
As her castle disappeared, Elgron snared

and widened a breach in the abyss, opened
a portal to the city of Adiska,
where Zane commenced his true apprenticeship.

And where he met his first true love, a student
who had been training at the Dremaan temple
since she was a child, azure eyes, fair skin,

wild, crimson hair, a smile that tremors him
like *Glymsen,* till he is like a Keth ring
tuning his dreams and the world around her.

Before he sleeps, he fashions a dream-bird
from breath and her scent, puts a gift inside—
the bauble seen in Shultar's trophy room,

which he took while she was crazed, though unable
to open it with what magic he knew—
and glitter-sends it to her room, to Jeera.

30

A Vision of Rescue

Jessie opens her eyes and finds herself
strapped to a bed. There are bars over windows,
walls covered in diagrams, edges dripping

with paint. Then she remembers. Not paint, blood.
Hers. The reason for restraint. Trapped once more
in the disbelief of uncaring jailors.

She too hadn't believed the nightly visions.
A dark man carrying a crystal sword,
climbing a mountain to challenge false angels,

thrusting his blade into the giant gem
that drained vitality from worlds below,
turning the angels to remnants of shadows,

the sword breaking in the process. A dream
sequence about her sexuality,
symbol books said, but she was sure the visions

were real. He was real, was seeking her out.
Or one like her. She could feel the connection.
Overwork, her doctor said. Too much study,

not enough sleep, no outings with new friends.
Yet, she was confident she'd found the source
of stories about wandering immortals.

Not just a lush character for adventure
tales, nor marked killer for morality
tales, nor banished tormentor of a saviour.

Or maybe all of these and more—the cauldron
of utter imagination and fancy—
composed in his own hand, apparently.

She'd even found traces of him in modern
publications. The strange thing was, his style
was fresher when closer to present day.

She named him Tamheduanna, Tam being
the name she gave to one of her childhood
imaginary friends, boy she could see

but never talk with; and Enheduanna,
name of the world's first non-anonymous
author, Akkadian High Priestess of

the Moon-God Nanna, whom Jessie felt sure
was inspired by the genius who
helped Hammurabi frame his legal code,

who had cast the questions for Nostradamus,
who had crept along the dank corridors
of Gothic thrillers, and who was now writing

mundane love-angst poems and fantasies
with trite-exotic imagery and symbols,
as though nothing worthwhile was left to write.

None of this made sense to her or to her
supervisors, who thought this research claim
a weak clutch at originality.

They recommended a long leave of absence,
rest for mind and re-creation of thesis.
She almost agreed, then saw a fan-photo

of a black-ink sketch the poet had auctioned
at a convention, recognised the dark
man of her dreams, both now and in the past.

She decided to meet the poet-artist.
John Linn was not the lithe man of her dreams,
was overweight, wore thick glasses, had acne.

Yes, he had started to write recently,
the weird texts were from his imagination,
as were his sketches, no dreams of god-heroes,

no dreams of her, and he'd remember if
they had ever met before. So polite,
except when he was leaving, and his manner

changed from hesitant bookworm to assurance,
with such focussed gaze she felt her mind open:
'Be careful later. Just show him your face

'and remember Jenny's lessons.' She gaped
after him, thought her doctor may be right.
Later that night, when she stopped at a corner,

a rasping voice ordered her to hand over
her cash. She spun around, threw off her hood.
The thief was so shocked by her albinism

she was able to kick him in the groin,
elbow-crunch the back of his head as he
doubled-over, foot-sweep him to the ground,

and run. Once home, her heart triple-time beating,
she recalled John's advice and shudder-chilled.
Her dreams that night were not of the dark man,

nor of John Linn, but of Jenny, the playmate
she invented when no one else would play,
the feisty girl who taught her to defend

herself against those schoolyard taunts and fights,
the Jenny who knew how to create blossoms
by breathing on a speck of dust and chanting,

who trained with twin short swords and could defeat
all other students in her school, who grew
faster than she and, when an adult, vanished.

By day, Jessie worried her manuscripts,
by night, she dredged her dreams and memories
or sought out John Linn. He had to know more.

When she found him, he denied warning her
of the attack, was thankful for attention.
Against her better judgement she agreed

to have lunch with him, then dinner, then more.
They were lovers only once, a strange night
of jasmine and haunting intimacy,

his gawkiness replaced by self-assurance,
an intensity not unlike that instance
of his defence advice, and his love-skills

more thorough, more thoughtful than he could know.
He left her the next day, her neediness,
her delusions, her theories, his excuse.

She returned to her studies more determined
to prove Tamheduanna had indeed
written or influenced the texts she read.

She recognised his themes, his leitmotifs.
The mountain of salvation. Broken sword.
Lovers torn apart. She became convinced

all major cultural ideas were his,
immortal lover, philosopher, muse
to male and female alike, who grew younger

the older the world became. She began
to take stimulants to pursue her studies,
and relaxants to make her sleep and dream.

This mania spiralled out of control.
The last thing she remembered was Tam's face
as John lifted her from the blood-swirl bath.

No doctor, nurse, colleague believed her now.
She could hardly believe the tale herself:
an immortal who went backwards through time,

who inspired art and idea because
he had already seen what could exist.
What about free will and linear time?

Soon, she stopped raging against the restraints,
agreed to talk with her psychiatrist,
admitted her dreams were delusional.

Weeks of such medicated grovelling
saw her discharged. The day she came home, bluebells
appeared in her garden. Winter had been

so dry blackbirds swarmed in surrounding trees,
on roof tops, numbers unseen in the city
for the twenty years her neighbours lived there.

Taking this as an omen, she collected
her research notes and sent them with a letter
to her supervisors: *If I survive,*

consider them proof of my theory that
the immortal will rescue me, through proxy,
as he did the first time. If not, burn them.

Then she arranged her pill bottles and filled
her bath with warm water once more. She lit
candles, swallowed the pills, prayed she was right.

As she eased herself in and closed her eyes,
breathing herself into that deep, still centre
she was once shown, faint music lifted her.

31

Facets of Awe

Remesh opens his eyes, steps back, then drops
to his knees. In front of him is a pulsing
simulacrum of one of his first paintings,

a twisted corpse surrounded by putrescence
and eviscerated remains. He gags,
empties his stomach, watches horrified

as the bile flows into the scene, which grows
life-size, each painted aspect separating
from perspective to dimension, each brushstroke

moulding to object, or dividing space
from surface, all beating faster than blood,
as though he were feeding it with his own

frenzied imaginings. A pus-filled wound
slowly widens to reveal a slate path
cut through dark mist, then curving beyond sight.

The acrid smell of smoke mixed with burnt flesh,
and he is sprinting through the mist. Flame-sizzle,
frantic screams, and the mist ripples away

from each side of the path, like parting waves.
Soon, he has crossed the horizon and is
approaching a cliff face. Wind howls from holes

in the middle of carvings on the rock.
The more he looks, the more the holes become
mouths, the carvings, blistered faces of children.

The stench thickens as mist darkens to smoke.
Ahead somewhere is the woman who set
the fire, who inhaled the same smoke and died.

On hands and knees, Remesh calls out her name.
He slams into rock, then presses along
the cliff until he finds an opening

with no smoke, little breeze. The passage walls
quickly narrow, so he shifts himself sideways
and squeezes through. Rock oppresses with weight,

air thins, darkness congeals, he feels himself
fading like imprint on sand under waves.
The tunnel turns upward and he smells musk.

He calls out to Nikolina, but echoes
settle on him like dirt on lowered coffin.
Hands, feet grope for crevices as he hauls

himself along. One second he is struggling
for breath, next he is falling down a slope
of loose soil and broken tree roots, and smashing

against the statue of a foot. He pants
for some time, then throws himself backwards when
the little toe, as big as he is, twitches.

For those of a thousand lives, memory
is rich between each life. The swift recall
of each moment, the stunned linking of these

with moments from previous lives, the endless
repetition of repetition, sudden
disengagement of pattern due to chasms

seen beneath the one pattern, growth as function
of leap, the realisation of double
vision as central plan, bliss, path and goal.

At first sign of distress, Rynobar leaps
into the air, but falls back towards earth,
wings no longer working, no longer there.

For an instant, she imagines herself
again in the night sky with other *hoya*
in their gyrating host of constant splendour,

the shapes they make, inspiration not only
for themselves, but for those who dare the dark,
who dare the dread chasm of themselves when

facing that dark—the trigger of raw change,
silent womb and tomb of thought, dream, sense, need,
all things spinning in and out of that nothing

that is and never is, like dragonflies
touching their reflection—though all she knows
is perpetual dance and blank rest after.

She now wishes herself to be much more
than foundation and goal, outcome of choice
when first she knew others had disappeared.

Instantly, two places fill her, the constant
night that ripples with origin and exit,
the narrow casket in between, where grows

a flicker of light through leaves, the bare touch
of tongue to skin, the first blush, the last breath.
The generation of poised blood calls her.

*In birdsong of early morning, clear grandeur
of prior sunset, certainty of more,
surprise at dawn itself, each breath as song.*

Azra watches the others wrestle with
Alyston's spell and be overcome, watches
each of their journeys into memory,

imagination, like moving tattoos
on his body. He perceives the whole garden
as body, knows where they are being led,

knows where he is being led, if he were
to deem himself the only one not caught
in Alyston's spell, not caught by desire.

A sigh explodes above him, air cram-shoves,
ground buckles, tilts, rolls, drops, counter-blast rhythms.
Azra recognises timbre of voice

as lover, mother, sister, brother, father,
child and friend over eons of fused lives
that exist in the time a dewdrop falls

from leaf to ground. They are a single dewdrop,
its condensation of moisture as fated
as falling masses, its pattern of structure

as distinct as newly-minted snow crystals,
lives as water mote joining water mote
and circling through earth and air, call of heat.

There is a groan, another juddering
of earth. He sees himself mopping the brow
of a woman giving birth, though her body

is as big as a mountain range, his cloth
as small as a leaf of grass. He has lost
his hold on perspective. He sees the others

waking from Alyston's game, wonders why
he is still trapped in the spell, size of sperm
standing between the legs of a huge woman.

He sways madly, feels hands supporting him,
hears two sounds: his voice repeating a name
in disbelief, a child's snide, gleeful laughter.

At noon, shadows again begin their preen,
sometimes a moon hardens its share of light,
flowers spark into bloom, eclipse of awe.

32

Birth of a God

The pregnant woman towers over them
as a range of bulbous hills, her skin mottled
like razed paddocks, pools of sweat like full dams,

the sutures in her groin thick as tree trunks.
Her plea-cries and crescendo moans are bellows
that maelstrom the air. Each contraction pitches

the garden through haphazard angles, tosses
people, trees, rocks like chaff. From deep within
her giant womb, wild laughter primes the rhythms.

Azra is repeating Devina's name
in a daze. Zane tries to calm him, while Jessie
helps Rynobar and Remesh to their feet.

'This can't be real,' Azra finally says.
'Such change is an outrage, even in Thexlan.'
He sighs, straightens his back. 'Or maybe not.'

Jessie considers this, then moves towards
Devina's seeping groin. 'But why do this?
What's to be gained by such abuse of nature?'

Remesh rocks his head sideways, to ease tightness
in his neck. 'Maybe some form of forced growth.
The longer birth is delayed, the more knowledge

'and power it acquires.' He points out tubes
hooked into her flesh and complex machines
humming and shimmering at eyes and ears.

Although pale and trembling, Azra surveys
the scene with that detachment of a monk
self-immolating to protest injustice.

'Remesh is right. Whoever arranged this
atrocious act wants to produce a god.'
He grimaces, then looks over to Zane.

Jessie returns from her examination.
'It doesn't matter who did this, or why.
Her pain is dire. We have to start the birth.'

'But how?' Zane says, as baffled as the others
by the panting monstrosity, more so
when her facial features begin to blur.

Azra points to Zane's sword. 'You need to cut
her stitches.' Another loud moan, another
contraction, and the landscape reels. Birds burst

into the sky and the companions struggle
to stay upright. Zane draws his weapon, steps
towards the giant's strain-dilating groin.

At once, the air before him splinter-opens
and Alyston appears. 'Leave her alone.'
He gestures, and a massive dog, all snarl,

quivering muscle, hunches between them.
Each time Zane moves, the creature rears its head.
'Your mother is suffering,' Azra shouts.

'This delay in the birth is dangerous.'
The boy stamps his feet. 'The longer it is,
the better for me.' Jessie stands near Zane.

'I don't know how this happened, but you risk
your mother and the baby.' The boy claps.
A second dog appears. 'You are all wrong.'

Convulsing, Devina screams through clenched teeth,
the garden lurches, light flickers through him.
Zane whispers. 'Did he grow taller just then?'

Jessie nods, realises the connection.
'I understand. You want to be a god.'
Alyston gives her a petulant look.

'I am already.' He gestures around
his sumptuous garden. 'How else explain this?
But it's still not enough. I want more power.'

Tugging Azra's arm, Remesh lifts an eyebrow.
The old man answers in a steady voice:
'He is the unborn child.' 'But who's the father?'

Alyston pricks his ears and smiles. 'I am.'
'That's not possible,' Zane says as he lowers
his sword to the dogs and, with his left hand,

begins a binding spell. Azra steps forward,
places his arm across the Dremaan's chest.
'Yes, it is. In Thexlan, time can fold back

'upon itself. And we all have descendants
and avatars who roam the braids of time.
I know this person. In another place

'he is Nikolina, loved by Remesh.
Elsewhere he may be any one of us.
But here, he is his self-engendered son.'

Jessie grimaces. 'A strange form of incest.'
Azra takes a step towards Alyston,
who glances sideways at him. 'We arise

'from our former selves. And we love these selves
in many other guises. There's no guilt.
The whole kosmos feeds on itself. We eat

'food grown in what remains of ancestors.
And we create ourselves through the next image
we crave or hate.' He takes another step.

'Alyston is a future me, as always
when my next lesson is humility.'
He puts out his hand, lets the dogs sniff him,

then walks between them as they settle down
and slowly fade away. Another groan,
and the boy is now a lanky youth, features

much like Azra's, though with dark, hooded eyes,
hair changing to raven-black with each second.
Dark shadows swirl within his golden aura.

Alyston bows his head, though Rynobar
thinks she sees a smirk on the youth's thin lips.
Another moan, and he grows taller, wider.

While Zane cuts the sutures, Remesh and Jessie
detach the rigging used to feed and train
the unborn baby and confine Devina.

Another contraction, and her brisk panting
is a windstorm in the garden. Within
a minute, the baby's head appears. With

the next contraction, the next push, the baby
gushes out in an amniotic ooze.
His body is normal size, but his head

is three times as big, the baby's dark orbs
wide open, gleaming with intelligence,
power and malice, his hands firmly clenched.

All at once the whole garden shakes itself,
like a dog after a swim in the ocean.
When everyone recovers, they are stunned

to see a normal-sized woman—Devina—
cuddling her normal-sized child to her breast,
no sign of Alyston. Azra joins them,

covers them with his cloak, regards them gently.
He turns back to the others, gives a bow.
'Thank you for your help. I will care for them.

This is my garden now.' He pauses. 'Maybe
this kosmos isn't as complex as I
once thought.' Tears rim his green eyes as he gazes

at the babe playing with Devina's pendant.
'But you will have to leave now. This birth will
not go unnoticed by Abzzu. Take Phaox

and return to your road. There is still much
to be done.' As soon as he finishes,
each particle in the garden begins

to blaze with its own iridescent colour,
like the first hues of creation, when there
is only that spark of sound that divides

into first light, first motion, first design,
themselves sparks for all that will follow, ground
of inspiration for return to sparks.

As the scintillations of light spin wildly,
the pitch of their pulsations soars and whines
until notes shatter neighbour notes, the shards

reforming into shriller notes that shatter
again and again, climb to higher octaves
until Zane and the others feel their ears

become fragile like drum skin overstretched.
Devina looks at Jessie, smiles, and pats
her stomach. Then she looks at the Dremaan.

Another smile, though with a hint of malice,
and for an instant Zane sees Shultar's face.
Someone laughs, and the whole scene splinter-flares.

33

Closer to Home

When eyes recover and their minds regain
the means to fashion dot, line, surface, texture,
Azra, Devina, Alyston are gone.

The travellers shuffle towards the gate.
Around them is the stillness of prey watching
the stealth of a predator, shiver-silence.

After they climb into the pannier,
Remesh takes hold of the reins. 'Where to now?'
Jessie peers along the length of the wall

in both directions, then back on their route.
She thinks she sees a black, flickering mist
creeping towards their overnight campsite.

She points to the right, where the land slopes up.
'I think it's time to leave the depths of Thexlan.
The one way to learn the truth of this journey

'is to cease hiding from ourselves, the dark,
and confront our fears from a place of strength,
so that everything else will be exposed.'

Remesh isn't so sure, but Zane stares deeply
at Jessie's face, sees the determination
and clarity in her eyes, and agrees.

Remesh turns Phaox around. 'Let's go then.'
As everyone settles into their seats,
Zane looks at the wall and recalls Adiska,

home of the Dremaan temple, his abode
for four years of training, skills of the body,
mind, spirit, from carriage of water bucket

down cobbled streets without spilling a drop,
to complex calculations of star movements,
to conjurations of demon and angel—

sometimes as mere facets of one's own soul,
loss, anger, bliss and hope; sometimes as those
imprints of communal souls that rule self:

parent, teacher, lover, trial and elixir;
sometimes glimpses into what dares creation,
that first cascade of nothing into something,

with its standing pools of will and awareness,
and prime governance of all things, the spark
sought for, the dread silence within that spark—

not enough time to learn all, master any.
The city was under constant attack,
not by armies or magic, but by nature.

The drifting hollow sands from within Chos
were on the march, desert that would not stop.
Everything covered turned to sand, as though

the whole world was fading, like Shultar's castle.
Only when the sands encircled Adiska
did Zane learn of the strong Dremaans called Kenri,

those who were destined to maintain not just
a part of Ghajat, like Elgron or Shultar,
but the whole world, though only for a time.

The current Kenri, Beraint, was near death,
his song-spark of power and vision fading,
though he doubted this, as all Kenri do.

Someone needed to challenge him, but those
who were willing to face him had already
failed the tests. Only the students were left.

But first they had to prove themselves Dremaan.
Being the last to commence training, Zane
was the last to be tested. He met Elgron

in the temple's central atrium, tiles
worn to dull sheen from centuries of feet
walking to lesson or *murga* or other

ceremonies in the service of fortune.
'What do you see here?' his master asked him.
Zane pointed to the statues of Dremaans

and Ghajat gods in their niches around
the large space and told stories about each.
Elgron smiled, merely repeated his question.

Zane pointed to the temple and the stars
seen through the open roof, and told those lessons
of the pattern-bonds between star and man.

Elgron frowned, pressed for a considered answer.
Zane looked down, eyebrows knotted with annoyance.
What hadn't he described? Around, above.

But not below. And not what was seen through
the eye rather than with the eye. He moved
to the side of the tiles, noted patched colours

like a child's finger painting out in rain,
focused his sight, relaxed his mind, to see
what had always been beneath sandalled feet.

Like a *murga*, the colours on the tiles
began to deepen, strengthen, form line, curve
and shape, an outer ring of painted figures—

boar, eagle, salmon, firefly, nubile nude,
breast-feeding mother, weeping ancient woman—
a central glyph: white feather, spiral web.

Elgron asked Zane to summon this same creature.
For three days he evoked spirits and souls,
demons and angels, for advice and power.

No food, no drink, no sleep, hallucinations
of vision and sound that wove through each other—
his mother's tales, his sister's screams, the touch

of Shultar's magics on his skin and mind—
but still he persisted long after others
had walked away. With an emphatic gesture

he dismissed all these fragments and wish-figments
of illusion, sat cross-legged, slowed breathing
to the light pant of autumn, sank his mind

into the pit of his belly, and waited
without consciousness of waiting, for entry
into whatever mystery remained.

For nine hours Zane sat motionless, while all
about him the clear sands of Chos formed shapes
to tempt or overwhelm him: smiling goddess

who disrobed and swung her breasts before him;
ogre brandishing in both hands war tools
that changed from spear to axe to bow to all

manner of shield and projectile machines;
thin, bleary-eyed scholar with book and chart
and promise of wisdom in symbols drawn.

Finally, Zane smiled. Through the depths of breath
he brushed the core of his song-spark, through breath
he realised the world was only breath.

As he stood, his eyes blazed with violet flame.
He told his master: 'The one creature who
can weave between all like the spider, who

'can see distance like the high eagle, who
can leap into the gap between all strands
and sight, is man.' The symbol rainbow-blazed

for an instant, opened into a staircase
leading down into darkness. Elgron pointed
the stump of his right arm towards the stairs,

told the new Dremaan to wait at the bottom.
There was one further feature to this quest
to find a new Kenri and save Ghajat…

An abrupt swerve in their steed's motion caused
by Remesh's lack of skill jolts them all
back to the present. He apologises.

Jessie studies the broad band of fringed light
on the horizon. Where is her bright sun
in its blue sky, the Milky Way at night?

If Thexlan was both ground and sum of all,
why did it not echo experience?
She doesn't know how obvious her thoughts

till Zane nudges her arm. 'If Thexlan is
all worlds at once,' he says, 'the light may be
purely spiritual, the means of substance.'

'But matter comes first,' she replies. 'The dense
sphere of energy flash-expanding, then
contracting into particles and gases,

'then slow accretion of elements till
suns and planets are born. Then life, then tools,
then cities, wealth, then destruction of life.'

Jiggling the reins, Remesh shifts in his seat.
'Yes, I believed in that. From dust to dust.
Nothing but, even if it gains the skill

'to fashion itself into its own vision.'
Zane catches the tone in his voice. 'And now?'
Remesh checks the road ahead. 'I'm not sure.

'Certainly there seems to be a state after
the dust of life, else we wouldn't be here.
But—' His attention is caught by the need

to navigate a series of haphazard
chasms and undulations. Zane takes on
his thought: 'But whether the spiritual is

'also the beginning as well as end?'
Remesh nods. 'I can't see the use.' 'Same here,'
Jessie says. 'Why return to what you've left?'

Zane stares out of the pannier to where
Mt Alkerii arises from the plain.
'Haven't you ever wanted to go home?'

They all fall silent and are so caught up
in their own thoughts they do not see the wall
slide into the side of the rising slope.

Until that moment, Zane has had no thought
of returning home, except for revenge.
He had hoped Shultar would destroy his village

during the madness of her last days, when
the poisoned *sorra* diminished her powers,
drove her to despair, and she lashed the land

about Aimal with continuous lightning,
which sapped her rage and skills to the point Elgron
could infiltrate the castle and help Zane.

Once she was dead, he was eager to ravage
Tarlkar himself, but Elgron restrained him
and whisked him to Adiska for his training.

Then came the challenge of the sands of Chos,
the battle with the dying, yet defiant
Kenri, and Zane's eventual acceptance

of the Thulsword, the prime symbol of change.
Once he wielded it, he thought of returning
to Tarlkar, but knew the task before him

so much greater, so much more elegant:
to discover the secret of unknowing
and not only destroy the village, but

everything else, while he remained outside
the unspell till he could remake Ghajat
into the place where his sister and mother

would never die, Jeera would never die.
He had no choice. Home was the feeling all
was back in place: his mother singing tales

of worlds within worlds, he and Kerrilea
competing for her attention, the two
of them eventually learning to cast

murgas, bring fortune to their family.
Home was the good past, where evil was not
what needed to be done to reclaim it.

He wipes his eyes, wonders if home could be
a place to return to, stories to tell
to loved ones, before setting out again.

Crack open a lump of rock and at times
there is nothing but dirt, at times a fossil,
at times the glitter-eye of a black crystal.

Jessie has never wanted to go home.
Not even if her father died. She wanted
to be far away from him and all others

who mouth God's words yet act with venom-smile.
One day, when Jessie was rubbing her eyes
after hours interpreting pictographs,

she saw the symbol for baby and thought
of her mother, an ache-throb at the belly
she was sure others would term homesickness.

She wanted her mother's arms around her,
like those days in church when Father was raving
about the world's decay and villainy

and she would lean on her mother to smell
the lavender in her crocheted jumper,
feel her hand pat Jessie's thigh and rest there,

cosy warmth that shields, soothes and does not judge,
like an arbour of roses, all thorns outward.
She was too young to know how harm could come

from one who said she loved you, then left you
to be hurt by others who profess love…
That day she blubbered hysterically, tears

almost ruining the ancient script—how could
she hope to see her mother again, who
had run away because of her afflictions,

according to her father? So now, Jessie
rubs temples and forehead, ache behind eyes,
that bearing-down-grief to tears or collapse.

Her mother is alive, somewhere. But Jessie
may not be, if she doesn't escape Thexlan.
Yet, why would her mother be at her side,

while she is in a coma, though she never
bothered when Jessie was grappling with madness.
That coma vision must have been a dream.

Home. She has not made one, except for lovers,
who murmur when inside her they have come
home, their lost home, but she is always silent.

Wandering through this vast unknowable,
ever-changing landscape of tale and soul
is the only home she may ever know.

White moth tears through silk to fire-husk air.
Orb-weaver mating voracious. Star eggs.
A dung beetle rolls black sun to its cliff.

Remesh doesn't care about home. He never
had one, except maybe at The Ice Temple,
and even then the place had turned on him,

as he imagines all homes do. He snaps
Phaox's reins, his confidence increasing
the more the creature comes under control,

like a brush stroke on canvas leaving paint,
shape first revealed in his imagination.
Remesh sees himself guiding them throughout

this lost and barren world, which would revive
with each step of their passage, into blooms
of all his flowers, painted and imagined.

All he knows is the comfort of these reins
in his hands and the impulse to outrun
not only Abzzu, but everything else

pursuing him: guilt, love, despair, that hunger
for what he knew the world could not deliver
and he struggled to depict. If he had,

such paintings would have been priceless, for he
is sure that what he craved was what drove those
who crammed The Ice Temple. Was it a sense

of home they, he, desired, or something else?
A sense of place, not to return to, not
for comfort, support, a handout before

being pushed back out the door, but a place
of purpose, of direction, which is what
Remesh feels now, even if the effect

of pursuit. Is there any other way
to engender purpose, a running keenly
towards a thing, instead of away from?

Maybe that's what Jessie meant when she pointed
uphill. He allows himself a tight smile.
Maybe these companions can teach him things.

Take the calliper to the world. Scoured brass.
Wing-beat tilts the clock into fire-works.
After the fall into dark, scaffolding.

Sitting at the back, Rynobar frowns as
she views the others muse on home, and listens
to the murmur of star-song above her.

She can never go home. Often she wonders—
whenever night arrives and the song beckons,
whenever the lights in her body echo

the patterns dancing above her—if maybe
she carries her home, her kin, within her.
But even if she is all the stars, all

hoya appetites, there is a contentment
lost to her, what her companions would call
a sense of home, replaced by a compulsion

of fate, the necessary joy of movement,
of widening her song into the world,
of glimpsing the birth of light from her wings.

Perfection of heat. Golden sphere. The strife
that impels separation, lust of union.
How water becomes earth becomes air. Hallow.

34

The Call of Dust and Flame

Soon they regain the grey road and their speed
increases. Jessie glances backwards, but
can see no more of the shadow miasma.

She wonders if Abzzu has jumped ahead,
waiting to pounce as they approach that dark
flat-topped peak in the distance, rising from

a rust-coloured plain their road snakes across.
She prays for no more detours and delays,
and a little later notices how

the passing landscape is gradually changing.
Gone are the massive cracks that hindered them.
Even the flat greyness has been replaced

by swathes of prickle-moss and clumps of heather.
The road is hard and smooth, with indentations
crossing it at regular intervals.

Nudging Zane, Jessie points to Mt Alkerii.
'What else can you tell us?' His temple twitches
as the Dremaan channels his memories.

'All I have is my mother's tales about
the creation of Ghajat, and those lessons
from Shultar and the Temple of Adiska:

'When the grains of the sea of Chos formed land,
it was still dust. Larandor, the first Kenri,
took dust, breathed on it, spilt blood, used the Thulsword,

'chanted a spell of making. The dust formed
a seed that turned other dust particles
into seeds of the world. All the dust danced

'to his song and formed shapes that flowed and grew
as the music split into melodies
that combined and split again and again.

'Soon Ghajat was a world of earth and sky.
Under it was Es Xayim, tree of lights,
its roots drawing sustenance from the rings

'Thexlan discharged from the first Mt Alkerii.'
He points out weathered craters far ahead
of them, two on each side of the grey road.

'Kenri and Dremaan have seen those in visions
and say they are remnants of former cycles
of existence. They also say the Kenri,

'who is the Dremaan for all of Ghajat,
becomes the keeper of the tree of lights,
which connects with Mt Alkerii, and listens

'to the music the land makes as it flows
and evolves, listens to the land's requests.
Each morning the folk of Ghajat make known

'their wishes for good fortune, some by prayer,
as I'm sure those of your worlds also do,
some by the sand pictures that imitate

'Larandor's first spell, and the mount sends forth
a Keth ring that not only contains answers,
but also the next challenge for each world.'

He slumps in his seat. 'That's all I remember.
And in this place, I can't even be certain
that what I recall is what truly happened.'

Remesh laughs. 'No memory ever is.
There are times I don't think it's necessary.
Animals don't need it, as they engage

'with the world through instinct. Maybe that's all
we ever needed: a good set of instincts
etched into brain and spine.' He pats their steed.

Jessie disagrees. 'Memory guides thought
and choice. Memory carries all emotions
of experience, those we either wish

'to avoid or to evoke. We are conscious
because of memory.' 'Or other way
around,' Remesh says. 'Either case, it's more

'hindrance than help.' Zane shifts so angrily
in his seat the pannier rocks and bounces.
'What of your paintings? Surely memory

'influenced them. Would you throw that away?'
'Yes, rather than have such pain before me
each day. Without memory, there's no pain.'

Jessie lowers her voice. 'And no joy, either.
You are denying that which makes us human.'
Remesh chuckles. 'You yourself have decried

'the destructiveness of man in your world.
You've called the human a plague upon life.
You deny the human in your own way.'

Jessie contemplates the changeable aura
of Thexlan. He is right. She hates mankind
for what it has done to her and her trees.

The world she faces now is a reflection
of how she saw her world developing.
Greed and lust had ravaged air, sea and land.

But the only way that mankind might die
is if it killed the world it has infested
and, so doing, destroy all other creatures.

Jessie finds herself crying. She is dead,
or nearly so, and still the schemes of craving
pursue her, as does her hatred of all,

including herself. She wants to be dust.
Yet, is such oblivion possible,
matter, soul, spirit always changing form?

Maybe oblivion cannot occur
because deep down even the most despairing
of souls has a masked urgency for life.

What will they find on Mt Alkerii, life
or another journey of life-in-limbo?
And how to tell one from the other? Faith?

Zane cocks his head. 'Does anyone hear that?'
Remesh slows Phaox to a walk. They hear
nothing, then a faint cry comes from a grove

to their right. They are too far to hear words,
but the tone of panic is obvious.
Remesh curses. 'But it's out of our way.'

Jessie glances at the meteor, then
Mt Alkerii, turns again to the trees.
She gives a little laugh. 'Everything is

'in our way and on it.' Zane shakes his head.
'What about Abzzu and that thing above?'
He takes out his sword. 'This may be a trap.'

He does not add that sometimes he considers
the whole of Thexlan as an endless trap.
Jessie taps Remesh on the shoulder blade

and nods towards the trees. 'And maybe not.
This journey is supposed to be about
gaining wisdom. How can we ignore those

'obviously in trouble?' Zane says nothing.
When Phaox stops at the edge of the grove,
his sword hums as though in anticipation.

The next time they hear the cry it is clearly
a plea for help. Zane takes the lead, with Jessie,
Remesh and Rynobar in single file.

Unlike the groves they have passed recently,
the trees are bare of leaves, trunks badly gnarled,
with motley-coloured bark, effect of blasts

by scalding winds, though now there is no breeze,
no sound at all, apart from scraps of sobbing
and that taut air full of sparks before storms.

They step over rotting logs and around
pools of rancid weeds. The smell is intense
with decay and from it their skins acquire

a film of slime that grows colder the deeper
into the thick wood they go. Jessie thinks
of the ghost stories she read with her mother,

almost laughs at the stereotype setting,
but when a pool ripples and a pale face
glares at her then fades beneath the black surface,

she chokes back her derision. Its eyes were
like her own when in strong light—purple flickers.
She stiffens her composure and walks on.

As they enter the clearing, gilded light
with shadow edges, the temperature drops
even further. A large stone altar squats

in the centre. Chained to it is a female,
legs apart, breasts exposed, coffee skin glinting.
Again, Jessie fights back a mocking jeer.

Surely, this must be someone's wish-fulfilment
and Remesh right to suggest they ignore
the cries. Then Jessie remembers the way

some men in her father's bible group leered
at her new church dress just before her father
banished her from the room. Fantasy or

reality, the woman deserves rescue.
As Jessie takes another step, a ring
of lurid flames bursts from the ground around

the altar and a low voice within thunders
with laughter. 'She is mine,' it declares. 'Leave,
if you value your souls.' Jessie laughs back.

'How corny.' She reaches out. Intense heat
sears the palms of her hands. She laughs again.
The heat drops a little. Zane grabs at her

to pull her back. She shrugs him off and glares.
He steps back. She sees Rynobar unfurl
her wings, and gestures her compliance too.

The flames crackle and spit more violently
and the voice becomes shriller. 'You must leave.'
Jessie can see a vague shape standing next

to the altar. Something gleams in its hand.
'I suppose you intend to ravish her—
before or after you offer her soul

'to the devil you worship in your weak,
childish way.' She titters, then starts to cackle:
'Mighty lord, I offer this sacrifice

'if you grant me my boon.' The dark shape blazes,
brings the blade closer to the woman's chest.
Jessie steps through the flames, then stagger-shakes

when she recognises the woman's face
as her mother's. The shape isn't her father,
but a more grotesque version, fire and smoke

and sneer, as when the layman gave his sermons.
'Whom do you serve?' it says, just like her father
each day, and for an instant Jessie sees

herself lying on rough stone, arms and legs
fettered, then gripping a small, sickle blade
while looking down at herself on the altar.

Regaining her mental balance, she senses
the heat now behind her. She folds her arms
and says, calm voice, 'I'm not afraid of you.'

The thing laughs and the intense flames press her
forward. She remembers the suffocation
outside the steel and ivory gate, knows

Zane had been right. This is a trap, of sorts.
She lifts her right arm, blue fire racing through
her veins. Nothing but pain will be spilled now.

Her father's face becomes hers for a second.
'It's not me you have to fear, little one.
It's much deeper. What have you always feared?'

She recalls her tree's rough bark at her back,
that comfort of knowing no one could find
her haven. She clasps those feelings to her.

'My mother leaving us was not my fault.'
Her father leans towards her and she suffers
that scorn of presence he always projected

when he towered over her. She stares up
at him, smells his sodden breath, does not flinch.
'And what you did to me...' She flicks her palm.

His form shrinks back, though the smile does not change:
'So what caused your affliction?' Jessie feels
her mind contract into a foetal ball

of shame. She has no answer. She knows whom
she blamed: her parents, the world. She now grasps
this isn't enough. What lesson is there

in her albinism? Was she to blame
because of sins in a past life? What god
would assign affliction here, fortune there?

Always her father's words: 'Part of His plan
for mankind. Do not judge His Mystery.'
Each time a stranger stared at her. Each time

a child gasped. Each time a so-called girlfriend
pointed at her while talking with the boy
Jessie had told her she liked, and they sniggered.

Each time she went to open her veins, smear
colour over her skin, say to the world,
'See, I am just like you.' Each time she breathed,

she cursed God's Mystery, cursed the idea
of Mystery. What use was life if one
could never unravel its rules, its reason?

But now, in the face of such a rejection
of Mystery in this rite she is sure
she has studied before, she has no choice

but to learn the motive of Mystery
or be condemned to stay within the flames,
watch her father cut her mother's throat, be

both of them in that stark instant of death—
holding the knife, feeling it cut her flesh—
awaken again, watch and do again.

Suddenly she hears music. Zane is playing
his lyre, and vital woe wells up in her
as in an instant she sees what he sees.

35

The Sacrifice

Zane waits at the bottom of the steps under
the temple. After a few minutes, Jeera
joins him there. She had also passed the test,

but Elgron told her to await Zane's efforts.
'Hopefully, together you will be able
to defeat the Kenri and save Ghajat.'

They wait in trepidation as a boat,
guided by a man in shadow, glides over
a silent underground sea towards them.

When the craft lands, he gestures them aboard
and they head back into an iridescent
darkness that quickly resolves into braids

of light high above them, like vaulted beams
in a cathedral, stretching into distance,
the length and breadth of the vast underbelly

of Ghajat, strands with running beams of light
that sometimes shimmer-join in one long burst,
but more often fade for long periods.

At random intervals, none ignite, plunging
this underworld into a mist-breath shiver
that would numb all sense if darkness persisted.

They travel for hours, then notice the strands
of light converging to a single pillar
flickering on an island before them.

They glide along a deep lagoon towards
the centre of the island. Massive mangroves
line the banks. Nothing moves. The only sound

is the sigh of their craft across the water,
which rejoins swiftly behind them and stays
flat and black even when the strands light up.

When their boat touches ground, Jeera and Zane
turn to thank the silent tiller man, but
he has vanished. They quickly make their way

to the massive trunk of light-braids awash
in halo swarms, the gaps between the flashes
less obvious, though their rhythm is speeding.

An old man dressed in tattered purple robes,
black sash, not Dremaan white, stands at the tree,
with fever eyes, swinging a crystal sword.

'More victims to be tested by Beraint.'
His words and the rhythm of the blade echo
each other, speech, man and weapon one fate.

Jeera remembers Elgron's stump, and others.
She offers her right arm. The sword arc-slices
the air and passes right through flesh and bone

without any damage. Beraint nods once,
turns to Zane, who offers hands clamped together,
proof of fate-strength, and smiles at his beloved.

Again the blade hums as it swings, again
there is no damage, again Beraint nods,
then says, 'There is one more test for you both.

'For one of you to take the Kenri role,
fate would have given you *Anen*, the jewel
that fits here.' He shows them the empty pommel.

Jeera and Zane look at each other, smile.
She takes the pendant from around her neck,
unclasps the small, silver sphere he sent her,

tosses it to Beraint, who inserts it
into the pommel, sighs, then bows his head.
'Now to find out who will feed Es Xayim.'

He charges them, sword-point nicking Zane's chest,
Jeera's left shoulder, as both students leap
aside, amazed the weapon can now hurt.

The old man pauses, blade above his head.
'You may have passed the Thulsword's Kenri test,
but with *Anen* it now can kill. Needs to.'

The students draw their own weapons, and watch.
Beraint starts chanting in time with his swings
and they realise he is summoning

the power of his song-spark, as well as
tapping into Es Xayim's fading strength.
As they dodge and parry the Kenri's blows

they chant their own inner songs and together
weave a simultaneous dance of strike,
block, counter-strike, wooden sword and short swords

against the crystal blade, until Beraint
withers under their combined attack, drops
his weapon, falls against the braided trunk.

'Do it,' he says, 'before the lights all fail.'
Zane takes up the sword and plunges it through
the Kenri. They watch as it drinks his blood

and flash-blazes with scarlet incandescence
while he fades into dust that swirls and rises.
A voice tells them to thrust the weapon into

the tree, but Zane pulls it aside and watches
the blood-light start to fade. 'Now,' Jeera yells,
then grabs him when he starts to walk away.

'Why?' she says. 'Because this world killed my mother
and my sister,' he replies. She shakes him.
'But you will die.' He wishes he had Shultar's

Keth shard and the knowledge to move outside
Ghajat, but resigns himself to this lack.
He shrugs. She peers at him. 'And I will die.'

He pulls away, his blazing eyes of fury
rimmed with tight tears. 'I pray Larandor will
forgive me and let our souls meet in Thexlan.'

'No,' Jeera screams, and attacks him. Again
there is clash of wood on crystal, again
song-sparks drive the fierce energy of battle,

again a Kenri is defeated, Jeera's
skill with her twin swords greater than all students,
including Zane, who ends up on the ground,

right arm aching from her disabling blows.
The Thulsword is dull-red and before Jeera
can plunge it into the tree—whose lights are

waning rapidly—the blade's song-spark vigour
fades with a sigh-tremor, as blade, tree, world.
She looks over at Zane, says, 'I love you,'

drives the sword through herself into the trunk.
Zane dashes to her, but cannot pull out
the weapon. He watches it fill with blood,

hugs her tight, begs her forgiveness, their tears
mingling. In seconds her body sags, but
does not vanish. Zane sobs as her blood flows

into the tree, strands of light shimmering
with renewed life and power, rainbow colours—
the island, the whole underworld, aglow

as rapid pulses of energy travel
along the humming braids to quicken breath
in Ghajat and dissolve the sands of Chos.

When the Thulsword is drained, Zane pulls it out
hacks and slashes the tree as it begins
to absorb Jeera's body. He wants her

alive, the tree dead, all of Ghajat dead.
Then the tree speaks to him, her husky voice.
'My sweet, you cannot destroy Es Xayim,

'nor can you bring me back. You are the Kenri.
Accept your fate. In that will be your healing.
I promise to be near you always, aura

'to guide and protect you, till next we meet.'
In his guilt and despair Zane ignores her,
slashes at nearby vegetation, screams

his defiance at Fate. He knows his task.
He will destroy Ghajat and remake it
with his loved ones returned, or destroy all.

With a single thought, he creates a version
of himself to guard the sacred tree, conduit
for his Kenri power. As Zane moves back

he spies something fluttering on the trunk:
long strands of Jeera's red hair, which he folds,
kisses, then pockets. He reboards the boat

and steers it towards Adiska, but not
before tossing *Anen* into the sea.
He will be the last Kenri of Ghajat.

36

To Unravel Herself

Jessie drops to her haunches, sobs for Zane
and his love of Jeera, whom she now knows
is Jenny, spirited childhood friend, sobs

for her sacrifice, though Jessie herself
cannot understand Zane's actions, blames him
for her friend's death, feels his grief, his remorse,

sobs too with the knowledge that even if
she can never escape the flames, the world
will constantly remind her of failed life.

How to find the secret of Mystery?
Part of her merges with Zane's music, plummets
and rises with gloom and blossom-bliss, while

another part tries to unstitch her musings.
She has read enough of fable and epic
to know how humans tackle and avoid

this question—clay figures, cave paintings, potions
of inspiration, degradation, flights
of dream, of amusement—without an answer.

She wonders if Zane's songs are attempts, not
to answer the question, but to evoke
an experience of core Mystery.

As with a music that starts low and climbs
in trills and cadenzas through pitch and rhythm,
then seems to disappear in silent quavers

of the highest note and pause, Mystery
is not a riddle to solve, but a state
to be keenly felt. So why her affliction?

Maybe, there is no reason other than
a trauma in the body caused by forces
beyond anyone's control, a chance change.

The only blame was how people responded
to her, though if she were to believe that
one chooses one's next life, the blame is hers.

Her head begins to throb under the strain
of such complex ideas. If one can choose
the next life, for those lessons contained there,

then it already exists, the choice also,
like a leaf buffeted by rain that falls
into a river. What use could there be

of a clockwork kosmos in which the end
is already known? Leaf tumbles to sea,
falls to the bottom, becomes mulch and fuel

for some future generation of tree
when the world axis shifts, sea vanishes,
leaf appearing once more to wait its fall.

She grips her temples and ignores the tread
of her father towards her. Jessie knows
he cannot hurt her now, and never could.

In a crevice of her mind is an image
that would open with an answer, if only
she could dive after it, become it truly.

She sees herself as a raindrop absorbed
in the river in the sea in the moisture
drawn up by sun, sees herself as the cycle,

without losing awareness of each drop.
She is each drop, can shift from any one
to any other, be all at once, be

the whole cycle at once and everything
the cycle caresses—soil, pebble, flower,
everything that laps, sips, gulps, or absorbs;

be tiny mote, be planet, be between,
be each thing at once, and all beyond each.
The Mystery is itself, as she is.

Jessie has ceased being Jessie, yet knows
which part of her sought such a state, which part
seeks to help others through that state, which part

blazes within all others and all states,
and how the illusion of state prevents
the spark being known, being fanned to breath.

Jessie not Jessie always Jessie always
not always memory of not and is
and is not yet can be if only now

only the flow of flow of thought of image
of sensation of insight of now of
then, flow of flow and behind flow of flow.

She blinks, finds herself nodding to the music
and watching tree and leaf and grass-stem glisten
in the middle of a rainstorm. The flames

are writhing into steam that thins and scatters.
The altar and its attendants have vanished.
Jessie begins to shiver, cold and shock,

till arms wrap her with warmth. Her body crumples
as weariness takes her, more dizziness
as rain slows and thickens like spider webs,

which splatter her cheeks with cold, snowflakes falling
in between skeins of rain. She grins and chuckles,
puts out a hand and watches snowflakes melt

as soon as they touch flesh, then fade to mist
that briefly forms the faces of her parents.
Jessie whispers her thanks. The mist unravels,

curls around her a moment, then is scattered.
She breathes deeply, allows herself to be
carried back to Phaox and wrapped in blankets.

37

A New Poise

When Zane looks back at Jessie's grove, the trees
have sprouted deep blue-green leaves and the hill
below is swathed in fine wavelets of grass.

A flock of bright parrots bursts from the trees
with constant screeching and much battering
of red-green to violet air, settle back

a little later, only to repeat
their spiral gesture, communal delight
in spontaneous weave of launch, flight, rest.

He wonders what really happened to Jessie
and why. Although exhausted, she is lighter
in some way, ease of aura, carriage, smile,

like one whose deep burden has been embraced
and revealed as an opportunity,
relief of fact, acceptance of fate's toil.

Remesh clicks his tongue at Phaox, steers it
to the road. Zane settles into his seat,
cradles Jessie's sleeping form, and begins

to notice how natural is the feeling.
Cold lightning strangles his spine for some seconds,
harrow intimacies, Jeera and others.

He starts to slide out from under her, but
she nuzzles into him and he relents.
The tang of her—a newborn's freshness edged

with zest for leap and lesson, bloom and blood—
shifts his gaze and he sees a brief smile play
on her lips. Like Jeera's. He turns away.

Jeera of the blue eyes glinting like ripples
on Lake Tarlkarni, unruly red hair,
smile of crimson lips as she chided him

about his lack of flexibility
his first morning of daily exercises:
smile when she first beat him in weapons training.

Jeera of the smooth, sweat-radiant body
a year after they met, the circle-dance
of glances and throat-tangled words, of dreams,

broken by her sly cheek-snuggle one day
in a library nook, that night the slow
press of hands to hands, slow lick at neck hollow,

nip of ear-lobe, blood quickening, the burst
to relentless dissolve of skin through skin,
rhythm cascades of heat and panting-bliss.

Jeera of the open gasp the first time
he fashioned a rainbow mist-bird for her.
Jeera of the wrenching-tears when she died.

Jeera. Jessie. The world is like a *murga*
unfolding before him, grain, pattern, fissure
within the painting, and maybe he is

back with his mother still learning the art,
like that time the urgency of his need
to prove himself an adept at this task,

rebel to his father's disdain, drove him
into fevered focus and chant on chant
early one day in his hideaway thicket,

sand grains jumping like boiling water, rhythm
of his breaking voice, flowing into pattern
as pinhole vision falls away to grey.

There was only silence, only a shiver
of presence as the silence opened into
deeper silence, like darkness fluttering.

He felt himself drawn further into silence,
presence fading to junctures of light-dark:
red-wild fecundity, blue-sear communion.

Then came a counter-song, a melody
of yearning and despair, a prisoner
looking at sky through a small, barred, high window.

Caught between two familiarities—
the first ancient, though only just met, like
glimpsing one's original face on water;

the other recent, yet vital for glimpses,
like those tears needed to clear dust from eyes—
Zane felt himself a moth between two lamps.

An instant later, he sensed desperation
of intensity in this second tug
at his awareness, knew the nuance there:

his mother singing him out of the *murga*,
drawing him home—smell of herbs in fish stew,
feel of bedding tucked around him. It worked.

How he missed her. But how he hated her
for leaving them to Shultar's moods and needs.
How he hated Kerrilea for being

the one chosen. How he hated the others
for allowing her to be the one chosen.
How he hated his guilt, hated his hate.

He swore there would be no more hate or pain.
For anyone. He would invoke the Spell
of Unknowing, no matter what it took.

When Jessie stirs and opens her pale eyes,
Zane doubts himself, his hate, his locked intent.
She looks at him. 'Have I been sleeping long?'

'Not long.' He gestures towards the far copse.
'Do you want to talk about it?' She shakes
her head, but smiles. He doubts himself still more.

Becoming conscious of his arms around
her, he lifts her slightly and slides away.
Though surprised by both his gesture of comfort

and his genteel retreat, she casually
mutters her thanks and brushes herself down,
before peering around to check their progress.

The road is still firm, though the soft verge shows
recent wheel marks and lines of footprints, all
leading towards the distant Mt Alkerii,

set in the middle of an ochre plain,
past a series of densely wooded hills.
Jessie squints towards the mountain and thinks

she can distinguish a complex of buildings
nestled in the gentle slopes at its base.
Her gaze drifts higher. The steep sides are creviced

by shadows. She shudders as she imagines
Abzzu lurking there, then regains composure
as though there's nothing to fear anymore.

She cranes her head further. The mountain rises
like an obelisk to the gods, but is
indented, like a target in the ground

for ball games. She wonders what they will find
at the top, which seems flattened by incessant
battering against the hard dome of sky.

Jessie turns to the Kenri. 'We still have
a long way before we reach Mt Alkerii.
I'd like to hear about your crystal sword.'

Zane looks up at the meteor, its speed
almost matching their own, its trail of dark
a little wider, then looks behind them

to where he can see Abzzu as a low
black cloud swaying over Alyston's garden.
'I suppose we're not in any close danger.'

'Worrying about Abzzu won't help us
confront it when the time comes,' Jessie notes.
Taken by the calm-logic in her voice,

Zane regards her and is surprised by her
graceful poise, her serene gestures, her aura
a bright mauve nimbus that stirs as she moves.

'Yet, you don't appear to fear it,' he says.
She shrugs. 'I do feel more centred, more certain,
yet Abzzu is a danger—it wants, needs,

'something from us.' Remesh turns from the reins.
'What would that be?' 'I'm not sure,' she replies.
'I do know we help ourselves through these stories.'

Zane stares at Mt Alkerii in the distance.
A shimmer about it brings to mind Jessie,
her aura a ripple of single colour,

like desert mirage curtains overlapping
each other in constant fluttering motion.
He closes his eyes and begins his tale.

38

The Gem of Synrath

'Since the first person saw patterns in stars
or wondered how to capture and use fire
or pleaded the return of some lost thing—

'a child in the forest, a parent crippled,
light vanishing from eyes and breath—or listened
to the wind chase its tail, then caress trees

'as if murmuring secrets of desire
and command, we have always wanted more,
have always dreamed of being gods or better.

'We dance, chant, draw patterns in sand, compel
breath and blood to wisdom, power, look upwards
out of the cramping dark from which we came

'and to which we wish never to return,
though the killing stroke is as close as laughter.
Something in us drives us beyond ourselves.

'Dust sculpted to land, broken by wind, moulded
to bricks, built into towers, into gleaming
cities, walls rising from loathing and fear.

'We are never satisfied. We are never
content with simple success. It has taken
many cycles of thought for me to dream

'the final dream, many more to decide
how that dream must be concluded, and why.
Now I shall tell you of the broken sword.

'The night I became Kenri, and lost Jeera,
my first love, who gave herself for Ghajat,
I had a dream, not blood, not shining swords,

'but a great tower gleaming in the distance,
tall like a spindle for the wheeling heavens.
I saw myself climbing the wooden stairs

'that coiled around the outside basalt walls.
At each turning, there were round window panes
through which I could see bird's-eye images

'of peoples and creatures thrashing and howling
and gyrating across landscapes of dream
and fate, displays of different sins and virtues.

'Through one casement I beheld myself peering
in a window looking at myself, saw
the tunnels of my eyes and the bright darkness

'keenly staring back at me. I awoke,
swore I would find that celestial tower,
swore I would find a way to topple it.'

Zane looks at the others, and perceives, now,
that in Thexlan the longer they have journeyed
together, the more open each one's dreams,

visions, memories become to the rest,
like salt dissolving into water, or
jewels reflecting their facets back and forth.

Rynobar sees most, for she had known him
in Ghajat; Remesh sees least; and now Jessie
can read what he allows himself to see.

'I wandered for years, loving no one else,
but always seeing Jeera disappearing
around corners, hearing her husky voice

'in market chatter and outside my window
at midnight. I studied mages and sages,
lived as mercenary or bodyguard,

'killed those who stood between me and more knowledge.
On the days I heard Kerrilea's laughter
and knew my guilt once more, I would drink, fight,

'drink again. One such night, I heard a legend
of a rich land where gods ruled from a tower,
overseeing the lightning and the seasons,

'a land where there was no hunger, no blight,
a land of fruitful harvests, bright lives, wisdom.
The man who told me the tale had white hair

'and the sign of the white snake on his cheek.
He sold me a weathered map, which I followed,
though always certain it was fake, like others.

'The tower was nothing like my dream, being
a squat temple atop a hill enclosed
by a wall that separated these gods

'from their people. I was warned not to enter
if not invited, but have never taken
such advice kindly. I climbed the low wall,

'which had no guards except the fear of power,
climbed the hill to the tower and its spread
of buildings, was greeted like a lost son.

'Though the world around the hill had all seasons,
the land of Synrath was eternal spring,
motley-gambol of creatures, blooms in nectar.

'Each day we feasted and fought, and each night
we feasted and loved. Whatever was needed
arrived out of thin air, much like my time

'with Shultar's spirits, but swifter. Not one
warrior died who wasn't resurrected
before the night's festivities began.

'Each dusk a golden method of bells summoned
these gods to their ancient temple, from where,
as told me by the tawny-haired, dark beauty

'I won as booty during tournament,
they would confer hopes and dreams on their subjects,
in the way of *murga* and Es Xayim.

'Not being subject, not yet god, I was
forbidden to participate or watch.
Such commands to me are like tests of fate.

'One day, I spelled myself into a dove
and watched their ceremony. They were gathered
around a massive mirror in the floor.

'Hands joined, they sang of health, wealth, and delight.
The air around them shimmered like fireflies.
Their chant reached a crescendo and the mirror

'became wildly phosphorescent, with rays
of energy shooting from it and circling
that chamber so fast and bright, shards of lightning,

'I had to cover my eyes with my wings.
When I could look, the gods were incandescent.
Those who had fallen in our games of war

'and lust were whole again, those who had craved
a new face or body were so transformed,
and I marvelled at how this crystal mirror

'aided both ruler and subject, a blaze
of compassion cleansing both man and god,
love of life drawing from itself for more.

'When they left I discarded my disguise.
As I circled the gem and studied each
gleaming facet, I remembered the portals

'in my dream and saw those crippled in mind
or body begging on the streets for food
or the means of oblivion. I saw

'those with clay masks for faces chained to plough
or rows of benches, rows of machines, rows
of weaponry, their children joining them.

'I saw infertile fields, saw savage storms
and sudden drought, saw crumbling homes, saw men
kill for nothing more than a scrap of pride.

'I knew I was not in the company
of gods but leeches. Like Shultar. I strode
to the centre of that mirror, in which

'was incised a dragon eating the sun,
and drew my sword. I would topple this tower.
The Kenri blade could reshape anything.

'The instant I started to chant, the gem
rippled with shadow-edged light, like lake waves
under stars, and the profane gods rushed back.

'When they saw me, they joined hands at the edge
of their gem and aimed their leech spell at me.
I raised my sword, plunged it into the lens,

'which fissured in a torrent of wild forces
that tossed me across the shrine. I awoke
and all the buildings were gone, the gods gone.

'I found the Thulsword stuck in rocky ground.
As I gripped the hilt I was mesmerised
by a vision of their deaths. I saw coils

'of light erupt from their bodies and swirl
around the room in a quickening storm—
high-pitched shrieks, boom-crack of lightning, air riven

'by ruptures like those below Shultar's keep—
then weave themselves towards the mirror gem,
a spiral of rippling intensities,

'my sword as focus. As power roared through
the channel made, the stunned gods shrivelled into
husks of skin that quickly dissolved to dust.

'With a sigh their temple, their waterfalls,
their pools of golden fish, their lavish gardens
with trees of speckled birds and silken blossoms,

their stone pagodas filled with jewelled divans,
their grottos of treasure and wine, their steeds,
their sundering wall, all faded from sight.

'The Thulsword, which seconds before had sizzled
with the power flowing through it, was cool.
As I started to pull it from the ground,

'I was aware of the surrounding land
and its peoples. Though I had no concern
either way for their health, I was content

'with my defeat of their malicious gods,
who had usurped a gift that could have been
used differently. I expected to see

'the returned energy restoring crops
and human faces, was shocked to see nothing
had changed, such good fortune beyond their grasp.

'With a wrench the sword came free. I fell back
and stared at the broken end of the blade.
I burrowed frantically into the ground

'for the missing shard, but to no avail.
It was only later I realised
I had ceased to age, and I often wonder

'if the energy of that event had
somehow been absorbed by me as a curse,
some sort of reprimand for my own actions.

'Not that it matters. There will always be
towers to climb, enjoy, deny, and topple.'
He strikes one last loud chord, palms the lyre silent.

39

Another Juncture

Remesh gives a little clap. 'A good tale.
Must be a wondrous thing never to die.'
His tone borders on querulous, as always.

'Actually,' Jessie says, 'the opposite.
In my studies, I researched every story
of immortal wanderers. They all spoke

'of elation at first, then learning gained,
delights savoured, the journeys and adventures,
sin without repercussion, then the boredom,

'the despair, the loss of loved ones, the constant
display of change while they remained the same.
And Zane in some way influenced those stories,

'maybe wrote some of them. Always alone
and never savouring the focus-tang
of the ever-present moment that only

'death inspires. There is no bliss in that type
of immortality for any person.'
'Are other types possible?' Remesh says.

Zane leans forward. Jessie may have divined
his despair, but what of his desperation?
Does she know anything of his true path?

Jessie considers her epiphany
before the altar. Immortality
is a condition that only the kosmos

could claim. She does not understand how Zane
can never die, unless it is a function
of never being born. He has not lived

in her real world, as though he were invented
for, or by, story, and condemned to wander
because his story is not knowable,

not just incomplete. Yet, he has affected
her own world, invisible traveller
reversing through time until…until time

itself is born. Where could he go before
time exists, and how is it possible
to be always there, yet here with them now?

Although immortal, he is singular,
the rock the stream flows over and around,
yet never worn away by such grave waters.

He can never be a part of the kosmos,
true punishment by the gods, bitter fate.
Her heart turns for him and she vows to help.

'The truest immortality is when
you give yourself to what is larger than
yourself, when you understand there is no

'you, never was, only the larger thing.'
Remesh snorts. 'And you could suffer abuse
by those in charge of this true, larger thing.'

Rynobar stretches wings, narrows eyes, smiles.
'I thought you once belonged to such a group.'
The artist glares at her over his shoulder.

'Yes, once. A home when the tavern burnt down.
A work that filled me with the same contentment
my painting used to give.' He drops his head...

When Remesh wouldn't turn up the last card
on the night of the fire, the seer said
one more thing as he gathered up his deck:

'I was you in another life, and Balis,
and the children Nikolina destroyed.
She loved them because she knew they were you.

'The cards have told me I will die tonight.
You will soon see your god and kill for him.
The world will kill you, a fate you will welcome.'

Then the man collapsed on the floor and died
before Remesh could summon any help.
When the last breath sighed to nothing, Remesh

felt a presence engulf him as he cradled
the man. A tender heat that grew much stronger,
wilder, the colder the dead man became—

razing every part of Remesh's being,
flowing into the dead man's gaping eyes
opening into a lattice of flames

connecting every life the man had been,
would be, always, knotted ribbons of lightning
extending the vast horizons within,

each knot a soul, all lives one soul, one god,
which breathed such fire along every soul sinew,
which palpitated with every life tongued.

When the spinning facets of vision-heat
became excruciating, like a million
bee stings on the eye ball, he gagged and blinked,

found the bar filling with smoke. Remesh crawled
out the front door and staggered down the street,
his mind whirling for more union with God.

Days later he joined the Monady Church.
He helped in soup kitchens, became a layman,
served on councils, played his part in salvation…

Remesh shudders, shakes his head, blinks, looks up,
realises the others are still waiting.
He jiggles the reins, keeps Phaox at speed.

'Sometimes such work is false belief. There is
no promise the larger thing will treat you
well when all that concerns it, is itself.'

Jessie conjures a long, smouldering branch.
'You don't see.' She swirls the wood in large circles
until aflame, light dancing in her face.

She offers it to Remesh. 'Take the flame,
yet leave the branch behind.' 'Not possible.
The flame is wood burning itself with flame.'

A gust of wind almost snuffs out her branch.
In that instant Remesh, Zane, Rynobar
see Jessie's body glowing from within,

a light more than the reflection of veins
showing through pale skin—trial and consequence—
an indigo radiance of calm power.

Then the branch roars back into flame and Jessie's
aura recedes, as though her lesson is
much more than even she would dare to know.

She snuffs out the fire. 'And so are we all.'
Zane stretches, then turns around to face her.
'But the flame will eventually consume

'the wood, and both will no longer exist.
Where is your immortality? The ash?
Out of which another branch is ignited?'

'The kosmos is an enormous flame-branch,'
Jessie says, then shrugs. 'I can't tell you how
it keeps burning, only that we and it

'are woven together.' Then she remembers
the sense of her insight. 'There is no we
and it, only the kosmos and its play.'

Again Remesh snorts, then thumps his chest. 'Well,
I only know this being. And each thing
out there is out there on its own as well.

'We have no ties with any other thing,
and then we die, always alone, no hope,
the utter knowledge that all faith is useless—'

'And end up in this nonsense place discussing
the mystery of life until we learn
discussion is also useless,' she says.

Zane moves over to her. 'I can't deny
an astonishing thing happened to you
back there.' He tilts her head with his left hand

and peers deeply into her pale blue eyes,
which do not flinch under examination.
'I can almost take on your certainty.'

He waves his other hand towards Remesh.
'But I have to agree with him. I haven't
had your experience, and never will.

The world is separate. Always has been.'
His conviction surprises him. 'The only
immortality is my life, my curse.'

Jessie stares back at him. His face is hard,
eyes the colour of the black trail above.
'While you believe that, you are indeed cursed.'

Zane turns from her at the sound of a snigger
from the front. 'Your derision is misplaced,
Remesh, for you're not beyond such opinion.

'You still haven't told us why we found you
almost lifeless by the side of the road.'
Remesh sighs. 'I wondered when you'd ask me.'

He clears his throat. 'A simple answer, really.
I was waiting for judgement. I had lost
my talent, my lover, my faith, had spent

'so long searching for them during my life
that when I arrived here, I was too tired
to continue. All that remained was judgement.'

He does not tell them how he had already
faced the mirror slab and been shown his sins,
how he had tried to recross the mist bridge.

His shoulders slump. 'I did search for them here,
for a while, but could find nothing,' he sweeps
an arm around, 'in this forsaken place.'

Jessie moves closer to him, rubs his back.
'So you allowed yourself to fade.' He shrugs
her away and raises his voice. 'Until

'you interfered.' Jessie slides back. 'But surely
you know nothing can disappear in Thexlan.'
He turns to her, face a rictus of anger

and perverted triumph. 'Why do we run
from Abzzu, if nothing is ever lost?'
Jessie keeps her own face full of concern.

'Essence isn't lost. Only our attachment
to things, which keeps us from expressing essence,
what Zane calls our song-spark.' He turns away.

She continues. 'I think we avoid Abzzu
because we do not want to sacrifice
what we think is our soul.' She stares ahead.

'You don't believe we have a soul?' Zane says.
'How can you be in a coma, and also
be here?' She shifts position so both men

can see her. 'Like everything else, the soul
is fleeting. When we are ready, it merges
into a thing much greater.' Remesh hisses.

'Why are you still here, if your revelation
has shown you this truth of reality?'
'Maybe there is something I'm meant to do.'

Remesh pulls sharply at the reins and spins
around as Phaox lurches to a stop.
'I'm tired of this gibberish, these puzzles.

'Everything here is a sham. We're all fake.'
He leaves his seat, starts to climb down from Phaox.
'I don't know why I bother with this quest.'

Even when he disappears behind trees,
the others can still hear him muttering
about the futility of their actions.

Zane moves to follow, but Jessie stops him.
'He'll return quick enough.' Rynobar offers
to watch the painter without being seen.

Knowing the ill-feeling between the two,
Jessie and Zane are unsure of this plan,
but when she looks at the star-demon closely

she sees an open caring in her eyes
and agrees. The great wings haul Rynobar
high above the forest of mountain ash

and keep her hovering there as Remesh
pushes his way through twisted undergrowth
to whatever haven will ease his mind.

'Remesh is such a fool,' Zane says, his voice
strained by exasperation. 'Can't he see
this self-pity isn't helping at all?'

He points back to Jessie's thicket of trees.
'Especially when that is on our trail.'
They see a swirling shadow smothering

the hill, the tops of its green trees like banners
tossing wildly in the middle of battle.
'How long before it gets here?' Jessie says.

'Three or four hours.' Zane scans the road ahead.
'And about the same to reach Mt Alkerii.'
He moves to the front seat. 'Remesh had better

make up his mind fast, or I will leave him
once I figure out how to control Phaox.
If you can, attract Rynobar's attention.'

40

Prelude to a Death

Remesh doesn't know nor care where he's going.
All he wants is to get away from words
and touch, from all those trials that brought him out

of his desired stasis, his stagnation.
Be nothing. Be still and empty. Just vanish
totally into dust. He doesn't care

if a Dremaan or a Kenri can take
such dust and fashion it into a world.
It wouldn't be his world, wouldn't be him,

just those parts of him without him. The dust
of dream and desire. Sorrow and despair.
Nothing of him, for he is truly nothing,

as Jessie has just pointed out to them.
What made her such an expert? Just because
of a lavish vision. Can she show proof

she saw anything at all, anything
worth listening to? He too had been gifted
with a vision of meaning, one confirmed

by the clergy at his new church, who claimed
similar visitations by the One,
who gave him tasks to benefit the One.

He shudders when he recalls Jessie's tale
of dancing universes. Not her words,
but their true speaker. When Rynobar's wingtips

touched her, their auras merged like coloured ink
in water—Jessie grew taller, more shapely,
her hair, her skin, her eyes becoming darker...

A large, cold shadow passes over him
and his drag-footsteps echo all around.
He blinks, and looks down to a hardwood floor.

He has walked inside a derelict building.
Or maybe it formed around him, some magic
designed by Thexlan to madden him further.

He notes rows and rows of wooden pews facing
away from him, and thinks of the old church
at the orphanage. He sees a red curtain

at the front and knows he is in a theatre,
much like the one Nikolina and he
visited at the start of their affair.

His eyes widen, breath spasms. The same hall,
same panelled stage, same sewn rip in the curtain,
same old-fashioned, suspended coloured lights.

That front pew was where they had sat alone,
no hands entwined, no knee pressing the other.
A small ensemble had played in that corner.

Now, nothing, not even their instruments.
All surfaces are covered in thick dust,
as if there had never been a performance.

What had they seen? Remesh sits down and cradles
his head in his hands. A short play about
a condemned prisoner the night before

his execution, how he argued with
the priest about last rites, how he turned from
friends and colleagues, blaming them for the crime,

the brutal rape and murder of a woman
picked up in a bar. The play shifted from
past to present, with lighting changes stressing

the hotel room of the murder, the cramped
confines of his cell, the sea-chest one foster-
mother shoved him into when she had callers.

Remesh glances up as the curtains part
with a rattling sound. The killer's still form
lies on the floor as it had at play's end.

From the musician's corner there arises
a weird sound, much like the wheezing of someone's
last breath, stretched to the upper registers.

The body rolls over, sits up, adjusts
its clothing and lifts its face to regard
Remesh directly. It is Nikolina.

He is desperate to touch her, but finds
he cannot move. Nothing moves in the hall,
apart from her lips and facial expressions.

'You could never leave me alone,' she says.
'I didn't want love, just oblivion
of lust and depravity. We were fire.

'Why did you spoil it?' He wants to tell her
it was the love she showered on her charges
that intrigued him and, yes, triggered resentment,

but his breath, lips and tongue cannot form words.
He wants to hold her once more, but no matter
how much he wills them, limbs refuse to move,

as though his body is chained and suspended
before the stage as before judge and jury,
like the prisoner during sentencing.

Nikolina titters. Remesh knows why.
He was the prisoner portrayed. The play
was written long after his execution.

'You couldn't kill yourself, unlike your mentor,
so forced the world to kill you. Who was she?
Did she look like me? Or what you recall

'of your lost mother? Or the female worker
at the orphanage who abused you when
you were sick with fever? Or all of us?

'Muddle of image and fact. You could never
tell the difference, part of the reason why
your work was so disturbing, so intense.'

His disembodiment intensifies
to the point Remesh feels his consciousness
spinning above the taunting ghost on stage.

What had she looked like? Every female face
he's ever known looks up at him, their strident
laughter echoing around and through him.

One face keeps appearing. He knows her now,
the daughter Zane saw being born to Jessie—
Keea, whose song-spark may be Rynobar—

and who Remesh knows he has killed, will kill,
eviscerated like his famous paintings,
details the police could not, will not, miss.

Had he really seen her, or anything
ever since Nikolina banished him.
Only his last paintings and the last card,

unturned, of the thin man. He painted evil
because he was evil. Flower and shadow
were his attempt at madness. Or were they?

Why did he really kill her? Chance or plan?
What was the difference to a world that needed
to protect itself so it could learn more

about its ways? Like Jessie's burning brand,
evolution from seed to branch to fuel
to flame to the invisible heat past

the iridescent edge of flame. His work
had tried to expose the world's dark regression,
its misguided retreat back to seed, back

to a garden of pleasure that could not
possibly exist, never did exist.
A burning was needed. His. Even now.

Looking down at the dark stage, Remesh sees
a bare room, a flickering candle and,
on a bed, two bodies writhing and moaning.

Two hands grasping two thin wrists. Two knees prizing
apart glistening thighs. Teeth clamping down
on birth-marked shoulder muscle. Haughty laughter.

Remesh feels the blood on his tongue, and spits
the same time the man does. Then his mind spins
into shock upon finding himself looking

up at his eyes, wildness cloaking dead depths.
He feels her body's excitement as his,
feels the hunger of the body above

hers flowing into desperation, rage,
into invasion of skin and breast when
she sees a knife in one hand, feels the other

clamped over mouth. Each plunge of blade is timed
with each thrust into groin, until he spasms.
She becomes numb to pain, but not to terror,

as she feels the point of the knife nick nipple,
ear, and eye-lid, lips and cheek-bone. Blood floods
her sight as though he knew that at some time

he would see through those frenzied eyes. The point
twists into socket in a desperate
venture to remove sight and memory,

but still she feels everything, even after
her lungs fill with blood and her heart is cut
from her mangled chest. Blood-drenched hands pull out

her entrails, array them on walls, his canvas,
map of life spiralling into sheer absence.
Somewhere there is manic laughter, then sobbing…

Remesh feels a hand touch his drooping head.
He looks up from the pew, sees Jessie next
to him, Zane in the aisle, sword at the ready,

Rynobar hovering nearby, her face
impassive, though with a glint of assessment
in sun-twirling eyes, knowing what he knows.

Remesh looks at the stage, the curtain still
unmoved since he entered, the only music,
the sound of despondent sobs, dying sniffles.

The light shimmers like purple seaweed swaying.
A shadow shivers him again, and contour
and texture waver and stream into soft

slivers as the theatre starts to dissolve
into grey powder, leaving a large cave,
slanting pale beams from a fissure up high.

Zane checks the crannied shadows, then rejoins
Jessie who is standing beside Remesh
still seated on a ledge near the cave entrance.

At her feet are the remains of a flower
crushed when he climbed to his perch. She knows it
as the inspiration for his last paintings,

fluorescent bloom in the middle of darkness.
She hands it to Remesh, who cups it gently
in both his hands and breathes on it. He waits.

Nothing happens. His body sags. He dangles
the flower from his hand, watches its petals
spill to the ground. All at once a wind draught

sweeps them aside as Rynobar comes closer,
wings ruffling the air. She prises the flower
from Remesh's hands, holds it to her chest.

Her body quivers as light emanates
from deep within her and flutters about
the trampled flower, which then swells with shape

that hints at rose, tulip, chrysanthemum,
a constant transfiguration of blooms,
the cave filling with multiple aromas

that intoxicate and cleanse and enliven
with each breath, with each particle of breath,
as when making love under summer skies.

Rynobar opens her hands and the flower
hovers briefly, then slowly starts to spin,
streams of rainbow light revealing red ochre

figures etched on the cave walls, a parade
of achievement—hunters with their spears, farmers
with plough and sprays of seeds, city-state builders

with charter, crane and plumb line, machine pilots
with fistfuls of lightning, flame eyes, dare-grins,
their wings obscuring all but a dark sun.

The primal flower travels once around
the cave, then Rynobar launches herself
upwards, enfolds it with her star-etched wings.

As she hovers, luminescence fills her,
flash-spears from feather tips and every limb.
Remesh reaches both hands towards her, but

Rynobar moves away: 'It is not time.
There are things I can do to help us all.'
Her body moulds itself to arrow, aims

for the roof fissure. The others rush out,
only to see a streaking burst of crimson
arc high and vanish in a squint of sky.

Jessie and Zane grab Remesh as knees buckle.
He waves them away—'I have to do this'—
and manages a few tottering steps

till Jessie brushes aside his objections.
'You have nothing to fear from any help.'
He takes another step, staggers, agrees

to her logic. During the return trip
he wonders why they had come after him.
As answer, Jessie points back down the road.

Some miles away, a sinuous black smudge
is widening as it moves towards them.
'I wanted to leave you behind,' Zane says,

voice even, 'but Jessie wouldn't let me.'
Remesh thanks her. She lifts her palms. 'Not even
Abzzu can come between us now.' He nods.

Just before they reach Phaox, something rustles
the nearby bushes. With sword and staff ready
Zane positions himself before the others,

but nothing happens. They continue on,
reach their mount and start to help Remesh climb
up Phaox's leg. A small shape cries out.

'It's Siraporn,' Jessie says as she rushes
to greet the animal, which purrs and preens
as she picks it up. The cat is well groomed,

fur fully recovered, with glossy sheen,
muscles lithe, eyes alert, purr strong, insistent.
'How do you think she found us?' Jessie says

as Zane helps her into the pannier.
He shrugs. 'Time is never sure here. Nor distance.'
He takes hold of the reins and they depart.

After a few moments of jerky movement,
Phaox eases into a steady rhythm
and Jessie is stunned to see the cat jump

onto the artist's lap, settle at once.
Remesh flinches at first, then rests his hand
on its back. Siraporn nuzzles and purrs.

'Well,' Jessie says, 'that's certainly surprising.'
She notes his red-rimmed eyes, sees calmness there,
glimmer of acceptance and innocence.

She wonders if hers had the same look after
her encounter with silence and herself.
Only Zane would know. She glances at him

and hopes fortune will favour him some way.
If this journey is prelude to an act
of discovery, when will Zane's occur?

She reflects on the landscape they are passing
through now, not thistles and thorns, but lush grass,
flourish of trees, green-gold facets of light,

wonders why such revelations occur
only around death, state of mind that never
truly exists if Thexlan is both ground

and parade of existence, maybe goal.
Were her companions also leading lives
in another realm, as she with her coma,

and dreaming such epiphanies that waking
would dismiss till the next big dream? A part
of her needs to dissect her revelations

and such matters, that part always divided
from the insights themselves, an eye exploring
all but the eye, all but the art of seeing,

while the rest of her, open to the act
of sight, and sight itself—what sees through eye,
mirror reflecting nothing but the mirror—

accepts the stubborn fact of Mystery,
which has her face, and those of everything
that existed, exists, or could exist.

Jessie has been graced a glimpse of that face
and can no more forget it as the tree
can forget the lightning stroke that scars it,

and branches change their course of growth and show
beauty beyond formulations of seed.
Then there is Abzzu. What part does it play

in revelation and choice? Is it truly
the locus of their fears? Does she dread it
or anything else? She looks at the mass

of flickering light, is filled with compassion,
much like she felt when she saw her companions
in pain. Maybe those gleaming energies

are a sign of its anguish—all it needs
is for someone to unravel its blight
of closed awareness, then frenzy will fade.

She taps Zane on the shoulder. 'Will we reach
the mountain before Abzzu catches us?'
Zane urges their mount on. 'It will be close,

'and we don't know if our arrival there
will deter it. Maybe that's been its plan
all along, to be guided there by us.'

41

The Song of Unknowing

A strange sound, more like rip than crack, more hiss
than boom, draws everyone's attention skyward.
The meteor is swiftly gaining speed

as it arcs across the sky, starving beast
abruptly unchained, while behind the sphere
the black wake widens, like Enheduanna's

trick—night without stars, the dark nausea
of bright nothing, bottomless well of silence
curving back on itself, swallowing echo.

They follow the tumbling mass as it drops
towards Mt Alkerii. It makes no sound
on impact, but the landscape buckles, shudders.

When they regain their seats and steady Phaox,
they see torrents of lightning, see smoke plumes
swirling from a crack half way up the mountain

and being drawn upwards into the wake,
which widens the more debris it receives.
Jessie's choked cry turns the others around.

Abzzu has reared its mass of shadow-sparks
through the black wake to the darkness beyond.
With each passing second, its pulses quicken

as it feeds on the abyss, and it swells
with turbulence, sends out thick tentacles
to encircle the world around the mountain.

Zane urges Phaox forward. 'There's no time
to unravel this meaning.' Jessie sees
a curious smile pass across his face.

As they race to Mt Alkerii, they notice
nearby plant-life instantly shrivel, crumble,
as though what was being sucked from the mountain

was the foundation energy of Thexlan,
blood gushing from a sacrificial carcass
above a gold ceremonial bowl.

How long before the road itself begins
to turn back to grey dust? And after that,
into what black furnace will the dust fall?

Much quicker than they expect—the destruction
to Mt Alkerii disrupting the weave
of time and distance—they find themselves hurtling

down a sloping highway past toppling buildings,
then slowing drastically as Phaox struggles
against the mob-flow trying to escape:

every dress from loincloth to powdered wig,
from tattooed face to soldier's garb, some screaming,
most silent, all holding to shapes they own.

What was once a bazaar is rubble—trestles
overturned, stalls collapsed, produce abandoned.
From nearby huts, people are loading goods

onto carts and rushing out of the city.
High above them, the wake is sucking gases
from the vent, while rocks of all sizes shower

the streets, each one caught in a fiery nimbus
that scatters when the debris strikes the ground,
which bends on impact before swallowing

the rock completely. With each scattering
of light, each rock fall, the nearby earth quivers,
then loses more consistency and colour,

like a wax landscape under desert heat.
Jessie grabs a woman running past, babe
in a papoose. Their clothes, once of fine cloth,

are in tatters, their faces streaked with grime.
The arm Jessie holds wobbles like soft rubber.
The woman keeps going and only stops

when her arm, already a bizarre angle
and stretched far beyond normality, seizes,
swings her to earth. Jessie rescues the child,

which has slid from its sling, observes the face
melting into itself, and hands it back.
'What's happening? Can anything be done?'

The woman looks blankly. Jessie shakes her.
The woman blinks, and her eyes show alarm.
Jessie repeats her questions and stands back.

Her face twisted, the woman answers slowly,
like talking in fluid. 'We are the guides
of the mountain and the sellers of dreams

'discarded each morning when Mt Alkerii
dispatches its welcome.' Her body wavers
in outline, and Jessie shakes her again.

'Whatever struck the mountain is releasing
all possible dreams from its care.' She shudders.
'Soon there will be nothing left. Nothing left.'

The woman stares around her one last time
and stumbles to an overloaded wagon
whose wooden wheels are more oval than round.

Zane stamps the earth with his foot. The depression
springs slowly back to place, but leaves an outline.
He smiles. 'I've seen this same effect before.'

'Where?' Remesh says, his eyes as filled with dread
as when he first met Rynobar. 'Adiska.'
Zane winces as shadows pressure his skull.

'When Beraint lost the strength of his song-spark.'
Jessie narrows her eyes. 'The tree of lights.
So Mt Alkerii can suffer like that?'

'Could be,' he says. Even with her composure
of insight, panic threatens to take over,
death of the kosmos no part of her vision.

'You became the Kenri. Can fix this, too.'
Zane's eyes glisten with concern and confusion,
yet still he has that enigmatic smile.

A new voice sounds behind them: 'I don't think
he'll be doing that, no matter how much
you may plea.' The group turns to face a youth

in burnished armour, holding a long spear
with two interlocking spirals of power,
one white like fresh snow, one red like spilt blood.

He is taller than Zane, with broader shoulders
and chest, black hair tied back, wide turquoise eyes,
and a poise Jessie knows she's seen before.

'Who are you?' she says. The youth smiles. 'You know.'
She takes a step and eyes him up and down.
'Alyston?' He bows low. 'At your command.

'But only this courtesy.' Levelling
his spear at the others, he looks to Zane.
'Isn't that so, Father?' The Kenri nods.

'What does he mean?' Remesh whispers, and pales
a little when Alyston swings his spear
towards him. But Jessie ignores the threat,

walks straight up to Zane. 'Your Spell of Unknowing?'
He peers at her. 'Yes, I can see you've known.
In fact, now I can see everything clearly.'

Straightening his posture, like one who's been
under a heavy load for centuries,
he places both hands on her shoulders, smiles

as if nothing strange has happened to them.
'You don't know how many cycles I have
endured being thwarted at the last second.

'Each time I make a small change in the world
and each time I am closer to enjoying
Thexlan vanish. Your presence is the latest.'

He grabs her arm and cuts it with his sword.
No blood. No mark. 'That you can be a Kenri
is the climax of all my plans, and soon

'we will be resting in oblivion.'
The vent's hissing makes it hard to note timbre
or tone of voice, but Jessie can see clearly

in Zane's dark eyes the cold determination
of his course. 'So I saved your life for this?'
'And I yours. The strange ironies of fate.'

She points to Alyston. 'Why do you need
a god? And I thought he was his own father?'
Zane smiles at him. 'Shultar is his real mother.

'I found her during one of my trips here.
She is Devina, too, as are we all
at some point, though I still don't understand

'that part of things. He keeps the plan in motion,
keeps us all off balance. Look behind you.'
Remesh and Jessie see Abzzu pulsating

just beyond the city borders, still reaching
to the ripped sky with a thick tentacle,
the rest of it blocking out the horizon.

All that is left of Thexlan is the mountain
itself, the damaged city below, and
a thin ribbon of land that disappears

into Abzzu: the sacred road, which glitters
and fades in succession. She realises
its grey dust contains the song-sparks of all

beings and stories belonging to Thexlan,
and soon they will lose all power to Abzzu.
Tears rim her eyes as she remembers those

she met. Then something deep flutters within.
'You won't succeed,' she states firmly. Zane sneers
at her. 'Why not?' She ignores his disdain.

'If what you say is true, that this endeavour
has been replayed millions of times, and always
with variation, then it will continue

'to replay. That is the bliss of the kosmos,
its eternal game. You're just as much pawn
as we are to you. We're all pawns, all players.

'The kosmos sings itself through us, is us.
Haven't you learnt anything yet?' Zane laughs
and slaps his son on the back. 'Except, each

'variation is not random. With each
I am closer to my goal.' Remesh brushes
aside Alyston's weapon. 'And that is?'

'As I said, absolute oblivion.
Isn't that what you wanted?' Remesh sighs,
massages his forehead. 'Yes I did, once.'

He looks up, conflicting emotions twitching
his face. 'But I've seen that's not possible.
Nor even desirable. We need life.'

Zane dismisses him with a wave of hand,
nods to Alyston, who nudges the others
towards a path at the side of the mountain.

42

The Rule of Fate

They climb steadily, the youth at the rear.
Zane rolls his neck now and then to relieve
doubt-tension of insight with dream and plan.

Could he truly be the instigator
of such evil—the dictator's design
when all else fails: destroy the universe?

Clearly, Alyston thinks so. Just as clearly,
Zane's memories, which once were jumbled like
the remains of a town after great flood,

are now filled with images of destruction
and repetition. Yet, if his plan works,
will not the nothing, the forever silence,

erupt into another sort of something?
There is nothing and there is kosmos. Which
is true? Are they goal and means for each other?

And what is his true part in this dynamic?
If he does nothing, will the kosmos find
yet another way to destroy itself?

At a cutting, Alyston calls a halt.
He tells the others to sit quietly,
approaches Zane. 'You're lapsing. You warned me

'about this, formed me to help prevent it.'
He lifts a pendant from around his neck.
'This should help.' Zane studies the smoky quartz

with its translucent veins that mesh and ripple
continuously, like lines of waves under
a shifting wind, realises it is

a Keth shard, a rare fragment of dream-ring,
which can reveal the prophecy of all
that befalls Thexlan, if read properly.

'Where did you get this?' Zane says. His son looks
at Remesh, who shakes his head. 'Not from me,
though I did give away something like that.'

Zane strides over to him. 'To whom, and when?'
Remesh looks away. The Kenri pulls him
to his feet, pushes him against a rock.

'Answer me.' The painter squirms. 'To a figment
of my imagination. A strange man
with the sound of insects all around him.'

Zane tightens his grip on Remesh's clothing.
'Why?' The man struggles to speak. 'I was tired
of searching and not finding Nikolina

'or anything of meaning. In exchange
for a crystal I received from the monk,
the man, who said he was a guardian

'of Thexlan, promised me what I desired:
dissolution.' Zane stares at him a moment.
'Then Jessie and I found you.' Remesh nods.

Casting him aside, Zane wonders what aspects
of his plans may still be hidden from him.
With relaxed yet focused mind, he looks into

the pendant, replays all the episodes
of his current journey. His body trembles
with thrill-panics of insights and escapes,

then calms as he concentrates on the scene
where he and Jessie cross the misty bridge.
The monk allows them each to choose a gift,

Zane's, the bent wood-nail that later turned out
to have been Remesh's before he died.
What did Jessie choose? He rushes to her,

drags her to her feet, and begins to search
her clothing roughly. 'How dare you!' she shouts
as she pulls away from him. 'I'll dare more

'before this time is done.' Remesh jumps up
to help her, but Alyston shoves his spear
at him. Zane grabs her again. She pulls back.

He cocks his fist. She stares coolly while reaching
inside her coat. 'I know what you want, Zane.'
She gives him the pouch with the spiral symbols.

He starts to apologise, but she turns
from him without looking, sits with Remesh.
Zane opens the pouch and tips out the gem,

which he immediately knows is *Anen*,
the gift he once gave Jeera and which fits
into the pommel of the Kenri sword,

though theirs was an unmarked silver sphere, not
this faceted jewel with its many etchings,
a new *Anen* conjured for a new cycle.

He unsheathes his sword and places the gem
into the pommel ring formed by the horns.
The blade starts to vibrate and tiny flames

flicker along its edges, quickly die
when they reach the broken tip. Still, the weapon
thrums louder and louder, rising in pitch

the closer he brings it towards the quartz,
which also begins to hum, relics cut
from the same source and welcoming each other.

Zane closes his eyes and lets the vibrations
permeate his body, ripples of sound
intersecting and cancelling each other.

He focuses on those places where sound
piles up on sound, and within each a scene
presents itself. He races point to point

as he tries to locate the one that tells
the fate of his plan. With a shock like sudden
blow in a dark alley, he realises

many scenes are variants of the one
he pictured the day when Shultar demanded
Kerrilea's death: he saw the Dremaan

stretched out above the mists of the abyss
and he standing there summoning up demons
and monsters to tear at her flesh and suck

at her soul. He had imagined her screams,
her cries for mercy, and the way he gloated
with his silence. Once she was dead, her soul

a tattered piece of fading mist, he had
imagined the same fate for those who stood
and watched Kerrilea burn. Everyone

would be destroyed as she had been destroyed,
and the more he discovered of Ghajat,
the more he saw the whole world was to blame.

One scene shows him singing a spell that draws
the darkness that is Ghajat and flings it
blazing into the mouth of Mt Alkerii,

to banish all dreams from Ghajat and every
other realm. Another scene shows him thrusting
a crystal sword into the sky and drawing

all energies to it till everything
is grey and he breaks the sword on his knee,
the released world-blaze consuming itself.

In one scene, a stranger, who may be Zane
or a wandering god of Thexlan, gathers
black song-sparks until he becomes all shadow.

A further scene shows Alyston and him
beside the lip of Mt Alkerii, with
a woman chained inside the cone, throat cut…

A loud blast from somewhere above disrupts
his musings. From the hole the meteor
had made, a crack is jagging down the mountain.

With rocks pelting them, they sprint up the path
hoping to reach the bend before the fracture
engulfs them in dream gases and debris.

A tumbling boulder strikes Remesh, but Jessie
grabs him and they stagger around the bend.
She sits him on a rock, stops the blood flow,

tells him the wound is minor. He thanks her,
then looks away quite suddenly. 'What's wrong?'
she says. He tells her that he is amazed

at her compassion, for Zane, and for him.
Jessie's stomach clenches. 'What do you mean?'
Again he looks away, then says, 'Your daughter.'

Ever since Jessie told the tale about
universes, Rynobar behind her,
with her, inside of her, the *hoya* speaking

with her, as her—no, as someone else, Keea—
she has known why Remesh and Rynobar
are wary of each other, has known what

Remesh will do to her daughter, has known
the painter's fate before and now in Thexlan.
Tears well up, though she finds it strange to grieve

for a being not yet born, not yet dead.
Then her mouth opens with a shriek. She beats
at his chest with her hands, falls back, kicks him

as he tries to comfort her, slaps away
any hand that comes near, then hugs her knees,
sobs wildly until Alyston jabs her

with his spear. She brushes it aside, glares,
then moves to her feet, breath centred once more.
Ignoring the orders of Alyston

and Zane, she approaches Remesh, who isn't
sure what to do. Jessie touches his arm,
looks at him, eyes now filled with understanding.

They both nod, then turn as Zane yet again
commands them to keep moving. 'I don't care
what happened between you'—he is red-faced—

'but the next time you ignore what I say
you will be punished.' Jessie smiles at him.
'I don't think that's really possible now.'

Zane slaps her. 'What about that?' She wipes blood
from her lips. 'I forgive you.' He cuffs her
so hard she staggers. Remesh catches her

and shoots a look of revulsion at Zane.
'I thought I was depraved,' he says, 'but you
are beyond me.' He dabs away her blood

and says to her, 'You don't have to goad him.'
'I'm not.' She straightens up, turns back to Zane.
'You do what you have to.' She stares at him.

'And I will do what I have learnt to do.'
'And what is that?' he says. 'Live my song-spark.'
He raises his hand, but his son stops him.

'Not yet. We still have a long way.' Zane wrenches
his arm away and glares again at Jessie
before turning back to the climb. He leaves

without looking around and is surprised
to find tears in his eyes. What is he doing?
Jessie once saved his life. *And you saved hers,*

another voice says to him, one that sounds
like a razor blend of Shultar and Elgron.
There is no debt. Only the rule of fate.

He remembers Jeera, her puckish laughter.
Her destiny was to love him and die.
Kerrilea too. Was Jessie to suffer

the same fate? Why did death occur to all
except himself? What gut-deep churning thing,
with talons, fangs, and eyes cold with disdain,

steel voice of rage and bitterness, drove him
to kill those he loves? *No,* that voice insists,
you have always listened to your song-spark,

always sought the deepest knowledge, and always
found it where death takes away those you love.
Because Thexlan killed them, it deserves death.

The Spell of Unknowing is now in motion
and the dissolving world will dissolve sorrow,
his and all that of others, leave behind

the momentary bliss of satisfaction,
before that also dissolves into nothing,
dead clamp of nothing from which nothing blooms.

43

Sparks Weaving

Once they reach the summit of Mt Alkerii,
Zane strides to the outer edge of the path.
Abzzu has swallowed almost all of Thexlan,

but when he stares into the greying cloud,
when he strains his ears to its moans and crackles,
he senses remnants of worlds he has travelled.

Nothing is lost, yet, not until the mountain
is totally destroyed. Everything else
is fractured, is despairing of links broken

and distorted, links to lives, to the objects
and emotions of lives, as though the cloud
were a giant tumbling puzzle awaiting

the end of its distressing disbelief,
awaiting the rebuilding of its parts
as affirmation of a faith that is

greater than destruction. Was not the highest
courage the belief in uncertainty,
the acceptance that Mystery is more

important than certainty, than control?
The greatest mastery is overcoming
fear of whatever is outside oneself.

The Kenri turns to his son, who has herded
the rest into an alcove overlooking
the enormous crater. 'I can't do this.

'Thexlan deserves to contemplate its stories,
live out its Mystery. We have to stop
this annihilation of Mt Alkerii.'

As he speaks, the grey cloud gives out a cry
of anguish, sound of space ripped into two,
which is reflected in Alyston's gaze.

Then comes anger, the youth's face turning crimson,
voice cracking with barely-constrained emotion.
'I was formed to destroy. You fashioned me.

'You trained and prepared me, while in the womb.
You crammed my mind with images and knowledge
from every cycle of your journey, every

'failure, poured into me your rampant zeal
to avoid repetition. Your doubt, too,
which battles my loyalty even now.'

His eyes cloud over briefly, a raw mixture
of that rage and frustration and despair
a child knows when spurned by judgmental parents.

Twice he rocks his head sideways, then exhales
with resignation. 'This is just another
failure scene, and I can't relieve your doubts.'

He levels his glowing spear at his father.
'Yet, this too you have foreseen, and made ready.
To defeat even you if necessary.'

Zane shifts swiftly into a fighting stance.
'If you kill me, how then can I enjoy
my success?' Alyston adjusts his posture

and breathing to match Zane's. The spear thrusts out
with no alert by muscle-twitch, eye movement,
or sharp intake of breath, swift as snake strike.

The point nicks Zane's sword arm above the wrist.
As the spear returns to its ready posture,
flash of flame, Zane senses he may have trained

his son too well. The youth sees this and smiles.
'You will enjoy your success, even if
I have to disarm your body '—the spear

flicks out and back again, a bicep wound—
'or bind you using your own spells.' He gestures
and a chain of energy spins around

arms and torso. But the Kenri is ready,
and his own gesture cuts the chain in half,
so that it falls to the ground and dissolves.

Movement blurs at the side, and Jessie shoves
herself between them. 'Stop this nonsense now.'
Alyston swings a gloved fist, but she ducks

with unexpected speed and skill. His eyes
widen with surprise, then narrow to scan
her combat poise. 'Clearly you can fight, but

'allowed my father to hit you. What's changed?'
She smiles, mind and body calm-vigilance.
'He has, as I knew he would. As will you.'

'No, I won't,' Alyston says as he thrusts
his spear at her body. She spins away,
dives back over the spear as he swings it.

'I was taught well, by a mentor of grace
and speed—she points skyward—and by my own
revelation of song-sparks and the kosmos.'

Rynobar glides towards them. In her arms
is a woman that, with a shock, Zane sees
is Jeera. She joins Jessie, twin swords ready.

'Zane may have trained you to fight him, but not
to fight someone like me.' Jessie steps back
from his lowered spear, senses fully open

to merest tremor of aura around
breath, muscle, glance, mental spark, her limbs primed
like bent-sapling snare. 'Or the three of us.'

Zane is too stunned to move, can't understand
why they would help when he had hurt them so.
Jessie's illumination at the altar

has taken her beyond his understanding,
has given her an acceptance of life
beyond individual self—her help

is not for herself, is not for the kosmos,
which she feels is endless. Must be for him.
Then there's Jeera, whose soul was never lost

at Es Xayim, whose presence has been near
throughout their travels, who always forgives.
Compassion shatters his last chains of doubt.

Yet deep inside, Zane knows even this turn
echoes in the crucible of all dreams,
seed of his story, seed of every story.

His knowledge opens infinite. He sees
machinations and beings slowly forming
a thunderclap of change—Larandor, Neshxi,

Shultar and Jessie, his Spell of Unknowing—
maybe far beyond his own dreams. He sees
future moments on Mt Alkerii weaving

and branching, blending and changing, forever,
yet constant, as with a jewel-labyrinth
of mirrors, each with a different small flaw,

but the final image perfect and pulsing
with the breath of itself, shimmering through
all possible scenes of despair and triumph.

Zane nods to the women and draws his sword.
Alyston backs away, swings his spear from
one to the other, sneer, then eager smile.

But Zane has no intention of confronting
his son. He leaves that to Jessie and Jeera.
Instead, he puts the Keth shard on his blade.

'You've tried this many times,' Alyston says,
his face now cheerless. A rising hum shrills
the summit, raising the hackles on all.

Zane yells to Remesh for his nail, and quickly
receives it. He pushes the blood-point into
the quartz's thickest vein, slices it open.

Jeera casts a lightning bolt at the youth,
knocks his spear aside with one sword and thrusts
the other at his throat. Alyston spins

and swings his spear towards her feet, then stabs
at Jessie who has moved in from behind.
She parries with a conjured staff and aims

a blow at his front hand. Alyston blocks
and mirrors her attack, his double-blow
numbing both her hands, and she drops the staff.

He grins, advances towards her. Just as
he thrusts his spear at her chest, Siraporn
leaps from a nearby rock, lands on his head.

He yells as she claws at his eyes, jumps backwards
to avoid Jessie's kick, somersaults over
Jeera's double sword thrust, lands on one knee,

swings his spear in a circle with one hand
while the other flails at the screeching cat,
rips her off, tosses her into the crater.

Throughout the swirling chess-game of the clash—
blow, parry, spell, counter-spell—Jessie thrills
in remembrance of combat drills she practised

with her imaginary friend so many
years before, one against one, one against
many, hand against hand, hand against weapon.

Jessie knows her actions are always centred.
When Zane struck her, she acted from an insight
deeper than memory and incarnation.

The pain in his blows was old pain transformed
into the locking away of old pain,
and her submission forced him to confront

and accept those things he had long forgotten—
even if they have done this countless times
before and barely survived such defeats.

Part of Jessie screamed when Siraporn fell,
but the song-spark within her, lost part quickened
by her vision at the altar, calmed her,

told her the cat will find itself, as always,
elsewhere in Thexlan, filled her with the flow
that comes when focus is beyond one's fate—

so now there is no awareness of skill,
only the instant of the thrusting spear
and her swivelling sidestep as it passes

her waist and Jessie grabs it with both hands,
the force of her spin and wrench of his weapon
tossing Alyston to the ground. He leaps

to his feet, sidesteps Jeera's attack, casts
a fireball, which Jessie blocks, grabs his spear.
As he starts to pull, she levers the weapon,

guides him off-balance in diminishing
circles till she has thrown him to his knees,
the metal shaft under his Adam's Apple.

Knee in his back, she arches him until
it seems the mountaintop is shuddering
with the tension of muscle bracing muscle.

Then, everyone realises the whole
mountain is vibrating haphazardly.
Alyston lets out a strangled laugh. Jessie

loosens the pressure at his throat. He laughs
again. 'You're too late. Mt Alkerii is
preparing its daily discharge of Orms—

'dreams, desires, needs. But when the Keth ring reaches
the fissure, Mt Alkerii will collapse,
Orms will fade. No dawn. Nothing. Only silence.

'Your wish is only minutes away, Father.
This time, you've won.' His laughter is cut short
by Jeera clubbing him over the head.

44

Always Choice

Zane peers inside the split-open dream fragment—
nothing but grey dust, with a hint of jasmine.
Has he destroyed all conceived destinies

or changed nothing at all? He understands
Alyston's sense of triumph, but is still
determined to undermine all such fate.

Inspiration leads him to smear the dust,
which pours out of the Keth shard in profusion,
near the broken tip of his crystal sword.

He remembers the vision of the woman
with her throat cut and knows that if he uses
Jessie's blood to repair his sword, the weapon

will allow him to survive the destruction
of Thexlan by hiding him in a pocket
of nothing, and he will emerge to make

not only a new version of Ghajat,
but a new Thexlan, a new Mt Alkerii,
to his own designs of justice and fate.

All at once he hears his mother's voice calling
to him from the middle of Lake Tarlkarni,
when the tribute ballots chose her for death.

He hears Kerrilea's screams as flesh bubbles
and sputters, as her clothes and hair flame-bursts.
He hears Jeera's words as the sword drains her.

'Do it,' says a voice behind him. He turns
and sees Shultar holding a struggling Jessie.
Rynobar is caught in a mesh of magic,

and Alyston is using his flame spear
to prevent Jeera and Remesh from helping.
'Did you think my son would abandon me

'to your ancient plan?' She twists Jessie's arm.
'This woman will die. It's up to you whether
her blood heals the sword, or is wasted. Choose!'

Jessie has stopped struggling, and Zane can see
her aura is deep and calm. He nods, turns
to watch Abzzu one last time, and is shocked

to see a curtain of mist form a figure,
a tall, thin man wearing robes decorated
with suns and lightning, who says, 'Yes, do it,'

then vanishes so fast Zane isn't sure
this manifestation of Larandor
actually appeared. He shakes his head, walks

straight up to Jessie, thrusts his sword through her,
all the way to the hilt. Rynobar screams,
Remesh hurls curses, but Jessie stares down,

sees the pommel ring empty, smiles, collapses.
In one swift action, Zane withdraws the sword,
inserts *Anen*, swings around and stabs Shultar:

'You had the *Anen*, but your vanity
wouldn't let you take the risk. So you failed.'
She clutches her wound, stares in disbelief.

Zane spins around to fend off Alyston,
parries spear thrust and spinning orbs of lightning,
slashes at his son, but doesn't wound him,

is relieved when Jeera and Jessie force
the youth back to where Rynobar can swoop
down, grab him, and drop him into the crater.

Zane kneels beside Shultar, her body ageing
quicker than when she needed *sorra* potions,
though the light in her eyes is still defiant.

He cradles her head, his feelings a swirl
of rage, relief, and something like affection,
though a wonder at all the waste numbs him.

Shultar coughs up blood. 'You still haven't won.'
The weight of her head lessens as her body
slowly fades. 'Thexlan is using you, too.'

Then there is nothing but a spinning spark
of flickering light that circles the clearing
and starts to rise. Jessie yells out to it:

'I want to ask my question now.' The spark
breaks open. The husk continues to arc
over the edge of the crater. The core,

more like a dancing flare of vital music
than solid light, drifts back down, lengthens, widens,
becomes a glowing human shape whose features

shift from male to female, from child to youth
to old, and those the companions have met
and been in their many journeys through Thexlan,

here and elsewhere. One form keeps reappearing,
Neshxi, and finally she says, 'I wondered
when you would take up that promise.' Her body

shimmers with the tints of all likely *Glymsens*.
Though awed by her raw radiance and power,
Jessie steps closer. 'How can we stop this?'

A shadow passes across Neshxi's face.
'All things that live will die, including Thexlan.'
'But Thexlan is everything,' Zane shouts out.

Neshxi nods. 'Mt Alkerii holds the seeds
of all things possible, all things imagined,
including the destruction of all things.'

Jessie glances at the cloud turbulence
around the mountain, then at Zane. She thinks
on all that has befallen them and listens

to what is unspoken in Neshxi's words.
'To destroy Thexlan was always Zane's fate.
Ever since Ghajat was an Orm sent out

'by Mt Alkerii. Even if he wanted,
he couldn't deny his fate. All those deaths
were a pattern to push him to this point.'

Neshxi strokes her skull staff and, as it fades,
another vicious tremor rocks the mountain.
'Every moment swings in and out of Nothing.

'If you have eyes to know, you would see how
Thexlan is substantial and insubstantial.
There is always choice.' Then she vanishes.

Jessie points to Zane's sword. 'Shultar was right.
My blood will be spilt whatever you choose.'
She pulls the weapon to her chest. 'Do it!'

Zane pushes her away. 'This isn't right.
My song-spark led me to this. Now it's time
to see if I can break through even that.'

He slices open his arm, wipes his blood
around the broken tip of the Thulsword,
weaves a spell to keep the others away,

then rams the dust-clad blade into his stomach.
Every part of his body screams and spasms
with the searing and clenching pain, but Zane

keeps the dark from flooding his mind by singing
the *murga* spell, as Kerrilea did
when the flames were consuming her. He watches

the sword fill with his blood, and sends his mind
into the weapon the same way he knows
his sister sent her soul out of her body

before the pain became unbearable.
He feels the blood and dust refresh the broken
structures inside the blade and when he senses

his blood loss bringing on the final dark,
hard temptation, he retracts his raw mind
and wrenches the sword from his sagging body.

He staggers inside his spell barrier,
struggles for breath, slowly steadies himself.
Then, he points the weapon skyward and chants

a spell of completion. Straight away, Abzzu
spasms and for an instant a rent shows
a giant eye staring impassively.

The rent closes, and Abzzu stretches out
a bulbous grey tentacle towards Zane.
The instant it touches the sword, its dust

starts to flow into the crystal, which flashes
with each beat of Zane's chant. The more he sings
the faster the flow, till the incantation

surges to a scream and Zane is hurled backwards.
When Jessie and the others reach him, Zane
is standing up, swinging the complete blade,

which thrums with each stroke. He smiles and hands it
to Jessie. 'This isn't mine now. Let fate
decide who will be its next rightful owner.'

45

A Surge of Silence

As the mountain pitches again, again,
Zane steps to the inner edge of the path.
He studies the bubbling and steaming lake

inside the crater, can distinguish Orms
of wish and need, of universe and tale,
every nursed sliver of imagination.

Suddenly, he hears Gedon's voice: 'It's time
to help you instead of hindering you.'
Zane turns to where his twin is offering

his right hand. 'You used some of your song-spark
to create me. And now you need that strength.'
Zane nods. He whispers a spell of reversal

and takes the hand. The air about them flares
and sizzles with energy. Gedon fades
and Zane's being quickens to bursting point.

Jessie moves beside him, nudges his hand.
He squeezes hers briefly, takes two steps, flings
himself over the crater's edge and arrows

his body for the plunge. Somewhere below
is the means for him to undo what was
begun so long between time. As he falls

he chants a spell of finding and, not knowing
how harsh the surface, weaves a magic armour,
which he discards moments later—the lake

being a liquid of honeycombed light
that parts easily. His dive takes him deep,
but not far enough. He tethers himself

to the current formed by Orms being drawn
to the rupture. What better way to find
the cure for his mistake than at its source?

As Zane swims down, he examines each Orm
that passes him in the swift chiaroscuro
of the approaching eruption, each one

a universe of thought and dream. He sees
strange beasts copulating under red suns
and eating their mates afterwards. He sees

tiny cells evolve into human beings,
into vast groups of creatures folding time.
He sees universes without life, just

revolving bodies of dust and rock glowing
and fading as darkness ripples the fabric
of their lost attraction for one another,

sometimes slow, sometimes rapid, like the rhythm
of seizure. Sees moments in a child's eye.
Sees moments in the fall of a tear. Moments

of a colossal wave circling a world
and engulfing everything, like a child
cupping its hands around a rainbow marble.

Moments of a luminous flame that never
flickers, even though there is only flame.
On pure instinct he reaches for this one.

As soon as he touches it, other Orms
are drawn to it, merge slightly like blow-bubbles,
are then popped free to spin into the flow.

In one, Zane reverses Larandor's spell
to fold back the dank roots of Es Xayim,
fashion Ghajat into a meteor.

In one, Jessie fades into butterflies
that blink into rainbows as she awakens,
her mother beside her, the other presence

Jeera, who smiles before fading in turn.
In one, nurses show Jessie the birthmark
of her new daughter, a winged sun. In one,

Rynobar gives Remesh his flower, then
the artist retrieves his nail, hurls himself
into a snaking whiteness that appears

while Abzzu shudders with the shaking mountain.
In one, the path of the meteor through
the bubbling Orms reveals what lies beneath

Mt Alkerii, a cavern filled with wings.
In one, Zane sees himself singing a *murga*
to increase the *sorra* harvest, but storms

wrack the lake and his mother drowns herself.
In one, Rynobar is given the Thulsword
and hacks off her wings, which fly by themselves

into the searing blackness above her.
She flings the glowing blade into the crater,
reaches inside herself, pulls out a sun

that opens wide enough for her to enter.
In one, Zane sees himself tumble through life
on a world not his own, sees hands that shape

with metal, with ink, with clay, with mud-brick,
sees cities dissolve into bracken lean-tos,
into campfires at junctions of rivers,

sees teeming creatures dwindle to one drop,
sees rock become blaze become spinning dust
become clouds of light-strings become balled heat

become a pin-hole flickering the dark,
sees his shadow on the dark, sees the dark
embrace him and smile. In one, he bleeds stars.

Then, Zane feels the current speed up and sees,
through the myriad colours of the Orms
below him, a dark rent that echoes elsewhere

in his own being, like loud double drums
that quiver the belly. He also senses
the Keth ring rising towards him. The rhythm

and melody of the wave as it gathers
its Orms is the same as the nonsense rhyme
Kerrilea sang to him during *Glymsen*:

Round to ground, inside down
Smile my cry, peel the crown
You're my sweet, outside drown

The upward rush seizes control of all
movement and he kicks hard against the weight
of dreams above him. He needs to be nearer

the rupture, though he has no idea what
he can do. Suddenly, his culling hand
strikes supple rock and he drags himself downwards.

He judges the speed of the rising wave,
with a shock realises he may not
reach the fissure in time. He wills himself

through threshing light and tumbling flows, left hand
still clasping the Orm with its constant flame.
Abruptly, his being quickens with power

and he plunges downward, mind fully focussed.
He stations himself alongside the rupture,
legs crammed into crevices widening

as the rock loses its rigidity.
The Keth ring surges towards him, a rhythm
that is so joyous, frantic, blissful, angry,

all those emotions wished for, feared for, by
everything that breathes, sings, weeps, curses, prays,
aurora of fulfilment rushing through.

Zane drives his right hand into the Orm, grasps
the flame. For a long instant nothing happens,
and then the blaze courses through him, so hot,

so fast, nerves sear and melt before they can
transmit the fact of pain, no time to name
the stench of consumption when silence surges—

If he is body he would sense and shiver.
If he is brain he would weigh and compare.
If he is mind he would invent and sing.

There is nothing. Not eye. Not sound. Not sense.
Not separation. Not fear. Not desire.
Not even the eye regarding itself.

Then something breathes. Air rippling with heat, damp,
and the tintinnabulations of sound.
He opens his eyes and sees his arm wreathed

with rampant flame, thrusts it into the rupture.
The flame ignites nearby wish globes in flurries
of cataract light…and when next he sees,

the rupture is fused shut and the Keth ring
is still rising towards him, the flame vanished.
He arches his body, lets himself fall

to greet the rising world. As it nears him
he feels himself dissolve into it, hears
a music much like the voices of women

chanting celebration and all fine things.
He suffers in this dance of dissolution
the rhythms of their song, the interplay

of melodies, some sorrowful, some joyous,
always in waves peaking higher and higher
as his body, his mind, his soul disperse.

He feels these intricacies of song gather
around him, fill him with the elegance
of feathers and that dawn-light dewdrops scatter.

He senses himself smiling somewhere, song
modulating to that smile. All sense fades,
yet he knows this termination is only

of history, not spark, imperative
to song. As the wave of the Keth ring surges
upwards, gathering Orms along its path,

the song scintillates frequency and pitch,
like bird-flock cries, bursts from the crater, climbs
and spreads throughout the sky, showering seeds

of dreams on the roiling grey shadow-grime,
sprouting imaginations of song-sparks
that unfold a bright landscape far below.

Zane opens his eyes to the hazy outline
of a pale face. As he strain-focuses
he sees faint figures dancing on the canvas

of her pupils. He sees the shapes of those
he loved: his mother, Kerrilea, Jeera,
and all their incarnations through each cycle.

Their hands are linked as they circle a tree,
wide branches, gossamer blooms, rainbow fruit.
Their singing kindles the tree, and he watches

one fruit fall to the ground and split wide open.
Light bursts from within. He blinks. Someone brushes
his lips with soft fire and intones a word

that will open. Already. Always.

Glossary

Abzzu: The sentient creature of shadow and lightning pursuing the characters in The Silence Inside the World.

Adiska: The jewel city of Ghajat. Home to the Dremaan temple.

Aimal: The abode of Shultar, directly above the mist edge of Thexlan, on Lake Tarlkarni.

Alyston: Son of Devina/Shultar and Zane. Trained by Zane to help him succeed in The Song of Unknowing.

Anen: The jewel that fits into the pommel of the Thulsword and which is always discarded into the streams of fate whenever a new Kenri takes command of Es Xayim.

Azra: The husband of Devina, father of Nikolina, and guide of Zane and the others. The answerer of messages.

Balis: The artist-savant who trained Remesh in painting in the country town where Remesh spent his childhood.

Beraint: The current Kenri, with whom Zane and Jeera do battle for the salvation of Ghajat.

Chos: The sea around and under Ghajat. The sands that come out of this sea first formed Ghajat yet also threaten the world whenever a Kenri loses power.

Devina: Wife of Azra, mother of Nikolina (with Azra) and, as Shultar, mother of Alyston (with Zane). The one who preserves.

Dremaan: Those who are highly skilled in the art of 'making'. A worker of worlds.

Dukor: Husband-son of Neshxi and maker of Turmas.

Elgron: The Dremaan in charge of the temple at Adiska. The teacher of Zane and Jeera.

Enheduanna: The name Jessie gave to Neshxi when they first met. Taken from the world's first known author, who was an Akkadian High Priestess of the Moon-God Nanna.

Es Xayim: The tree of lights beneath Ghajat, which is the power foundation of that world through its 'root' connections with Thexlan.

Fable, Lie or Life: The story game played by the travellers, usually when they are resting for the night. One of them tells a story and the rest choose if it is unreal or made from life, or is something else.
Forii: The ancestral rule-voices of the denizens of Tarlkar, composed of the commands and rulings of all headmen and other authority figures of the village stretching into the past.
Gedon: The gold-skinned version of himself that Zane created to guard Es Xayim. He appears at crucial moments to hinder, help and challenge Zane.
Gem of Synrath, The: The giant leech-jewel that allows the false gods of Synrath to maintain their realm of perpetual spring.
Ghajat: Zane's home world. A realm quite close to Thexlan in the hierarchy of worlds. A realm of archetypes.
Glymsen: The eruption of Orm rings from Mt. Alkerii that signal (and create?) the new day, and which also resound throughout Ghajat.
Haal: The goddess of Lake Tarlkarni. Possibly Shultar.
Hoya: The star-demons of Ghajat.
Ice Temple, The: The house of decadence run by Nikolina.
Jeera: The first lover of Zane. A student of Elgron in the Dremaan temple at Adiska.
Jenny: Jessie's spirited childhood imaginary friend who teaches her some fighting skills and is actually Jeera.
Jessie Willis: A 21st century albino student of ancient languages and literatures who suddenly appears in Thexlan and must journey through this strange land to find out why she is there.
John Linn: The over-weight poet-artist that Jessie met while researching an immortal wanderer she had named Tamheduanna.
Keea: Jessie's daughter, whose song-spark may be Rynobar and who may be destined to be murdered by Remesh.
Kenri: The first Kenri sang Ghajat into existence. Those who follow are Dremaans who pass the Kenri Test and then become the 'dream sentinel' of Ghajat by looking after Es Xayim.
Kenri Test: All those wishing to be the next Kenri must open the staircase into the region below Adiska, must be accepted by the Thulsword when wielded by the current Kenri, and must have been drawn to the Anen during their life before the test.
Kerrilea: Zane's sister. Given by the villagers of Tarlkarni as

a sacrifice to Shultar.

Keth Rings: The rings of Orms projected into Thexlan by Mt Alkerii during Glymsen.

Keth Shards: Gem fragments of Orms that drop out of Keth Rings and can be used to predict the future or find the past.

Larandor: The first Kenri of Ghajat.

Makir: The women (generally) of Ghajat who are trained to perform the *Murga*.

Monady Church, The: The sect Remesh joins after his revelation, with a theology based on one world, one god, one way to rejoin god, one heaven.

Mt. Alkerii: The dream mountain in the centre of Thexlan, from which all things arise, to which all things return. The source of the rings of Orms generated each morning.

Murga: The sand song ritual (path of prayer) performed by the Makirs of Ghajat before and with every Glymsen, in an attempt to ensue good fortune for the coming day and to summon from Es Xayim the fulfilment of their desires.

Neshxi: Goddess of Thexlan. Also known as Enheduanna.

Neti: The god of the character in Remesh's tale who quests to retrieve the soul of his lover.

Nikolina: The daughter of Azra and Devina. The owner of The Ice Temple. The lover of Remesh.

Orms: Those wish-globules, or world-bubbles, containing the prayers, dreams and hopes of the inhabitants of Thexlan, cast out from its depths by Mt. Alkerii during Glymsen.

Phaox: The long-snouted, eight-legged beast of burden owned by Azra.

Remesh: A painter from the early to mid 21st century of Earth (or a parallel Earth) who is executed for murder and finds himself in Thexlan.

Rynobar: A hoya (star-demon) from Ghajat who has journeyed to Thexlan to discover the reason why other hoya have disappeared.

Scylarii: The non-human dreamers of Thexlan. The fashioners of Time. What our nightmares experience when they have nightmares.

Shultar: The Dremaan mistress of Lake Tarlkarni and the surrounding lands. Orchestrator of the deaths of Zane's mother and his sister, Kerrilea.

Siraporn: The current name of the animal companion of Azra and Devina, who travels with them during their various cycles of existence. She is a chocolate-eared, battle-bred cat.

Song of Unknowing, The: The spell that undoes the creation of Ghajat and possibly the existence of Thexlan.

Sorra: The purple plant from the bottom of Lake Tarlkarni that Shultar distils to prolong her life.

Star-demon: Hoya. Beings of the Ghajat sky who come down from the stars at night and kill those who are unprotected.

Synrath: The realm of those false gods who use a giant leech-jewel to maintain their power over their peoples.

Tam: The name Jessie gave to the childhood 'imaginary' boy whom she could see but to whom she could never speak.

Tamheduanna: The name Jessie gave to the immortal wanderer who apparently influenced the major cultural ideas and texts of human history and who moved backwards through time. Name is a combination of Tam and Enheduanna.

Tarlkar: The name of the village where Zane lived his childhood.

Tarlkarni: The lake on which Tarlkar is situated.

Thexlan: The creator and final world of all possible worlds. The world of all worlds, of all potential worlds, of all possibilities of existence. The womb and home to all dreams, all stories.

Thulsword: The blade of Ghajat's Kenri, both test and badge of office.

Turma: Map-portal—large, round, white disks of swirling vapour in a thin border of whorling flame, constructed by Dukor.

Zane: An immortal wizard and seeker of wisdom who is striving to invoke The Song of Unknowing in order to destroy Ghajat and possibly Thexlan.

About the Author

Earl Livings has published literary and speculative poetry and fiction in Australia, Britain, Canada, the USA, and Germany, and has publicly read his work at venues in Melbourne and overseas. He has a PhD in Creative Writing and he taught professional writing and editing for almost 20 years. Earl has also worked as a freelance editor, a manuscript assessor and a Writers Victoria mentor. His writing focuses on science, history, nature, mythology and the sacred. Ginninderra Press published his second collection of poetry, Libation, in late 2018. He is currently working on an historical fantasy series set in 6th century Britain and new poetry and short story collections.

See Earl's website: https://earl-livings.com.

Acknowledgments:

There are many people I wish to thank for their help during the long journey from idea to publication. First of all, the late John McLaren, who was my PhD supervisor at Victoria University, with an early version of *The Silence Inside the World* forming a major part of my thesis. Second, John Jenkins, who helped me refine a draft of the verse novel to its final PhD form. Third, Albert Sommer and Joel Martin, who read the manuscript and gave me valuable feedback when I was preparing it for submission to publishers. Fourth, Liz Bright and Edwina Harvey, for welcoming me into the fold at Peggy Bright Books and for guiding me through the publication process with timely patience, humour and expertise. Fifth, Manabu Takeda, for his striking cover illustration. Sixth, those friends and family who have encouraged, supported and championed me over the years of this project, especially Astrid and Bill Bahr, Catherine Bateson, Mary Bratton, Veronica Calarco, Harley Carter, Michael Crennan, Nadine Cresswell-Myatt, Nick Engelman, Peter Farrar, Garry Fay, John Irving, Ray Liversidge, Chris Millar, Pheroza Rustomjee, Soni Stecker, Tricia Steer, Elly Varrenti, and Cathie Walsh. Finally, my wonderful and talented wife, Joanna Steer, who has endured my anxiety while I waited for her to read and annotate the manuscript at various stages, who has reassured me and emboldened me, and who has been a bright and constant loving presence.

 Peggy Bright Books: Proudly publishing square pegs for round holes.
See www.peggybrightbooks.com for more Peggy Bright Books titles.

Lightning Source UK Ltd.
Milton Keynes UK
UKHW021146170622
404578UK00009B/2046